"With its colo... ng, and
well-plotted ... perfect

—Ellery Ad... author

"Using a palette of clever plot twists and intriguing characters, Cheryl Hollon creates a richly drawn world that's both bucolic and dangerous in *Still Knife Painting*. Readers will take a shine to this addictive new series!"
—Agatha Award–winning author Ellen Byron

"Set against the blazing backdrop of an Appalachian fall, *Still Knife Painting* serves up a tasty stew of murder and moonshine. In this series debut, Cheryl Hollon weaves a tale as complex and country as the antique braided rug that figures in the story."
—Barbara Ross, author of the Maine Clambake Mysteries

"This book is well paced, anchored by an excellent central character, and infused with a keen sense of place. Veteran scribe Hollon makes it all look easy. Rocking in Miranda's chair on the porch, sitting under a quilt and taking in the view sounds like a plan to me. Pass that moonshine."
—*Mystery Scene* magazine

The Webb's Glass Shop Mystery series

"The novel's pace is leisurely, built around character interactions, travelogue and lots of information about glass art and its history."
—Colette Bancroft on *Cracked to Death*, *Tampa Bay Times*

"A zippy read. If you like cozy mysteries, you're gonna devour *Pane and Suffering*."
—Creative Loafing, Tampa Bay

"There is plenty of variety and not just workbenches in the lively story by Cheryl Hollon."
—*Fresh Fiction* on *Pane and Suffering*

"Webb's Glass Shop is certainly a place where you'd want to hang out."
—*Kings River Life Magazine* on *Pane and Suffering*

"A fresh and original new series! Well-crafted with smart and intriguing clues."
—Krista Davis, *New York Times* best-selling author on *Pane and Suffering*

Also by Cheryl Hollon

Webb's Glass Shop Mystery Series
Pane and Suffering
Shards of Murder
Cracked to Death
Etched in Tears
Shattered at Sea
Down in Flames

Paint & Shine Mystery Series
Still Knife Painting
Draw and Order
Death a Sketch

Published by Kensington Publishing Corp.

Cheryl Hollon

Death A Sketch

Kensington Publishing Corp.
www.kensingtonbooks.com

KENSINGTON BOOKS are published by

Kensington Publishing Corp.
119 West 40th Street
New York, NY 10018

First Printing: August 2022
ISBN: 978-1-4967-2528-8

ISBN: 978-1-4967-2529-5 (ebook)

10 9 8 7 6 5 4 3 2 1

Printed in the United States of America

Dedicated to my parents,
Wendell Eugene Hollon
1927–2019
Dorothy Marcella Hollon
1926–2021

Acknowledgments

This third book in the Paint & Shine series has been a challenge to complete. I almost didn't start it at all. My dad died in the middle of writing the second book, and it affected my writing. Then, tragically, my mom passed in May of 2021. Because the setting for this series is the family farmhouse he grew up in, and they lived in during their first years of married life, it was agony to go back to those beloved rooms and haunting wood trails. I'm delighted to complete a story they would have loved.

Then, of course, you have to add the disruption of COVID-19. I was ordered to "stay at home" by not only the governor of Florida but, more importantly, my physician daughter-in-law. Guess whose advice I follow to the letter? Yes, if you guessed Jennifer, you're right!

My editor at Kensington Publishing Corp. is the charming and patient Elizabeth Trout. She has managed the Mount Everest of details that have allowed this book to land safely in your hands. I'm grateful for her encouragement and understanding during the creation of this story. She's a delightful star!

Thanks to Larissa Ackerman, advance copies of this book were sent out for early reviews and a local television spot. Kudos to her and Michelle Addo for wrangling bookstores and authors for the four amazing Kensington CozyCons that occur every year across the country. Her job was even harder this year, with a massive rescheduling of all the events for the following year because of COVID-19. It's a lot of work to pull off, but readers are enthusiastically supporting these events.

I'm one lucky author to be a client of literary agent James McGowan. He has enough energy to step in as a relief pitcher for the sun itself. He's also an excellent sounding board for proposal packages and a magician with social media. He helped me extend my reach without spending more time on social media. Now, that is magic.

There are four incredible independent bookstores within five miles of my apartment. How can a writer be so lucky? Haslam's Book Store was established in 1933. When we moved to the St. Petersburg area in 1975, we haunted their aisles, searching for affordable used books for our two young sons. It's lovely to host a book signing event in the very spot where they learned to love books.

The second is Books @ Park Place, owned by Nancy Alloy and her guardian dog, Watson. The newest independent is Tombolo Books, owned by Alsace Walentine. In downtown St. Petersburg, there's a new Book + Bottle bookstore and wine shop. We're so lucky to have a community that supports them all.

Erin Mitchell is a guardian angel for all the writers who need that special touch. She lives just up the street from me, and I was lucky to snare her for my website relaunch for this new book. Friends are even more important in this daring new post pandemic publishing world.

I wouldn't be published if I hadn't found the online chapter of the Sisters in Crime organization. The group is called the Guppies, which stands for the great unpublished. That's the way it started out. Members would share publishing information, critique query letters, sharpen up those first five pages, and spread the good news and cheer with a virtual kick line with flying boas. The magic of this chapter is that after getting published, we hang on to help those who have just started and need a little help. Thank you, Guppies!

An online tribe of support comes from my fellow bloggers at The Booklovers Bench (www.bookloversbench.com). It's a group of seven cozy authors. One of us posts an essay every Thursday on a topic of interest to our readers. We support one another in promotion, publishing issues, triumphs, as well as setbacks. Many heartfelt thanks to Terry Ambrose, Nancy Cohen, Debra Goldstein, Dianna A.S. Stuckart, Maggie Toussaint, and Lois Winston. Stop by for the free book contest every month.

I also blog every month with Raquel V. Reyes and Tara Lush on the Cozy Florida blog. I usually give away a signed book, along with some swag (www.cozyflorida.com).

My baby brother, Mark Hollon, and I have been conducting weekly conference calls for about five years. It started when he decided to write a business plan for his start-up company, 3DCincy. He designs and produces 3D-printed parts. We've helped each other tackle the down and dirty decision-making side of our respective businesses.

My beta reader is Sam Falco. This is an author name I think will become famous for his intricate plots, sharp dialogue, and skillful storytelling. I'm grateful for his guidance in the early stages of each new book.

I always thank my muse, Joye Barnes, for her unstinting delight in encouraging me when my spirits are low— usually when I'm in the valley of the shadow of the middle muddle.

There are so many friends who keep me going. I'm absolutely sure I'm going to miss someone. I'm so sorry if it's you. Howard and Kate Finberg, JD Allen, Gale

Massey, Carol Perry, Martha Reed, Edith Maxwell, Ellen Byron, and my dearest work-friend, Sarah Weist.

I have talked to so many writers whose families have never read a single word they've written. How heart-breaking. Thank you to my big family for encouraging me in this journey. I've learned a lot about supporting dreams from those who have encouraged mine.

My ninety-four-year-old mother was able to take me back through her childhood memories of a time when life was simple and basic. Still scary is that my grandfather's older sister and her new baby died of the Spanish Flu. We've spent many hours discussing country manners, favorite recipes, social disasters, and places for gatherings, reunions, and also the ever-present church life of her youth. What a blessing to be able to share these rich memories with her.

My husband, George, is my rock and a guiding light through the many triumphs and challenges of publishing. He's got my back. I couldn't write at this pace without his full and unstinting support.

I especially want to thank you, the readers, for embracing this series in so many wonderful ways. You've blogged about it, written reviews, talked to your friends, preordered the new books, and most important—read it. Thanks for your support. It means everything. It's worth repeating. Readers mean everything to me.

CAST OF CHARACTERS

Local Characters in Order of Appearance

Miranda Dorothy Trent	Protagonist (recurring character)
Sandy	Miranda's puppy (recurring character)
Dorothy Marcella Trent	Miranda's mother (recurring character)
Ron Rose	Miranda's handyman (recurring character)
Gene Buchanan	Late uncle, Mom's bachelor brother (recurring character)
Doris Ann Norris	Receptionist (recurring character)
Austin Morgan	Local forest ranger (recurring character)
Kevin Lovelace	Rescue team member
Sheriff Richard Larson	Wolfe County Sheriff (recurring character)
Felicia Larson	Wolfe County Coroner (recurring character)
Iris Hobb	Older sister cook (recurring character)
Lily Hobb	Younger sister cook (recurring character)
Tyler Morgan	Austin's sister (recurring character)

Employees of BigSky

Rowena Gardner	BigSky administrative assistant
Terry Burns	BigSky VP of operations /victim
Frank Tobin	VP of human resources of BigSky
Carol Hampton	Team Leader of Firehawks
Lisa Porter	Member of Team Firehawks
Janice Utz	Member of Team Firehawks
Eileen Hoffman	Member of Team Firehawks
Xavier Johnson	Member of Team Firehawks
Jeffrey Nelson	Team Leader of Sweatsocks
Oliver Young	Member of Team Sweatsocks
Victor Zane	Member of Team Sweatsocks
John O'Reilly	Member of Team Sweatsocks
Sheila Collins	Member of Team Sweatsocks

Chapter 1

Late Friday Afternoon, Miranda's Farmhouse

"I have a bad feeling." Miranda Trent rocked gently in the front porch swing, her hand wrapped around a hot cup of mint tea. "What a mess. I shouldn't have accepted a big contract from that horrible man and his horrible company. A four-day workshop is a big leap for my new business." She drew up a handmade quilt and tucked it around herself and Sandy, the sleeping puppy in her lap. "Have I made a dreadful mistake, Mom?"

"There's no way to tell, honey," said her mom, Dorothy Marcella Trent, who was tucked into the other end of the quilt, one booted foot touching the plank boards of the porch floor to keep the swing moving. "You need the business."

"I certainly do. Tourist season is virtually shut down for the winter. There won't be anything happening in these hills until spring. Well, except for a few Christmas events up at Hemlock Lodge," Miranda said.

"I've been so busy going back and forth to Dayton trying to sell my house, I haven't paid much attention to you." Dorothy tapped Miranda's toe with her own. "What's so special about this upcoming workshop? I don't understand why you're so worried."

"I'm expanding into a new, outdoor-based training service to support corporate team-building workshops."

"You've been doing your cultural tours for a couple of months. So it makes sense to expand. I'm sorry to be so preoccupied when you needed to brainstorm."

Miranda felt a relaxing warmth spread through her chest. She had been upset by her mom's distance. It wasn't deliberate. Her mom was spinning a lot of plates at the moment. "I got a call a couple of weeks ago from a sportswear company headquartered in Lexington. BigSky Corporation is known for its popular graphical designs. They're really gorgeous. Anyway, they asked me to provide a four-day team-building workshop based at Hemlock Lodge in Natural Bridge State Park."

"That sounds like the kind of challenge you love. What's the format?"

"Basically, it's a series of games, competitions, and challenges. On the first day, we hike the trail to Balanced Rock and draw with charcoal. We lunch here at the farmhouse, then tour the distillery and make up the mash for moonshine in my brand-new, tiny, one-gallon sampler stills. That's followed by a nature photography event, then some outdoor stew preparation."

"That sounds like something that should suit you right down to the ground. I don't understand why you're so wrought up."

Miranda pursed her lips. "That's just day one. On day two, we tackle a rope bridge challenge, have a boxed lunch followed by a watercolor lesson at Rock Bridge, then everyone makes chicken pot pie here at the farmhouse and checks the flavoring of the moonshine mash."

Dorothy shook her head. "My, oh, my. That's a lot to get through. No wonder you're feeling stretched thin. What's on for the third day?"

"We start off with an aerial rope event at that zip line roadside attraction over in Slade. Then we have an eco-friendly scavenger hunt. For the artistic event, we make table centerpieces with the items collected. The cooking events are pie baking and then using your precious sourdough starter for dinner rolls."

"You mean Viola?"

"Yes, although I'll never get used to the way you treat that starter like it was alive."

"It is alive! Family tradition demands that you name it after the person who gave it to you. That's a way of sharing the love in the bread."

"Then, on the last day, everyone pulls together to create a traditional Thanksgiving dinner where we celebrate the team and finish off with the moonshine that everyone helped to create."

"I'm exhausted just hearing about it. You do see the irony here, don't you?"

Miranda pouted. "What on earth are you talking about?"

"It's so funny. You, who are a world-class worrier as well as an introvert, are teaching a team-building workshop when you're not sure if your Paint & Shine business will make it."

Miranda gave her mom a sad smile. "Nailed it. Well, it's also one of my strengths. I relate to loners. You remember that's what Grandma used to say: 'What doesn't kill you makes you stronger.'"

"I think this might be a bit too far. Do you have enough help? Should I postpone my trip to Dayton? I could do that."

Miranda grabbed Sandy and snuggled him up under her chin. "No way. You need to get that house sold. I won't risk it. You've got a terrific offer for that house. I'll have the Hobb sisters for kitchen work. The BigSky Corporation is sending a manager to assist with wrangling the candidates. The participants are supposed to be in line for a special, fast-track management program, depending on their performance in the workshop."

"So why are you worried?"

"I don't know. Sometimes I think I worry just to feed my habit of being a great worrier. You know that."

"Yes, but this business is all about what you enjoy. You should be enjoying it."

"When I stop to think about it, I am." Miranda paused for a few seconds. "I've been working on my people skills, and the art gallery jobs I had up in New York City were super for learning how to approach people and close sales."

"That's right, you are more confident. So, why are you so worried?" Dorothy asked again.

"It lasts four days. Four whole, long days. I've never done anything like it, but because the tourist numbers were falling, it seemed like a gift."

"This is normally a slow time for sightseers and tourists. It's the weekend before Thanksgiving. Lots of folks are already on their way to family gatherings, not company team-building adventures."

"I did wonder why they wanted this particular time.

Although most of the fall colors are still on the trees, one heavy rain will strip them down to bare branches."

"It's already cold up on the ridges and cliffs right now," Dorothy said.

"Right. I'll know better when I've been in business for a couple of years." She sighed deeply. "If I last that long. Who knows if I'll even be in business a year from now— or even a month from now? Most new businesses fail in the first year. These last few weeks have been a whirlwind introduction to cultural touring."

Dorothy patted Miranda on the shoulder. "Dear, I know you think you're the cause of the tragedies surrounding your new Paint & Shine business, but violence is a natural part of living out here in the highlands. We're from a rough and determined stock of Scotch-Irish. The Hatfield-McCoy feud is not a fairy tale. Some say it's still running."

"I'm learning that," Miranda said while scratching Sandy's full belly. They sat swinging with the only sounds coming from the country night. She picked out a barn owl, a coyote, and, finally, the cricket from inside the house. She had been trying to evict him for several weeks with no luck. Was he good luck or bad? She couldn't remember.

Dorothy took a long sip of her tea. "I feel bad about going back to Dayton right now. It's even worse since Ron Rose the handyman—" She stopped and smiled when she said his name—"has taken a big job over in Jackson. I think you are going to need all the help you can get."

Miranda mirrored her mother's smile. Ron had somehow captured her long-widowed mother's heart. They were as cute as high-school sweethearts with their lovey-dovey ways.

"It's not a problem, Mom. You're lucky the house sold so quickly. Going back and forth is just too much hassle. Especially since Ron proposed."

Dorothy began folding the quilt off her lap. "Are you sure? I could change my plans."

"Don't make me repeat that whole string of reasoning. We've already been through that. When is your closing?"

"Monday morning." Dorothy drained her cup. "In fact, I'd better get on the road. Friday nights are always a nightmare going through Cincinnati. It used to be that the backups were for those coming south. Now, it seems just as bad whichever direction you're going."

Miranda glanced at her wristwatch. "Right, if you leave now, you should be just ahead of the rush." She took Sandy in her arms and walked down to the driveway with her mom.

Dorothy tickled Sandy under his chin. "You be a good puppy, now, okay? Watch over Miranda for me."

With a feeling of intense isolation, Miranda watched her mom's car drive away. She hadn't fully considered how much she would miss that her mom had been helping her with the tiny tasks that kept a household going. While Miranda concentrated on her small business, like laundry, dusting, and keeping food in the refrigerator.

The phone rang. Miranda felt annoyed, but pushed that aside. She was determined to secure her ownership of this homestead farmhouse. All she needed to do was keep her schedule full enough to make a decent profit. Her uncle's will stipulated that she needed to pay her taxes and establish a licensed moonshine distillery before the end of the year. She was very close to achieving both, so she could enjoy this wonderful country life without fear. She went inside, put Sandy down, and picked up the handset.

"I've got more suggestions," said Mr. Tobin, vice president of human resources of BigSky, the world-famous manufacturer of sportswear.

"Good evening, Mr. Tobin. More changes? It's a little late, don't you think? The workshop starts tomorrow morning."

He paused. "What did you say? Is this connection bad? I need more changes."

Miranda sighed. He wasn't listening to her at all. "What kind of changes?"

"Two things. First, I want to split the workshop into two teams. Then I want them to compete against each other for a big reward. That should elevate the focus with the workshop participants. This is not going to be merely a fun time in the mountains."

Miranda thought about the activities she'd planned for the workshop. Grudgingly, she admitted to herself that those were really good ideas. He might be annoying, but he was a creative businessman. "I agree, Mr. Tobin. A competition will add some spirit to the events, but won't there be some sort of scoring and evaluation tasks? I'm not set up for that kind of paperwork, and I couldn't just add that without significant extra fees."

"No, I see that. Don't worry, I'll handle those processes."

His tone made her feel like a dolt for mentioning it. It was demeaning.

Mr. Tobin continued. "Also, because there's going to be some scoring and assessment tasks, I'm going to send my administrative assistant. She'll handle all the paperwork."

"That's good. What's her name?"

"Rowena Gardner."

"Rowena Gardner? That's an unusual name. I think I know her if she's from Dayton, Ohio."

"She commutes into the plant from Winchester, but if I remember from her application, I think she got an associate degree from a junior college in Dayton. Anyway, she doesn't have a local accent and she's an efficient admin."

"Rowena was the star organizer of our class back at Colonel White High School. If I remember right, she was president of the Honor Society, captain of the cheerleaders, and also our class president."

"That sounds like her."

Oh my goodness, if this is Rowena, it's bound to be an omen that this workshop will be a fantastic success. She's a little odd, but a good organizer. We were great friends.

Miranda frowned. "Wait, that means you're adding a person to the total number of participants?"

"You don't need to charge me for that. She won't be participating in the events."

That weasel. He's trying to lowball me on the price. He's not getting away with it.

"Well, that's fine, but she will need to eat if she's going to tag along with the competitors to make scoring assessments. In fact, it will be the same as your special meals-only fee. Right?"

There was a short pause. "Oh, very well. That won't cost much. She'll join you tomorrow morning for the eight o'clock orientation meeting at Hemlock Lodge." There was another pause. "Hold on for a second. I've got another call."

He switched her to Hold before she could agree. She thought that if this was how corporate types ran things, she was glad she didn't work for a big company. Not her cup of tea at all.

"That was bad news. I won't be coming out tomorrow to lead the workshop. I've got a labor union emergency over at the manufacturing plant in Louisville. They've chosen the holiday rush because they know we can't afford any production losses leading up to Black Friday. I've got to handle it in person."

Miranda raised her eyebrows. Things would go much smoother if he weren't around. "That's too bad, but I've got everything all lined up. It will be fine."

"Oh, not to worry. I'm sending over a substitute manager to take my place."

Miranda gritted her teeth. *Just how many last-minute changes was she supposed to deal with*?

"Perfect! Who is it?"

He ended the call.

Miranda replaced the handset in its charger. "It would be nice to know who this new supervisor is," she said to the empty room.

She started back out onto the porch as the phone rang again.

"Hello, this is Paint & Shine, your source for cultural tours in the Kentucky Highlands."

"Hi, Miranda. It's Rowena Gardner. You sound just the same as you did in high school. Way more professional, though."

Miranda laughed. "Hi, Rowena. It is you. I couldn't believe it when Mr. Tobin mentioned your name. You sound the same too."

That voice brought back a memory of them trying out for the cheerleader team in their high school gym uniforms. Rowena's long dark hair and olive skin in the school's salmon suit fit her curvy shape in all the right places. On the other hand, back in those days, Miranda's figure had yet to appear. In fact, she didn't actually blossom until the following year.

"It's great to hear that we'll be working together. Although Mr. Tobin didn't seem to know much about your background."

"I am not surprised. He doesn't see any of his underlings as worth getting to know. Anyway, he's sending me over to help manage the workshop. Mr. Tobin is going to make this workshop competition a strategy for his recruitment goals for the new year. I'm not sure what he had in mind, but I'm sure it will be a passel of trouble."

"Are you staying up at the lodge?"

"No way. Mr. Tobin won't spring for the extra expense. I'll be going back and forth from Winchester every day. It's not a problem. I'm used to driving into the Lexington office. Driving to Hemlock Lodge will be quicker."

"That's nonsense. You can stay with me."

Sandy had patrolled all the rooms in the farmhouse as soon as Miranda set him down. Now he was back at her feet and nipping at her ankles. "Stop that."

"Stop what?" Rowena asked.

"Sorry, it's not you. It's my puppy, Sandy. He wants some attention. Where was I? Oh, if you stay here, you'll be right on the spot for any problems that might come up. Plus, we can catch up on old times before the event gets underway. I think it's going to be fantastic, but I expect we'll be run off our feet. Please come."

"Really? Do you mean that? Are you sure I won't be putting you out just when you'll be busy keeping all these candidates focused on your workshop?"

Miranda laughed. "Actually, I would be taking advantage of you in helping to keep everything running smoothly. My mom has gone back to Dayton to close the sale of her house. You could take her room."

"I'm not sure."

"Come on. We have so much catching up to do. It would be more fun to do that before the madness begins. Please come. Pretty please?"

"Well," chuckled Rowena, "how can I possibly resist a pretty please?"

"Great. Come on over tonight and we can have a nice, long chat before the workshop starts. Mom's bedroom is upstairs, so it comes with some privacy. It also has a desk, and I finally have great Wi-Fi connectivity. You'll love it."

"Perfect, but I'll bring over some wine. Luckily, I brought my laptop home from work today. Somehow I knew I might be required at the last minute. Mr. Tobin is not big on well-thought-out plans, as usual. I'll pack up and be at your place in a couple of hours. Text me your address."

Miranda sent the text, and then she refreshed things in her mom's upstairs bedroom. She changed the sheets, replaced the quilt with a fresh one, and cleared out a space in the top drawer of the dresser. She also removed a few of her mother's clothes to give Rowena a slim slot in the closet.

In order to chase the lingering scent of her mom's cologne from the bedroom, she opened the front window. It looked out over the dirt road that ran by the farmhouse. Her last touches were to set out fresh towels, put a carafe of water on the nightstand, and set a vase of wildflowers on the desk. Miranda dusted all the furniture, then gave the floor a quick sweep. All was in visitor-perfect shape.

Rowena arrived at the farmhouse a few hours later in a clean but elderly blue Ford Fiesta. Miranda ran to the car. They squealed their delight. She gave Rowena a giant hug standing right in front of the open car door.

"Rowena! You look wonderful. What have you done to your hair? My memory might be tricking me, but I thought it was straight—stick straight, in fact. Now it's curly and absolutely gorgeous."

"I stopped trying to make it stay straight. This is my natural hair, and I'm happier not worrying about it. It takes me no time at all to get ready for work now."

"I love it. It suits you," said Miranda. "Let's get your luggage put away." Rowena pulled a small, wheeled suitcase out of the trunk. She also had a backpack that held her work laptop and its electronic paraphernalia and a large black handbag. Then, finally, a special office box containing hanging folders of papers for the workshop participants. Miranda picked up the file box. "Head into the house and up the stairs in the dining room. Go right on through the storage area. The bedroom is at the front of the house. There's a small desk right in front of the window for you."

Miranda followed a few paces behind. Rowena stood in front of the desk and looked around the room. "This is delightful. So cozy. Is that one of your grandmother's quilts?"

"Yep, I'm knee-deep in them. That sounds like I'm complaining, doesn't it? I'm grateful she's still able to keep up with her main pleasure in life." Miranda placed the box on the small desk. "Would you like a worktable as well? I have several sizes."

"I can see you're used to working out of the office. Yes, please. I could use a small table, thank you very much." Miranda went to get it while Rowena opened her suitcase and stowed away her clothes in the mirrored dresser and in the small closet.

After she set up her laptop and work materials on the desk and portable table, Rowena pulled out a bottle of Shiraz from her suitcase. "I just grabbed this from my wine rack. It's an Australian blend that most people like." Then she lifted her eyebrows for a moment. "Plus, it has a screw top, and I don't have to show you how terrible I am at opening a bottle of wine."

Miranda smiled. "Perfect. I'll rustle up a charcuterie board. I have some local cheeses, sugar-cured ham slices, homemade peach marmalade, and some crackers. Come on down when you're settled in. We'll snug up on the living room couch in front of the fire."

Rowena came downstairs. "This is a beautiful farmhouse. So cozy, with real country touches." She pointed to a runner rug in the dining room and a matching circular rug in the living room. "They're gorgeous. They match everything perfectly. Your grandmother again?"

"Yep. She's a real dynamo. I just gave her the remaining fabric from my new curtains, and she braided these up in only a couple of weeks." Miranda smiled. "It's nice to have her so near. She loves her life at the Campton Rehabilitation Center."

"What? Do you mean a nursing home? She's happy there?"

"Yes, very happy, but this one is different. All the residents are from this area, and they all have known each other since childhood. Every time I visit, I drag her away from some kind of activity. I've learned to check the website before I visit."

After a couple of hours, most of the bottle was gone and they had polished off all the meat, cheese, and crackers. They caught up with each other's families, covered Rowena's training as a secretary, and Miranda's art education in Savannah. Then Miranda outlined her unsuccessful stint in New York City, trying to break out as a landscape artist.

Rowena frowned. "I've had more than my fair share of boyfriend issues. I broke off a five-year engagement last year, so I ran from that. Unfortunately, I also had to leave a good job in marketing. I was lucky to find work at the BigSky Corporation. Stupidly, I've fallen into another bad relationship. At work again, of course. I'm such an idiot."

"You mean with someone you work with at BigSky?"

"I'm hoping not to repeat that experience anytime soon. Not the getting engaged part anyway. I still like going out dancing. Never mind me. I don't want to talk about it. What about you?" Rowena raised her eyebrows at Miranda,

"Well, I'm not married, but I must say, a forest ranger lives next door. He is not only a pleasure to look at, but he's kind. That and, of course, he makes me laugh."

"Is it serious?"

Miranda looked at her former classmate and scrunched her brow. "I think there's some sign of it, but I'm so focused on getting this business up and running, I'm not really thinking about that. That might be a mistake."

"It feels as though we graduated from high school last week. How nice to reconnect." She looked down into her empty wineglass. "Let's not lose each other again."

Miranda collected their glasses, plates, knives, and napkins and piled them on the empty charcuterie board. "I feel the same, and I don't intend to lose track of you either." She looked at the empty wine bottle. "Would you like to have a sample of my moonshine? It makes for a great nightcap."

"You make shine?"

"Yep. That's a condition of my uncle's will. In order to keep the farm, I need to have a distillery up and running within the first three months."

"What happens if you don't make the deadline?"

Miranda stood stone still with her blue eyes open wide. "The entire property reverts to my second cousin." She shrugged her shoulders. "He owns the adjoining property, so it won't exactly go out of the family. I've been so focused on getting things running, I didn't realize how fast the date is coming." She headed into the kitchen.

"What is the date?"

"I think it's either Christmas Eve or New Year's Eve. I'll find out from my uncle Gene Buchanan's executor on Monday. I also want to find out how I prove that I've met the conditions." She looked over her shoulder. "Come on back. We'll sit in the kitchen."

Miranda put the charcuterie board on the counter. She motioned for Rowena to sit in one of the oak chairs at the little enamel kitchen table. After she had dealt with the dishes, she got out two small mason jars and put two ice cubes in each. She got a lime from the refrigerator and sliced it into wedges. Then she filled the jars with equal measures of Seagram's ginger ale and her latest batch of moonshine. She swiped the rim with the lime wedge and dunked it in as a garnish.

Sitting down at the table, Miranda raised her jar. "A toast to a rediscovered friendship. May we not get lost again." They clinked their jars, and each sipped the cocktail.

Rowena's eyes widened. "This is wonderful! It's smooth, fresh, and not a bit harsh going down."

"Thanks, that's exactly what I was going for. I've finally replicated my uncle's famous recipe, and I've got the making of it down to a manageable job."

Rowena took another sizable sip. Then leaned back in her chair. "It's just lovely. I'm not a real fan of hard liquor. I prefer my red wines. What are your overall plans for the property?"

"Nothing simple, of course. I'm struggling to finish getting the distillery in the barn approved. There are still some licensing issues, but I'm making do with my uncle's original still until the construction stage is complete. Big projects out in the country are a complete nightmare."

"Better you than me. I'm happy to work for my bread in the corporate world. It's safe and predictable." Rowena downed the last of her cocktail. "I'd better try to get a little sleep. I'm happy about the overtime, but the workshop will be stressful. Everything is always stressful with this company."

"Really? I had hoped for a nice group of outdoorsy types eager to learn something about art as well as cookery."

"Not this time," said Rowena. "Hey, is that your boot?"

Sandy was standing in the doorway to the kitchen with a hiking boot hanging by its tongue from his mouth. He tilted his head sideways, and the boot clomped to the floor.

"Oh, Sandy!" Miranda lurched out of her chair and grabbed up the boot. "Oh no. This is one of my new boots."

Sandy looked up with adoring puppy eyes.

Chapter 2

Saturday Morning, Hemlock Lodge

Miranda parked her van in front of the historic Hemlock Lodge in Natural Bridge State Park. She grabbed the lint brush and swiped down her tan skinny jeans topped by a white logo golf shirt and also a serviceable black, all-weather coat to handle the unpredictable November weather.

She never tired of the feeling of wholesome warmth and comfort she associated with the sixties-style stone and wooden lodge. It was perched on a dramatic ledge overlooking a deep valley complete with a small lake and a resort-style swimming pool. Her mother was terrified of heights and would insist that the table for their Sunday buffet dinners had to be as far from the floor-to-ceiling glass windows as possible.

The first person she saw was the lodge's longtime receptionist, Doris Ann Norris. She had been working at the lodge for so many years, no one could remember who she'd replaced.

Miranda walked over to her desk just beyond the foyer and across from the fireplace lounge. "Hi, Doris Ann. Have you seen my group yet?"

Doris Ann tucked a strand of silver hair back into a small bun at the nape of her neck. "Sweetie, they've been straggling in by onesies and twosies since I got here at seven. I been tellin' them how to get to the private area in the dining room."

"You're a star. Thanks for your help. There should be a total of ten participants with a manager and an administrative assistant. So, including me, it's a total of thirteen."

"That's bad luck!"

Miranda laughed. "Not always. I love the number thirteen. Some of my luckiest days have fallen on the thirteenth."

"Like what?"

"My first day on campus at the Savannah College of Art and Design was on Friday the thirteenth in September of 2013. My first large painting sold on Friday the thirteenth in November of 2015. Sorry, I'll catch up with you later. I need to meet my clients before the orientation starts at eight."

She waved a hand at Doris Ann and made her way to the far end of the dining room. The lodge didn't have a conference room, but Doris Ann was able to rustle up a few felt-backed partitions to mark off an area at the back of the large hall. A delightful bonus was access to the nonstop breakfast buffet.

The temporary conference room provided plenty of seating, and there was a whiteboard on wheels at one end with loads of markers. The conference table was set with writing tablets, pens, folders with the Hemlock Lodge logo that were probably left over from some past event.

Doris Ann has outdone herself.

Each setting also had a glass, and water pitchers were placed on folded napkins down the center. A side table was set up with coffee, tea, orange juice, and a plate piled high with fresh doughnuts, along with biscuits, butter, and honey.

Miranda smiled as she mentally thanked the receptionist. Doris Ann had gone the extra mile to help her clients feel welcome during the orientation presentation of this four-day workshop.

There were six people standing around with the lodge's thick white coffee cups, enjoying a jolt of caffeine. Rowena had claimed a spot down at the opposite end from the whiteboard. She had a row of badges lined up and a sheet of paper with names listed for checking off.

"Hi, Miranda. Here's your badge. I hope I didn't wake you this morning. There's so much to set up for these off-site corporate events. I wanted an early start."

"No, you managed to get away without even bothering Sandy. That's quite a feat." Miranda pinned the badge just above the Paint & Shine logo. Her name appeared under the BigSky logo. "How many are you expecting? I was told there would be ten."

"Right, there are ten participants. So that adds up to a total of thirteen, counting you, whoever is Mr. Tobin's replacement, and me as the administrative assistant." Rowena tilted her head, and her smile indicated satisfaction.

"I'll let my cooks know. I would have liked to have known that earlier. You know, like, when I was ordering the food." Miranda gave Rowena a stern look but couldn't hold it long. She grinned. "Right, it's not a problem. I always have extra food."

As the time drew towards eight o'clock, all the badges were given out to participants, but there was a lonely badge still on the table. The name read Terry Burns.

Miranda looked out into the dining room but didn't see anyone, so she walked over to the lobby area and stood in front of the reception desk. "Thanks for the extra effort with the conference room, Doris Ann. I truly appreciate it. It's going to work perfectly for presentations."

"You're more than welcome, Miranda. We want you to succeed. Every tourist you bring makes a big difference to our local businesses."

"Thanks. That makes up for some of the worrying." She furrowed her brow. "I don't think I told you, but there's a substitute manager who should be arriving any minute. Have you seen anyone?"

"No, but I did get a call a few minutes ago for directions. He was a gruff feller—very impatient—like it was all my fault he was lost."

"That must be him." She looked at her watch. It was already fifteen minutes past eight. "I think we'll start anyway. This workshop is packed to the brim. Send him in when he gets here." She started to turn back, then stopped.

Miranda inhaled a long, deep breath to relieve her stress. Not an ideal way to start her first corporate event. This wasn't actually her fault, but she was prone to feeling guilty about anything that went wrong that connected with her business.

I need to lighten up.

She walked back to the partitioned section and stood beside the whiteboard. Around the table were five men, five women, and Rowena. They looked at her with some curiosity, and she felt a little anxiety, too.

Miranda cleared her throat and began. "Welcome to the first Paint & Shine Team Building Workshop. My name is Miranda Trent. I will be leading you through four days of exciting activities, challenges, and learning experiences. They will range from art projects to physical feats to culinary events, along with brewing your own moonshine."

There were lifted heads, nods, smiles, and smirks among the participants. Just the reaction Miranda was hoping to see.

"First, we need to get to know one another, so if you please, state your name, where you were born, your job and how long you've been with BigSky, and, finally, one interesting fact that no one would guess about you."

There was a din of chatter around the table. She thought she would wait until they quieted, but the more aggressive members were still trying to establish dominance within the group rather than settle down.

She rapped her knuckles on the table and cleared her throat.

"I'll start. My name is Miranda Trent. I was born not far from here in Hazel Green, Kentucky. I'm not an employee of BigSky, but I am a new subcontractor with hopes of making this workshop a permanent part of your management training program. As for an unusual fact, I play the mandolin just like Ricky Skaggs, except I'm not as good." She pointed to the tall blonde on her left. "Now you."

"Good morning. I'm Carol Hampton, originally from Troy, Ohio. I've been working as a benefits specialist in human resources for a little over a year. I was the cheerleader captain in high school." She tossed her long blond locks and turned to the petite redhead next to her.

"Oh, hi. I'm Lisa Porter," she said in a hoarse whisper. "Sorry, sorry. I'm having a bit of voice trouble because of the pollen out here." She paused and took a drink of water from the glass in front of her. "That's better. Sorry. I'm from Cincinnati, Ohio, and I've been a cost clerk in the accounting department for about three months." She coughed, then took another sip of water. "I collect rare teacup sets."

The next woman was writing furiously in a small black notebook. Lisa nudged her with an elbow, causing her to drop her pen.

"What?" She looked around at the participants and tucked a stray brown hair behind her ear. "Right. I'm Janice Utz. I'm from Maysville, Kentucky. I work in the purchasing department as a buyer. I've been with BigSky for a little over three years. During that time, I have completed my master's degree in marketing at the University of Kentucky." She pushed her tortoiseshell glasses back in place with a finger that showed clear evidence of nailbiting. "I'm an instructor of Taoist Tai Chi at the Friends Meeting House in Lexington."

The next woman, ivory-skinned, with a jet-black undercut bob, and wearing black from head to toe, stood up, waited until she made eye contact with everyone, then smiled.

"Good morning, everyone. I already know most of you, but my name is Eileen Hoffman, from Brooklyn, New York. I work in the marketing department and specialize in promoting our company using social media campaigns. I've been with the company for about five years. I am a lawn bowling champion and raise prize-winning Wyandotte chickens." Eileen sat and waved a hand like Vanna White for her neighbor to talk. "You're next. Speak up so we can hear you."

The young Black man blinked deliberately with a pained look. He sighed nearly soundlessly, but Miranda caught the inference that this wasn't the only time he'd received a thoughtless barb from Eileen.

He looked up at Miranda and spoke with a clear but soft voice. "My name is Xavier Johnson. I'm a newly hired graduate with a master's degree in international marketing. I'm from Birmingham, Alabama, and I guess my unusual fact is that I play the five-string banjo like Earl Scruggs."

The next participant opened his mouth to speak, but a harried, slightly overweight man burst in around the end partition. He was dressed in a crisp navy suit with a white shirt and a blue-and-white University of Kentucky Wildcats tie. "Hold everything. I've got some announcements." He marched over to the whiteboard and stood in front of Miranda.

He must be Terry Burns. This can't be good.

The man puffed out his chest. "This is no longer an individual player competition. Mr. Tobin directed me to split you into two teams to more accurately predict your behavior when working within BigSky."

Miranda stepped beside him. "Good morning. You're Terry Burns, I presume." Miranda reached out her hand. "Your boss told me to expect you in his place."

He ignored it and frowned. "He's not my boss. I am his senior. This workshop was my idea. Understand?" Then he abruptly shook her hand with a soft grip. "You must be the organizer."

"Yes, I'm Miranda Trent. What a nice surprise for your

employees." She stepped right beside him and indicated the empty chair right beside Rowena. "We've set aside a place for you to observe. As soon as we've finished the introductions, there will be plenty of time for announcements." She glared at him. His company had contracted her to conduct this workshop. She was going to do just that. Her way.

She stood even taller. "Let's pick up where we left off, shall we?" She looked down at the conference table and noticed that Carol was staring at a man with a shaved head. Her face had turned a mottled shade of red.

Miranda was puzzled by that reaction, but she pointed to a short, stocky man who appeared to be the youngest in the group. "I believe you're next."

"Yes, I am." He was a bit chubby, and his voice was pitched high and scratchy, as if he had been up too late at some smoke-ridden party. "My name is Victor Zane. I'm originally from Bowling Green, Kentucky, and I like living so close to my family. I'm a recently hired clerk in the shipping department. I don't really know why they sent me, but I'm really glad to be here. Really."

There was a short silence.

"Oh, I almost forgot," said Victor. "My hobby is flying radio-controlled airplanes, and I play the drums for a local garage band."

The next man stopped scribbling notes and put down his pen, then ran both hands through his red, curly hair. "Hi, I'm Oliver Young. I'm from Laguna Beach, California. I've been working in the legal department for about three months. As you might guess, my hobby is surfing, but since I've been living here, I've taken up cliff climbing in Red River Gorge."

"I'm John O'Reilly," said the tallest of the participants. Even sitting, he was an impressive, athletic figure. "I'm from Tampa, Florida, and I've been working in the quality assurance department for almost six months. My unusual trait is that I love baking bread. Mostly sourdough. I'm not vegan or anything, even though sourdough bread is vegan. I just like baking it."

Miranda felt her eyes widen and a catch in her throat. *Oh, heavens to Betsy! I haven't given a single thought to a vegan participant. I'm escaping this time, but I've got to add dietary issues to my sign-up form.*

"My turn." The next participant displayed a tooth-dominated grin that looked a little sharklike. "My name is Sheila Collins, and I'm a new employee with the IT department. I've mostly been going through the Microsoft certification process so I can take over the training modules we send our employees to off-site. That will save the company a lot of money as soon as I pass my tests. I'm from Centerville, Ohio, and my hobby is singing in a gospel quartet. I also play the organ—a little." She flushed at this last statement.

"Thank you. Now I think there are a few announcements from your company representative, Mr. Terry Burns." She waved a hand for him to join her at the whiteboard.

"Wait, wait. You skipped me," said the tall, well-muscled man with the shaved head.

"I'm sorry," said Miranda. "I apologize. Please introduce yourself."

He stood up and scanned the group. "My name is Jeffrey Nelson. My parents are from Canada, but I was born in New York City. I got a football scholarship to the University of Kentucky. I studied global marketing and finance. BigSky hired me for their new outreach initiative to succeed in the competitive international sportswear arena." He gave a long stare at Mr. Burns. "I don't have a fun fact." He sat.

Mr. Burns made his way down the room and sedately nodded at each employee like royalty. He stopped at his chair and folded his arms. "The good news is that the winning team will be assigned to our progressive, Fast Track program for management stars. There is a lot at stake here." He sat down. "Your whole future depends on the outcome of this competition. This is not a company-paid vacation."

There were rumbles of protest around the table.

"I didn't think so," said Sheila.

"Of course not," confirmed Victor

"Who would think that?" Xavier leaned back to show his shock.

Rowena sighed wearily and pulled out a stenographer's pad and pen from her laptop bag. She spoke loud enough for everyone to hear. "How did you want to choose the teams?" Her words were clipped and her jaw tight. Miranda was irritated as well. She didn't even work for their company.

Mr. Burns pulled a folded slip of paper from his suit jacket and gave it to Rowena.

Rowena opened it, scanned it, then placed it face down in front of her. Then she resumed writing on her pad.

"That note lists the members of the two teams," Mr. Burns continued. "Each team needs to elect a leader and a team name. Rowena will take care of scoring the two teams and keeping everyone apprised of the scores."

Rowena was sipping on her coffee. She put down the cup and showed the group a tiny smile. "Absolutely, Mr. Burns." She returned to taking notes.

Mr. Burns continued without even glancing at Rowena.

"I've got two sets of the latest designer BigSky golf shirts for the participants to wear. HR gave Mr. Tobin your sizes, and he had them pulled from the stockroom."

He looked down the table to Rowena, then continued when she looked up to make eye contact. "I've left the boxes with the lodge receptionist. What's her name?" He snapped his fingers. "Oh, Doris Ann. You can hand them out after I leave."

Miranda twisted her head towards Mr. Burns, her brow creased into a frown. "You're leaving?"

He turned to face her. "I have an important conference call that couldn't be rescheduled. I expect you'll be able to continue with the orientation. That is what we contracted you to do, right?"

Miranda displayed a tight smile and pressed her lips into a straight line. "I require a private word before you go." She motioned for him to follow her through a door that led to the outside balcony that circled the entire lodge on the cliff-view side.

He raised his eyebrows, but he followed.

He's obviously not used to having his underlings challenge his actions.

Miranda turned to face him. She could feel the blood flushing up from her neck to her ears. "I'm quite comfortable giving the orientation your company insisted in our contract be given by a company executive." She stepped in front of him with her back to the glass windows and spoke in a crisp tone.

He folded his arms. "Plans change."

"Mr. Burns, I understand that plans change, but don't expect that I will accommodate them in silence if I don't have the proper resources. I'll tell you upfront about my concerns and will let you know if it changes my price."

"That's not a problem. Frank Tobin and I agreed that Rowena would do the paperwork for human resources. She will also take care of recording all the scores, so there's no extra work for you. Your contract stays the same." He looked back at the attendees and then stared at Rowena, as if daring her to challenge him.

She stood tall. "Rowena explained how she was handling it last night. She's staying with me at the farmhouse. We're old friends."

"That's perfect, then. You won't mind telling her, will you?" He turned and walked back into the dining room, leaving Miranda with her mouth open.

"Of course. I would be happy to do that," she said to his rapidly disappearing form. "No problem. I'll take it from here."

Miranda returned to the conference room and looked at the participants. She could feel that her own eyes were wide with all the organizational bombs Mr. Burns had just dropped on her and Rowena and the participants.

How are we to provide a focus on team building when there are so many changes? This is not the right message.

In the back of the room, Rowena had turned pale, but her eyes were narrowed in determination.

"Thank you for your patience while we rearrange some of our plans to accommodate the competition twist," said Miranda. "Hopefully, with Rowena handling the scoring, we can make this a life-changing experience for you. Oh, for Mr. Burns, too, of course."

On cue, he stepped to the front of the conference room, then glared at each participant around the table. "Don't forget. This is a test of your management potential. Are you good enough to help catapult BigSky to the leading sportswear graphics designer in the world? Do you have the spirit, energy, and creativity BigSky needs to win? That's what I need to know." Then he waved his hand for Rowena to join him outside again on the balcony.

Her face lost even more color, but she grabbed up her pen and tablet and trotted after him.

Miranda started up the projection system as it displayed the first slide, its heading indicating it was the Health and Safety Briefing. "While they're working out some administration details, let's get our housekeeping done. I know you're all athletic, but I still want to cover some trail basics."

The slides reviewed the commonsense things to do while out on the trails. Miranda covered those issues quickly but thoroughly. "Any questions?"

Silence from the group.

"Fine, let's take a fifteen-minute comfort break before I lay out the plans for the rest of the day."

As everyone filed out, Rowena returned with a chalky look around her mouth.

"What's wrong?"

Rowena inhaled a shaky breath. "You can't tell anyone. Promise?"

"Of course I promise." Miranda gave her friend a side hug. "You're upset. Tell me. I won't say a word to anyone."

"I've just talked to Mr. Burns. He says that all the members of the losing team will be fired."

Chapter 3

Saturday Morning, Hemlock Lodge

"You can't take this personally," whispered Miranda. She gave Rowena a shoulder rub and led her back to the foot of the conference table. They sat together for a few seconds in silence.

Rowena scrabbled in her laptop bag and drew out a packet of tissues. She blew her nose and dabbed delicately at her eyes with a corner of a tissue. She managed it without smudging her mascara. She sniffed and mumbled, "I don't think this is a proper workshop at all."

"What do you mean?" Miranda drew herself upright. "I worked hard on making this workshop part fun, part adventure, and a big part educational. It's going to be a great team-building experience."

Rowena sniffed. "That's not what I mean." She looked Miranda straight in the eyes. "I think this is just a way to get rid of employees without having to worry about getting sued by them."

"How does that work?"

"Look at the list of teams that were drawn up by Mr. Tobin." She handed over the slip of paper. "What do you notice about the team assignments?"

Miranda crinkled her brow and scanned the names. "I don't see anything. It's just a list of five names in two groups."

"Right. But now look at the lists through the eyes of a manager who doesn't want to include diversity in the management ranks."

Miranda looked at the list again. "Oh my goodness. I see what you mean. One team is mostly women and the other team is predominately men."

"Exactly," said Rowena.

"But why?" Miranda splayed her hands wide. "This is supposed to be a team-building experience to reveal unknown skills and talents."

"Well, it struck me as an easy way to get rid of women and minorities without having to actually go through a paperwork process. Although, conversely, it appears to me that this paper trail could leave them wide open for the very lawsuits they want to avoid. I don't think they've consulted anyone. They think they're clever, but because the teams were created by management, there is evidence of bias—putting women and minorities in one group."

"I understand your reasoning, but I'm not convinced. It seems such a convoluted way to cull the herd."

"Convoluted is the perfect word for management. I'll be documenting the scores for your challenges. I think they will be used to justify why those candidates aren't suitable management material for BigSky. They'll be fired."

Miranda shuddered. "Good heavens. That's horrible. How on earth can you work for them?"

Rowena shrugged. "It's not easy to get a good job with only a junior college associate degree. I took some adult night classes in secretarial skills. Honestly though, they pay really well, they have a comprehensive university tuition refund program, and they have a wonderful benefits package. Most of the managers are good people. You know, the outdoorsy, ecologically green, quirky kind of folks. If I walked out now, I might never get a job this good." She shrugged again. "I'll put up with a lot to have job security."

Miranda didn't bargain for this kind of career-killing result to the attendees of her workshop. Could she play this so that everyone's scores were high enough to keep their jobs?

"Listen, Rowena, let's get around this. I'm clever, and so are you. We're going to beat this nasty little management game. We should be able to manipulate the results into a tie. We'll have to be a little clever about it, though. That'll fix their wagon."

The participants returned and resettled in the conference room. Miranda stood at the front of the room with the slip of paper with everyone's name assigned to a team.

"As you heard from Mr. Burns, there are to be two teams competing against each other. He has assigned the following members to what I'm calling Team A. Carol Hampton, Lisa Porter, Janice Utz, Eileen Hoffman, and Xavier Johnson. That leaves Jeffrey Nelson, Oliver

Young, Victor Zane, John O'Reilly, and Sheila Collins as the members of Team B."

There was a moment of silence and then a chattering of protests and objections. Miranda was beginning to wonder if maybe she might need a whistle to get their attention.

She stood tall and squared her shoulders. "Attention, attention, attention." She waited a moment, then tapped her knuckles on the table. "I need your full attention." She waited until the hubbub died down and they were all looking at her.

"Now, let's get back to the workshop." She used both hands to point at the opposite sides of the table. "Let's reconfigure ourselves to have Team A on this side and Team B on this side. Before you choose a seat, you must select a team leader and then choose a team name. The team leaders will sit up here in the first seats." She looked at her watch. "You have ten minutes."

The participants stood and organized themselves into the two groups and started the noisy process of deciding leadership roles.

"Hey!" Doris Ann bellowed over the din from the entrance to the makeshift conference room. "If y'all don't quiet down, you're gonna get thrown down the mountain for the bears to eat. This is a civilized dining room and we don't hold with that kind of behavior."

There was immediate silence in the conference room.

"Doris Ann, I am so, so sorry," said Miranda. "I apologize. We were just given some unsettling news. We certainly know how to behave in polite company, don't we?" There were nods of agreement around the room. "It won't happen again."

Doris Ann gave each participant a look that would have sent a hardened criminal slinking under the table. "This is your only warning. Next time, out you go." She turned on her heel and disappeared behind the partitions.

Miranda inhaled a huge breath and puffed out her cheeks in an exasperated sigh. "That was close." She looked at the participants. "If she wants to close us down, I'm in big trouble, but you'll be in bigger trouble."

There were murmurs of varying apologies around the room.

"I'm sorry."

"No excuses."

"I didn't mean it."

"Didn't want to cause trouble."

Miranda rubbed the back of her neck. "I'll give you an extra five minutes."

The two teams gathered in tight groups. Each stood on their side of the conference room table, whispering as forcefully as possible.

Miranda found the situation absurd and glanced over to Rowena. It looked like she had the same issue. Miranda bit her lip. Bursting out into giggles would not help the situation at all.

At about the ten-minute mark, Miranda announced, "This is your five-minute warning. You need to come back to sit where your assigned leader is at the head of the table."

Both teams arranged themselves around the conference table. Carol Hampton was sitting in the team leader seat of one side, while Jeffrey Nelson was sitting in the team leader spot on the other side. All the participants relocated themselves and appeared ready for the challenges ahead.

"Thank you for your cooperation. I see you've made your team captain selections. Congratulations, Carol and Jeffrey." She led a polite round of applause. "I would like each captain to stand and tell us your team name and then describe the motivation that inspired it. Carol, please start."

Carol stood, then cleared her throat. "Our team name is Firehawks. We feel that it represents our burning passion for providing the best outdoor garments coupled with a fierce loyalty to the environment. It describes the way we intend to lead the BigSky corporation to success not only financially but also ecologically. We can't lead on a global level without addressing global issues."

"That's a great name." Miranda looked over to Jeffrey. "And you?"

He stood and shifted his weight from one foot to the other. He gulped down the last dregs of his coffee. "We picked Sweatsocks as our team name."

Miranda tilted her head. "I'm sorry, what was that?"

"Sweatsocks," repeated Jeffrey. "We spent most of our time figuring out who was the leader. So I just picked the last thing we shipped out of the warehouse   sweat socks."

Miranda was struck by the difference in maturity between the two teams with the naming decision motivation. She wondered if Mr. Tobin's elimination scheme was going to backfire on him. That would be just deserts.

She smiled, then resumed her announcements.

"Our first competition of the day is to hike to the overlook at Lover's Leap. We're all going to do a sketch of the rock formation. I will lead by example and give you detailed instructions. Each team will submit all their drawings for a blind critique."

"Who's going to do the judging?" asked Jeffrey.

"Good question. Your drawings will be judged by our local forest ranger, Austin Morgan. He's an expert on the local lore of that area. He'll give us one of his famous ranger talks, and then he'll choose the sketch that best portrays the historical setting."

"What does the winner get?" piped up Sheila.

"Rowena, could you address that?" said Miranda.

"Sure." Rowena came to the front of the conference room with her stenographer's tablet. "Each drawing will be judged on three factors." She referred to her notes. "One for drawing technique, the second for geographical accuracy, and last for atmosphere and emotion. The winning sketch will earn a point for their team."

The participants began to ask questions all at once.

"Quiet," said Miranda. "Raise your hands. We'll get to all of you, but we only have ten minutes before we need to get on the trail." She pointed to Sheila.

"What do we do if it snows?"

"Snows? It's too early in the season for snow." Miranda looked around the partition and out through the tall windows of the dining room. She stepped back into the conference room.

"Well, no one told Mother Nature." She looked out again at the soft, fluffy flakes. "It will make footing a little tricky and visibility challenging, but not really impossible. Those flakes actually mean it shouldn't last long. Hang on, let me see if we can cancel this event." She texted Mr. Burns:

Miranda: Snowing. There's a chance we'll cancel.

Mr. Burns: No. Fantastic first challenge.

Miranda: Risky trail conditions could cause an accident.

Mr. Burns: Are the trails closed?

Miranda: Not at this time.
Mr. Burns: Proceed, or I'll have Rowena take over.
Miranda: Will safely continue if the trail is open.
Mr. Burns: I'll see you on the trail.
Miranda: Not if it's closed.

For a moment, she stared at her phone.

He has no clue whatsoever.

Miranda looked out the window at the cotton fluffs and at her anxious participants, then back at the snow.

"We're going ahead. Everyone needs to follow my instructions carefully." She planted a huge smile on her face. "It's going to be exciting."

Chapter 4

Saturday Morning, Natural Bridge State Park

Everyone grabbed up their Paint & Shine backpacks loaded with art materials and water bottles. They started out on the trail that began from the back door of the lodge and led straight up the rugged bluff.

They started out in one massed group but slowly sorted themselves into their two teams. The Sweatsocks bulldogged in front of the Firehawks until they were several hundred feet ahead.

Miranda placed herself and Rowena in between in case there were any trail questions or injuries. She didn't really know how wilderness savvy these folk might be.

Apparently, the Sweatsocks weren't aware that sound traveled in weird ways in the gorges and cliffs. You could scream at someone ten feet from you in order to be heard, yet someone a quarter of a mile away could whisper and be understood.

Jeffrey and Oliver were at the back of the Sweatsocks group.

Jeffrey spoke under his breath. "I just don't see how Mr. Burns thinks he can get away with this. You know that he's loaded the teams in an obviously sexist and prejudiced way. You know what that means, don't you?"

Oliver huffed his disgust. "He's so obvious. You would think at his management level, he would have a little more finesse."

Jeffrey laughed. "Finesse. Mr. Burns will never be accused of that."

Oliver joined him in a round of stifled laughter.

Although the trail was steep, it didn't take long to climb to their first remarkable site.

"Whew!" said Carol, panting like an overheated Labrador. "That was steep, but this view is totally worth the climb. Is the whole area like this?"

Jeffrey grinned and stood beside Carol. "Stunning."

One by one, Carol's team straggled in and joined Miranda, Rowena, and the Sweatsocks. Already they were behaving as two competing teams. The Sweatsocks grouped at the top end of the Balanced Rock Trail, while the Firehawks stood next to Miranda, slightly below the rock.

Rowena gave Miranda a tiny wave and moved to a spot at the far edge of the trail. She put down her small daypack and pulled out a pen and her stenographer's notebook. It was a not-so-subtle reminder that her job was to observe, not participate.

Silence followed, except for the heavy breathing. That finally ended after a few minutes as both teams stood gazing at the view. Just as Miranda had predicted, the fluffy snowflakes lasted for about ten minutes, leaving behind delicate patches of white highlighting the bright red, yellow, and orange foliage.

It was a meditative silence. The kind where you believed your soul could drink up the spirit of the mountains. No one wanted to break the spell.

"We're not there yet," said Miranda.

Thirty minutes and six hundred climbing steps later, both teams joined up at the park's largest wooden shelter.

"Holy cow," Victor panted, "that was awful." He dragged himself over to the wide steps that led up to the wooden shelter and crashed down on the second step. Sweat dripped from his nose onto his BigSky golf shirt. He took the shirttail and wiped his face and neck. "How many of these challenges involve dragging ourselves up a freakin' mountain?"

"I can't say." Miranda folded her arms across her chest. "Mr. Burns has forbidden me to tell you about any of the challenges in advance. He's concerned that you might find some unfair advantage." She shrugged.

"That's harsh," said John.

"So, he already doesn't trust us?" said Sheila.

"Brilliant," said Janice.

"Congratulations," said Miranda. "You've climbed the steepest trail in this park. The sandstone block we passed is the reason it was named Balanced Rock Trail. It's also the best trail for stunning views of the iconic Natural Bridge. Your first challenge is to sketch the arch from any angle you choose."

"But I don't know how to draw," whined Janice. "That's not fair."

"Don't worry. No one is expecting Leonardo da Vinci sketches here. That's not—"

Janice interrupted. "Not a problem." The group laughed.

"The challenge isn't for the best drawing." Miranda caught the eye of each member. "The winner of the challenge will be for the sketch of Natural Bridge that represents the essence of your strongest leadership skill."

Jeffrey frowned. "Can you explain that a bit further?"

"It's not the artistry that will be judged. It's how you present your choice and how it relates to you as a future leader."

"Pffft," said Victor.

"Remember the purpose of this workshop," said Miranda. "It's to test your creativity, communication skills, leadership potential, and problem-solving abilities."

Miranda took off her backpack and pulled out ten thin drawing tablets. She gave five to Carol and five to Jeffrey. "Pass these out to your teams."

Carol and Jeffrey exchanged a long glance, then distributed the tablets.

"Now," continued Miranda, "let's all find a place to sit."

"On the ground?" Eileen looked around at the stone floor of the shelter. "This has probably never been swept."

Miranda tilted her head. "You are working for the leading manufacturer of outdoor gear, right?"

Carol moved to stand by Eileen. "Some of us work only on the construction and design part of product development." She coaxed Eileen to sit. "It's dry. Sit and be grateful it's not two inches of mud. Oh, and also be very glad the snow stopped."

Miranda continued. "We've hiked to this shelter where you have a chance to creatively interpret the iconic Natural Bridge. First, I'll give you a few pointers about landscape drawing. After that, you can go anywhere on the trail to sketch whatever inspires you."

"Oh no, I didn't bring a pencil," said Janice.

"What are we drawing with?" Victor whined.

"Oops, sorry. I forgot." Miranda pulled out ten packets from her backpack that each contained three drawing pencils, a soft white eraser, and a smudging stick. Again, she gave the packets to Carol and Jeffrey to hand out.

Then, everyone just looked at her, completely clueless as to what to do next.

You would think I asked them to skin a skunk. They're terrified of art.

"Go on, sit, sit." She waved her hands like shooing chickens. "It's a shelter. Make yourselves comfortable. We're going to do a practice sketch. It doesn't count in the competition. It's to get you familiar with the materials and learn some basic skills."

The two groups sat on opposite sides of the large shelter, and Miranda stood in the center. She explained the hardness differences between the 4B, 2B, and HB drawing pencils. Then she plunged into the five important drawing skills, including the ability to recognize edges, lines, and angles; recognize proportion and perspective; decipher shadow, highlights, and gradations of tone; and, lastly, the ability to unconsciously tie them all together.

"I understand that this is a lot to throw at you, but if you are open to drawing freely, it will be easier for you with practice."

She looked at the participants. Their reactions ranged from clear-eyed confidence to deer-in-the-headlights terror.

"Carol and Jeffrey, take your teams out to draw. Stay on the trail. You must all be back in this shelter in one hour. One hour exactly."

Everyone bolted into action with a flurry like flustered pigeons.

Miranda waved her hand at their disappearing backs and yelled her final instructions. "Be careful out there."

The two groups scattered in both directions up and down the trail.

Again Miranda yelled, "I'll be by in fifteen minutes to check that you've found your inspiration and give each of you a progress critique. Be ready."

Miranda motioned for Rowena to join her at the entrance to the shelter. "How do you think that went over?"

"About as well as it could." She nibbled at the little finger of her left hand, then realized what she was doing and quickly put it behind her back.

"We were lucky the snow stopped right after we set out on the trail. If it hadn't, I was going to call it off and take my lumps from Mr. Burns."

Rowena exhaled a pent-up breath. "Yes, I'm glad it stopped. For me, the consequences are losing this job."

"Really? You would get fired?"

"Yes. I'm convinced that Mr. Burns would have me fired." She nibbled on her right little finger again. "He's unpredictable. I don't know why he's still with the company after last year's disaster."

"What disaster?"

"There was a manufacturing error that cost the company millions. The sizing measurements for our most popular hoodie were transposed. Worse, the error wasn't discovered until they landed in our stores right before the fall college rush."

Miranda frowned. "How did he avoid getting fired?"

"He blamed it on the foreign manufacturer, but it

should have been caught during the quality check of the specifications."

"Why wasn't it?"

"He had decided to send out the order without that step."

Miranda shuddered. "I'm not very impressed with his management style, but then, I don't have to work for him. Are you going to be okay?"

"He always manages to have his way. He can be ridiculously charming at times. That usually works." Rowena smiled weakly. "If I can just survive these next few days, I think I can transfer to the Cincinnati division in the company."

"Is that possible? I would think you might need to leave the company altogether."

"The thing is, I love working there. Most of the people are wonderful. You see a mini version of the kinds of staff the company has. Most are fantastic, but some are awful."

"Well, it might be a financial hardship, but I can absolutely cancel this workshop at any time." Miranda patted Rowena on the shoulder. "Don't worry, we'll get through this. Come on, let's see how they're doing. Let's climb up first and be done with the uphill part of the day."

Rowena giggled. "So, even you get tired of the endless climbing?"

Miranda returned her smile. "Yes, it does seem that these trails are all uphill. Both ways. Even for me."

Rowena laughed.

They walked around the next bend and found Oliver sitting on a medium rock with his drawing pad. The sheet of drawing paper was completely blank. "Oh, I'm so glad to see you. I've never been good at drawing, but I can't even seem to get started."

Miranda squatted down next to him. "Don't panic. Representational images are just fine. This competition is more about your leadership style than artistic competency. What management skill do you want to illustrate?"

He scratched his scalp with the pencil. "I think I'm a free thinker with a great attitude."

Miranda nodded. "When you look around you, what shape or form do you think represents that kind of thinking?"

Oliver tilted his head, and then a warm smile lit up his face. "Oh, I see. It's what the drawing represents. Gotcha." He started rapidly sketching an amorphous, infinity-like shape. "Thanks."

They left him with his pencils flying and his head bent down to his work.

Next up the trail, they found Lisa leaning over her drawing pad on a boulder. She had brushed away the snow and was happily drawing one of the maple trees that spread its limbs out over the trail. She looked up and frowned.

"I'm not ready to show this to anyone." She lifted up her drawing pad and held it against her body. "I'm even less ready to talk about it."

"No problem." Miranda held up both her hands in a stop signal. "I'm here to help, but not if you don't want any." She stepped around Lisa and turned to Rowena. "Let's keep on with the others. Is she insecure?"

"She doesn't interact much with anyone at work."

That's an inconvenient trait for a prospective manager," said Miranda.

Rowena lowered her voice. "There've been a lot of rumors about her and Mr. Burns."

"Really? They don't behave like there's anything between them. In fact, I haven't seen them within yards of each other."

"I think it ended." Rowena frowned. "I also think it ended badly."

At the next turn they found three more members of Team Sweatsocks. Jeffrey, Victor, and John were standing in the middle of the trail arguing.

"That drawing is terrible," said Victor pointing his finger at John's sketch.

"It doesn't have to be that good," John shot back and stepped towards Victor.

"Then you've got it nailed," snapped Victor and stepped towards John.

"Hey, hey, hey," Jeffrey grumbled and put his drawing materials down on a rock. He stepped between the quarreling men and placed a hand on each chest. "This isn't a fighting matter, guys. This is supposed to be a team-building activity, not an excuse to get in a fistfight. What are you thinking? Rowena would be within her rights to report this to Mr. Burns."

Victor and John stepped back and looked straight at Rowena.

Victor tilted his head back. "Just great. Thanks, John. You've gotten us in trouble again." He shook his head from side to side. "Why do I do this?"

John bit his lip and turned to Rowena. "You're not going to mark this down in your book, are you? Victor and I are friends. You know that. We argue like this all the time. It's not serious."

"I know, I know," said Rowena. "Don't worry about it."

Miranda pointed to their blank drawing pads. "However, this is indeed an event that will be scored. You have to complete the assignment or you will get a zero. There is a style of art called nonrepresentational. It is a complete abstraction, where the lines, colors, and shapes themselves are the focus of the artwork, rather than any existing *thing*. As long as you claim that is your style, no one can challenge it."

Victor and John grinned like toddlers. Then nodded their heads and gathered up their materials. They sat on a nearby log and started to work.

Jeffrey folded his arms and spoke in a whisper. "Thanks, ladies. These two are loose cannons. They have some sort of political currency within the organization that I haven't figured out yet."

Miranda pressed her lips into a tight line. "You need to stop wandering off and keep them under control. These trails are beautiful, but Mr. Burns doesn't realize they are also dangerous."

"Dangerous?" asked Jeffrey.

"I warned him that our hike might be canceled or at least delayed because of the snow. Oddly, Mr. Burns wouldn't hear of it. In fact, I think he was thrilled that there might be harsh weather."

Jeffrey's eyes narrowed, and he swallowed a cough that he covered with his hand. "Got it," he said in a tight voice.

Miranda and Rowena turned back and walked down the trail to find Carol with three of her team members either sitting on or near one of the resting benches with their sketch pads balanced on their knees. Carol and Xavier sat on a large rock beside the bench. Each team member worked silently as they stared at the view that stretched across the Natural Bridge. Their sketches showed the whole team walking over the sandstone arch. The point of view was from the back. The near side of the bridge was barren and stark, while the far side was lush with pines and maples.

"It's only been twenty minutes," said Miranda to Carol. "Your team is doing a fantastic job. Great start."

Carol stood up and motioned for Miranda and Rowena to follow her down the trail.

Rowena gave Miranda a little shoulder shrug, but they both followed.

"I'm deeply concerned," Carol said in a low voice. "I'm afraid this competition nonsense violates a ton of employee rights laws. What on earth do Mr. Tobin and Mr. Burns think they're up to?"

Rowena shook her head slowly. "I don't know what's gotten into them."

"Is this a new behavior, or is it typical of their management style?" Miranda looked from Rowena to Carol and back to Rowena.

Carol lifted up both palms and shrugged. "I don't know either of them well enough to figure out their goals here. In fact, this is the first time I've met Mr. Burns. You'd think I would have by now. He's the vice president of operations."

Rowena sighed. "Sadly, this is pretty typical of Mr. Burns. Even as a vice president, he's very hands off. I haven't seen these kinds of shenanigans from Mr. Tobin. So far anyway. But the two of them have been holding a lot of meetings together now that there's an opening on the board of directors."

"That might explain their sudden collaboration," said

Carol. "But I don't understand how destroying this workshop helps them."

Rowena frowned. "Neither do I, but I can try to find out."

"Keep doing what you're doing, Carol."

Miranda motioned for Rowena to follow her. "Let's get back on track here. After dinner tonight, when the workshop is over for the day, I wonder if we can do some research about the legality of handing out a promotion to a special group as a result of competing in a workshop environment. There's bound to be someone I can ask."

"We can at least search the internet."

"I might give my uncle's estate executor a call. He's mostly retired and loves to research unusual points of law. If he finds this interesting, we'll have an answer in a few days."

They walked back up the trail to wait at the shelter. Rowena raised an eyebrow. "Everyone is just sketching away, exactly as you asked. You're an awesome teacher."

Miranda smiled. "Thanks. I work hard at that." She checked her watch. "We'll give them a few more minutes and then call time."

Rowena checked her watch, too. "I think there's more to this than a guaranteed opportunity to get into the Fast Track program. This feels more serious."

"Serious how?"

"There seems to be a lot of animosity towards Mr. Burns. More than I've felt back in the office."

"That could be the stress of the environment along with the competition."

"This is a serious, career-limiting pivot point. It's a serious business to place everyone's careers at risk," said Rowena.

Chapter 5

The team members returned to the wooden shelter showing varying levels of satisfaction with the exercise.

Miranda smiled both inside and out when she saw a tall man in a tan uniform leaning against the peeled log railing at the back of the shelter. Austin's arms were crossed over his wide chest. His eyes lit up when he noticed that she had seen him.

Miranda waited until everyone was seated on the stone floor of the shelter. She scanned the competitors for a head count. She counted to nine.

"Someone is missing. Who is it?"

Oliver pointed to the Firehawks. "They have no leader. Carol has abandoned her team."

Miranda rolled her eyes. "I'm sure that's not true. Has anyone seen—"

"Sorry, I'm right here," said Carol. She sounded out of breath and scrambled to sit with her team. "I got distracted by the view."

Miranda frowned and waited until everyone was quiet. She glanced at her watch. "We are running a little bit late. But if you've been to other national or state parks, you know that ranger talks are always a treat. I am pleased to introduce our local ranger, Austin Morgan of the Daniel Boone National Forest."

Austin tipped his flat-brimmed brown hat. "Happy to be here."

She waved for everyone to gather around Austin, and then she went to the back of the crowd. Rowena followed and stood beside her. Miranda could see the tension in her eyes and the stiffness in her stance.

Miranda whispered, "I expected to see Mr. Burns by now." Her phone pinged. "Right. He just texted that he would meet us on the trail." She looked back towards the trail. "I think even he would agree that this is a highlight of our experience out here this morning."

Rowena's phone pinged. "Well, not in his view. He's sent me his thoughts about even more challenges. I'll have a look down the trail to see if he's close by."

"Thanks, but I think—" Rowena slipped out of the crowd and trotted down the trail.

That was a very quick exit.

She turned to watch Ranger Morgan's program. She gave him a little hand wave and was pleased to see that he noticed.

He turned up the volume of his smile. "I want to thank Miss Trent for holding these outdoor trail experiences. She's helping our parks to entice visitors away from their screens into the natural beauty of Kentucky." He focused his gaze on the participants and scanned from left to right. Some seemed comfortable and interested. Some looked uncomfortable and irritated.

"I'll keep this short as I understand you have a set of challenges associated with your team-building workshop. I'm sure you noticed the unique formation called Balanced Rock on the way up here." He stopped and let the silence grow. "Right. It's impossible to miss. But a curious fact is that at a certain angle, it looks like a fuzzy imitation of the Sphinx in Egypt. Some old-timers have called it the Sphinx for decades.

"Although it is now called the Balanced Rock, it is, in fact, a pedestal rock—a single piece of stone that has weathered in such a fashion that its midsection is narrower than its cap or its base. This is one of the biggest and most perfectly formed examples of a pedestal rock east of the Rocky Mountains. We're proud of that."

Ranger Morgan grinned. "I don't want to just feed you facts. I'm here to answer your questions about the forest and the incredible sandstone arch, Natural Bridge. We also enjoy a microclimate that provides faster weather changes than you can track with the app on your phone— like our snow this morning, followed immediately by an Indian summer afternoon. Questions?"

Janice raised her hand. "Do you have bears?"

Ranger Morgan nodded. "Yes, we do. We have black bears that are very shy of people, so I doubt you'll see one. In 1900, black bears disappeared from this part of Kentucky. Logging destroyed the forests and also their den sites. Prior to that, more than one hundred fifty years of unregulated hunting. They left. But when the forests recovered and matured, they started to make a comeback in the late nineties. Now we get from twenty to thirty sightings a year."

"What about poisonous snakes?" asked Sheila.

Ranger Morgan put his thumbs in the armholes of his puffy brown jacket vest. "That's a smart question. You're here at the time of year when they're mostly in hibernation. Of the thirty-two types of snakes in our area, there are four venomous ones. Those are copperheads, cottonmouths, timber rattlesnakes, and pygmy rattlesnakes.

"That said, given our erratic weather, they could come out to warm up on a sunny rock. It pays to make lots of noise when you're on the trail. Not only to warn the snakes, but to give the other wildlife plenty of notice so that they can avoid you."

Ranger Morgan scanned the group. "Remember, stay on the trail. Leave nothing but footprints and take nothing but memories. Thank you for your attention."

Everyone applauded. Ranger Morgan tipped his hat at the group, then, hidden by the brim of his hat, he winked at Miranda. "If you don't mind, I'll tag along behind you back to the lodge. I've got to check in on a few vandalism reports."

Miranda stood in the same spot where Ranger Morgan had given his talk. "Let's get ourselves back to the lodge." She scanned the group. "Has anyone seen Rowena? She left at the start of the talk, but I want to make sure she won't be left up here alone. Has anyone seen her?"

Jeffrey quipped, "I would have escaped at the first chance. I hope that's what she's done."

Carol gave him a scathing look. "And leave the competition open for my team to take the prize? Not likely."

She turned to Miranda. "I haven't seen her, and I was watching."

"Why?" asked Miranda.

"I wanted to make sure she would be giving honest appraisals. She works directly for management, and I wanted to understand if there was any way to cheat her system." Carol looked directly at Jeffrey.

He shrugged his shoulders.

"Not likely," grumbled Miranda. "But it's odd that she didn't come back."

Sheila spoke up. "But if she ran into Mr. Burns, he probably gave her fifty million things to do in the next five minutes." A chuckle passed through the group like a wave in a sports arena.

"You're probably right. Carol, follow me down the trail with your group. Jeffrey, you and your group can fall in next, and then Ranger Morgan will act as our rear guard—watching for bears, of course."

Miranda led them down the trail. They made fairly good time even though the participants were distracted by the fairyland effect of the melting snowfall. In addition, Miranda felt that they were in no real hurry to rush into the next competition.

As they approached Balanced Rock, Miranda had planned to reveal the view that identified it as the Sphinx, but she saw two forms lying across the trail.

She held up her hand. "Wait, everyone. There's something ahead that doesn't look right. Stay here." She took a few steps closer and saw someone lying prone, and someone bent over them.

She called back, "Have Ranger Morgan come down here. It looks like someone has been hurt. Everyone else, stay back here until I come back with the all-clear. Carol and Jeffrey, I expect you to manage your teams. Stay here."

She sprinted down the trail as fast as she could while slipping and skidding on the damp and mucky trail. She had only gone about ten yards when she heard Austin's boots pounding right behind her. She risked a glance back, and his eyes were focused ahead in a concentrated, take-no-prisoners look.

They both stopped about five yards away from the two figures.

Terry Burns lay sprawled across the trail, his face pale, his mouth slack, with blood seeping from a head wound into a patch of snow and rocky rubble. Kneeling beside him, Rowena was weeping in great, chest-racking sobs.

She held a bloodstained rock in her hand. She looked at the rock and then up at Miranda. She slowly set the rock down on the trail, then asked in a childish voice, "Is he dead?"

Chapter 6

"He's still breathing," Miranda said to Austin.

"Good." He pulled out his phone, glanced at the signal strength bars, and quickly dialed 911. "Hey Sue Ann, this is Ranger Morgan. We have an injured man up here in National Bridge Park on the Balanced Rock Trail. He is unresponsive and bleeding freely from a head injury. Send the rescue team with a litter. He's quite heavy and will probably require a neck brace."

Of course he would know the dispatcher by her first name.

Austin listened to Sue Ann for a few seconds. "That long?"

There was another pause while he listened again. "Good. Thanks."

Austin stowed his cell phone and turned to Miranda. "They'll be here in about twenty minutes. Meanwhile, let's see what we can do to help his chances. What's his first name? I need to try to get him to come to."

Before she could answer, Rowena broke out of her stillness, glanced at the rock beside Mr. Burns, and looked up at Austin. "I know. I know who he is. His name is Mr. Burns. Terry Burns, the vice president of operations at BigSky Corporation. He was supposed to be joining the workshop group up at the shelter." She looked at Miranda, then back to Austin. "Is he dead?"

Miranda remembered that she had asked that question before. She took Rowena by the elbow to help her stand. "Let's move over here at the side of the trail, out of everyone's way. You've had a terrible shock." Miranda quickly took off her own outer jacket and wrapped it around Rowena.

"What's going on down there?" yelled Jeffrey. "What's blocking the trail?"

Ignoring the commotion, Austin was feeling the fallen man's arms and legs for breaks. "It looks like his injuries are mainly the head wound. It's a deep gash. Have you got your first aid kit with you? I need a thick compress."

He took off his outer jacket, rolled it up, and tucked it lengthwise around Mr. Burns's chest and down to his legs.

He then opened a pocket flap on his pants leg, pulled out an emergency foil blanket, and spread it out to its full size. He spread the blanket over Mr. Burns and tucked the edges in to cover the jacket as well. Then he took the compress pads from Miranda and pressed them to Mr. Burns's wound.

"Mr. Burns," he yelled into his ear. "Terry! Terry Burns! Can you hear me?"

There was no response.

Meanwhile, Miranda went back to Rowena and led her over to a smooth boulder beside the trail. "Sit here. The rescue team will be here as soon as they can. We need to stay out of the way so they can get Mr. Burns out of here and to a hospital as quickly as possible."

"Hello?" yelled Jeffrey. "We're still here."

Miranda held Rowena by her upper arms and looked into her unfocused eyes. "Rowena, snap out of it. I'm going to need your help with everyone. Rowena!"

Miranda released Rowena and snapped her fingers several times.

Rowena slowly raised her head and looked into Miranda's eyes but didn't speak, and it didn't look like she would.

"You stay right here. I'm getting someone to sit with you." She ran up the trail to meet the BigSky participants.

"Finally," said Jeffrey. "What's going on?"

"Mr. Burns has a serious head injury and is unconscious. Ranger Morgan has called 911. The rescue team will be here shortly. Make yourself useful and hold back any other tourists." She shook her head slightly. "Not that this trail is crowded, but we don't want to interfere with the rescue effort."

Carol moved through the group and stood beside Jeffrey. "What about Rowena? What's wrong with her?"

"I simply don't know. She hasn't said a word." Miranda looked around at the group. "Stay up here until they've taken Mr. Burns down the trail. I'll be back with more information as soon as I can."

Miranda returned to Rowena and then heard the run/walk noise of the rescue team long before she saw them. As she looked down the trail, two men and one woman jogged a quick step up to the scene. They left the litter propped against the cliff at the side of the trail.

While two of them knelt beside their patient, the tallest man approached Austin. "Hey, buddy, what do you know?"

It struck Miranda once again that she was still an outsider in this part of eastern Kentucky. She had only spent her girlhood summers at the family farmhouse. The kids she occasionally played with, including Austin, had grown up together. The adage was true. In a small, rural community, everyone knew everyone.

"Hey, Kevin. This is one of Miranda's tourist clients. He's a big shot from that sporting goods place over in Lexington."

Miranda stepped forward. "His name is Mr. Terry Burns. I'm Miranda Trent, the owner of Paint & Shine, in charge of this cultural adventure."

"Hi, there, I'm Kevin Lovelace, from Stanton." He reached out, and Miranda shook his roughly callused hand. "I've heard about your tours up here. People are saying good things." He turned back to look at his partners working on Mr. Burns. He pointed to the bloody rock. "Was that there when you found him?"

Miranda and Austin looked at each other. Austin tilted his head towards Rowena, and then he gave Miranda a look that implied he was on duty. "When we arrived that woman was bending over Mr. Burns with that rock in her hand." He pointed to Rowena, standing, pale and silent, with her hands clenched into fists by her sides.

Kevin smoothed his beard with a hand. "I see. Do you want to make the call to the authorities?"

"Yep, you guys get him to the hospital. I'll call it in to the authorities."

Kevin turned to Miranda. "Do you know if Mr. Burns has any health issues, allergies, anything?"

"No, I don't have a participant form for him. He arrived this morning as a substitute for the HR vice president. I hadn't even thought about the paperwork." She palmed her forehead. "I should have."

"Don't worry. We have his insurance details from his wallet. We'll take things as we find them." He pointed back up the trail to the rest of the participants, who had drawn closer while they were talking. "You can help by making sure the public doesn't get any closer. We should be able to get this guy out of here pretty quick."

He was right. In the few minutes Kevin had been chatting with her and Austin, his partners had applied an extra-large pressure bandage to the wound, inserted an IV, put him on oxygen, affixed a neck brace, put another blanket over the foil one, then transferred Mr. Burns into the litter.

Kevin grabbed the handles at the head of the litter and turned down the trail while the woman carried the lighter foot end. The third rescuer gathered up the medical trash, quickly packed up the medical case, and scurried down the trail to catch up.

"Kevin," yelled Austin. "Call me after you get him admitted in Lexington."

"Sure 'nuff," replied Kevin from over his shoulder.

Miranda watched them for a moment. "Where will they take him?"

"The nearest Neurological Intensive Care Center is in Lexington. The main reason is that he hasn't regained consciousness. This is definitely not good."

"Right. I'm calling BigSky to report it, and tell them to get his family on their way to the ICU. At least there's cell signal up here." She made the call, and while she was speaking to the receptionist, she saw Rowena with her hands over her face, sobbing.

By the time Miranda finished, Austin had called the nearest authorities.

"The Powell County sheriff is on sick leave. He won't be back for three months. All major incidents are being handled by the Wolfe County Sheriff's Office. I called it in. We have to wait here until Sheriff Richard Larson arrives to look at the scene and talk to you and Rowena."

"Great. I can't see that the whole group needs to hang around here on the trail. I'll send them down to the lodge."

"Agreed." Austin looked at the narrow trail. "I'll make sure they don't step near where it happened."

Miranda slipped back up the trail, formulating what she was going to say to her clients. How could she explain this in a way that would inform but not alarm?

She stood in front of her workshop members. "As you saw, there's been an incident. Your company's vice president of operations, Mr. Terry Burns, has been grievously injured. Carol and Jeffrey, I would appreciate it if you would lead your teams back down the trail to the lodge. Settle everyone into the conference room. I want each participant to make another drawing."

Jeffrey frowned. "But—"

Miranda interrupted him by holding up her hand. "For this drawing, I want each of you to sketch what you saw of the incident up here on the trail. You were all right here this whole time, and what you observed might be important later on."

Carol pressed her lips together. "You also want us to document what we saw because you think this was no accident. In fact, you didn't call it an accident. You called it an 'incident.'"

"Interesting observation, Carol," Miranda said. "It's also a good way to focus everyone's attention on a helpful action rather than get in the emergency responders' way."

Miranda and Austin stood next to Rowena as Carol and Jeffrey led the group back down the trail that returned them to Hemlock Lodge.

Rowena blurted out, "I didn't kill him."

Chapter 7

Saturday Morning, Balanced Rock Trail

Sheriff Richard Larson plodded up the trail, huffing and puffing like an underpowered steam locomotive. He had unbuttoned his coat to cool himself. His beer belly stretched his uniform shirt so tightly that you could see the waffled thermal undershirt underneath.

He stopped in front of Miranda and Austin and held up one finger for them to wait. "I haven't . . . been up here . . . since . . . I was a . . . kid."

Austin covered his mouth and snickered as quietly as he could. When he regained control, he said, "You asked us to guard the site and keep hikers from this part of the trail. We've done that."

Miranda felt sorry for the sheriff. Mostly he worked in his office in Campton, filling out reports and mediating disputes between the citizens and the city council.

The tiny town was set within a small, flat valley, so

very little uphill walking was required. "Hi, Sheriff Larson. It's nice to see you again. So sorry to bring you up on the trail."

Sheriff Larson frowned at her. "Thanks. This is a terrible time for the sheriff of Powell County to be out of commission." He put his hands on his hips and looked around at the ground, at the rugged cliffside, and then he finally spied the bloody rock. "Is that the rock you think caused the injury?"

"Yes," said Miranda. She signaled for her friend to step forward. "This is Rowena Gardner. She is an administrative assistant for the BigSky company. She found Mr. Burns. Right, Rowena?"

Rowena visibly swallowed hard and spoke barely above a whisper. "Yes, sir. I found him."

Sheriff Larson pulled a notebook and a pen out of his jacket pocket. "Thanks, miss. Can I have your full name, please? Your complete address, too."

"Rowena Kay Gardner, 2525 South Maple Drive, Winchester, Kentucky, 40391."

"Thank you. From the beginning, tell me what happened as clearly as you can."

Rowena again gulped before she could speak, but her voice was louder. "I was hurrying down the trail to get to the lodge to find Mr. Burns. He was expected to participate with the employees who were in the workshop, but he didn't show up. Miranda asked me to find him and bring him back to the shelter."

She hesitated.

"Fine. Then what?"

"I saw him lying across the trail. I called out to him. But he wasn't moving. When I got closer I saw the bleeding coming from underneath his head." She stopped and began to hiccup. "Sorry, I"—*hic*—"get the hiccups"—*hic*—"when I get"—*hic*—"nervous."

"Now, there's no need to be nervous, Miss Gardner. I just want to know what happened to Mr. Burns."

"Does"—*hic*—"anyone have some"—*hic*—"water?" Rowena was beginning to turn pale from hyperventilation.

"Hang on a second." Miranda rustled in her pack and pulled out an eight-ounce, aluminum water bottle and handed it to Rowena. "Drink it all in one go."

Rowena sighed with enormous relief, removed the cap, then downed the entire bottle. She replaced the lid and handed it back.

"Do you feel better now?" asked Miranda.

Rowena stood quiet. She waited for a long minute for the next hiccup. None. She smiled. "Thanks. That did the trick. Now, what was I saying?"

Sheriff Larson clicked his ballpoint pen. "You had just seen Mr. Burns. Then what?"

"I didn't know what to do. His head looked awful, but I could see his chest moving, so I knew he was still alive."

She squinted and looked at the spot in the trail where Mr. Burns had been. "I'm not entirely sure, but I think I yelled for help. Given how dehydrated I was, it couldn't have been very loud." She looked up at Miranda. "Yes, I think I yelled."

Miranda was puzzled. "Why were you dehydrated? There were bottles of water for the taking in the conference room."

"I forgot to get one."

Miranda couldn't understand why Rowena was dragging out what should be a straightforward recollection of her actions once she found Mr. Burns. Miranda stared at Rowena. "What about the rock?"

"Rock? What rock?"

"Rowena, are you okay?" Miranda looked into Rowena's eyes. "You were holding a big rock." She pointed to the side of the trail. "That rock."

Sheriff Larson hurried over to where Miranda was pointing. He used his pen to point at a rough rock about the size of a softball. "This rock. Ranger Morgan, I thought you said she had it in her hand."

Rowena turned to Miranda. "I don't remember that."

Sheriff Larson began furiously scribbling in his notebook. "Hang on. This rock is too small to cause much damage if it slipped down the cliff. It would make more sense if someone used it to hit him."

He took out his cell phone and took a few quick snaps of the rock and the stained area where Mr. Burns had bled on the trail. Looking up, he took some pictures of the cliffside. Then he took an evidence bag from the inside pocket of his jacket and secured the bloody rock.

"It also doesn't look like he was struck down by a rockslide. There aren't any other rocks or debris on the trail. It's hard-packed, so any new material would show up." He put away his phone.

"I didn't hit him," Rowena squeaked. "I would never do that." She began to back away down the trail towards the lodge. "He was hurt when I found him."

"Wait just a minute." Sheriff Larson took a few paces to stand in front of Rowena. "I think we need to take your statement back at my office. Come along."

He firmly clasped Rowena by the upper arm, then marched her down the trail.

Chapter 8

Saturday Noon, Sheriff's Office

Rowena followed Sheriff Larson into his office. He motioned for her to sit in one of the guest chairs that faced his desk.

"Can I get you a cup of coffee? It's bad stuff, but you look like you need something."

Rowena sat and folded her hands into her lap and stared at them. She sniffed and refused with a little head-shake.

"How about a soda pop? I've got Coke. No? What about an Ale-8? It's a local ginger soda and might settle your nerves."

Rowena lifted her head. "Yes, please."

Sheriff Larson left and walked towards the kitchen and met Austin just coming in the front door.

"Richard, I would like to be with you when you question her."

"What in the dickens do you mean?"

Austin squared his shoulders. "It's my territory. I was working there with those folks. I need to report what happens now."

Sheriff Larson puffed a frustrated breath. "Fine. I'm getting her an Ale-8. Want one?"

"Yep, your coffee tastes like river mud."

Sheriff nodded. "I won't argue that. Get one out of the fridge, then come on into my office."

Rowena took the green bottle from Sheriff Larson and downed a generous gulp of the fizzy ginger soda. She coughed and looked around for somewhere to put the bottle. A glance at Sheriff Larson confirmed that he didn't want her to set it on his desk. She ended up setting it on the floor beside her chair.

Meanwhile, Austin walked in, took a giant swig of his soda, then plopped down in the other guest chair.

Sheriff Larson fidgeted in his creaky old chair, leaned forward, and steepled his hands. "Now, young lady. I know this has been upsetting, but I really need you to tell me exactly what happened up there on Balanced Rock Trail."

"I'm not sure I can help. I've already told you everything I know. I don't remember anything else."

Sheriff Larson frowned. He didn't like being taken for a fool. He threw a look at Austin, who stared at Rowena in confusion.

Austin splayed his hand wide. "You were right there on the trail. I saw you standing over Mr. Burns."

Rowena looked at each of the two large men and began to shake. It started with her hands and moved up to her shoulders. Her neck and head quickly joined in. She put her hands over her face and began sobbing like a two-year-old in a supermarket. "I just don't"—*hic*—"remember."

"Not again." Sheriff Larson puffed out a frustrated breath.

Austin quickly handed over his clean red bandana and looked directly at Sheriff Larson. "Get your wife down here. We're just making things worse."

"I'm"—*hic*—"sorry." Rowena blew her nose. "I don't know"—*hic*—"what's wrong with me!"

Sheriff Larson grabbed up his telephone receiver. "Hi, honey. I've got a situation. I'm interviewing a witness to an incident up at Natural Bridge State Park. She's very upset. I think you can help. Can you come over to the office right now?"

He listened for a few seconds, then stood and turned his back to the others. "I know what I'm asking. If I didn't really need you, I wouldn't be calling. I'm desperate."

Another pause. "Yes, I understand, and I'm very grateful."

He replaced the handset. "She'll be here in about five minutes."

Sheriff Larson and Austin didn't speak to Rowena. They sat quietly while her sobs ran the course to loud gulping. Then her hiccups stopped until there was finally just some intermittent sniffing.

Rowena saw a slender woman stamp into the building and head straight for the sheriff's office. The dark-haired woman threw a stern look at the two men and waved her hand for them to leave. They both scrambled out. She shut the door.

"Hi, there, my name is Felicia Larson. Before you ask, yes, I'm married to the sheriff. I'm the county coroner as well as a clinical psychologist. My husband tells me that you've had a traumatic experience this morning. He felt you would be more comfortable talking about it with me. Is that true?"

Rowena looked up at her and tipped down her head in a tiny nod.

"That's good," said Felicia as she sat in the visitor chair Austin had so quickly vacated. "May I?" Felicia took Rowena's hands and began to rub them vigorously to bring some warmth and color back. "Trust me, you'll feel better once you've talked about what happened. Start anywhere you like, but you need to start talking about it."

Rowena removed her hands from Felicia's and folded them in her lap. "I remember leaving the shelter just up the trail beyond Balanced Rock and starting to walk down towards the lodge. I was shocked at how quickly the snow disappeared. It had been coming down so hard you couldn't see two feet in front of you. I thought that was odd."

"That happens here sometimes. Go on."

"I also remember admiring Balanced Rock. In fact, I think I took a picture of it on my new smartphone." She rummaged around in her purse and pulled it out, then pressed the photo gallery icon. "See, here are the last pictures I took." She handed the phone to Felicia.

"Yes, very nice." She handed the phone back to Rowena. "Continue, please."

Rowena dropped her phone back into her giant handbag and put it down beside her on the floor. "That's just the trouble. I remember seeing Mr. Burns just after taking that picture. I remember feeling panicked and disoriented. Then, nothing at all until the sheriff and the ranger put me in his patrol car."

"That's very unusual."

Rowena looked Felicia square in the eyes. "I simply don't remember."

Chapter 9

Saturday Noon, Hemlock Lodge

Miranda walked into Hemlock Lodge and headed down the hallway towards the Sandstone Arches dining room. She could hear the group's chattering from the moment she entered the large open space. The dining room manager gave her some serious stink eye and waved to Miranda to come over quickly.

Miranda faced the manager. "I'm so sorry about this. I'll handle it. Don't worry." She turned and quickstepped into the makeshift conference room and stood in the front by the whiteboard.

"If you can hear me, sit down and be silent," Miranda said in a moderately soft voice. Then waited for about ten seconds.

Then she spoke in a quiet, conversational voice. "Everyone. Sit down and be quiet. There'll be no information until everyone is seated and perfectly silent." Miranda repeated that in an even quieter voice to the workshop attendees.

Her technique worked as she continued to speak in a very low voice. "As soon as everyone is seated, I have some announcements, then you can ask questions."

In less than a minute, everyone was seated and you could hear a pin drop.

"As you saw out on the trail, Mr. Burns was seriously injured." She looked over to the team leaders. "Thank you, Carol and Jeffrey, for taking your roles and responsibilities seriously, and for leading everyone back here."

"No problem," said Jeffrey and Carol at the same time. They looked at each other, and Carol flushed and looked down.

Miranda paused. "The paramedics took Mr. Burns to the Neurological Intensive Care Unit in Lexington. I'm waiting to hear about his condition. I'm not an expert, but it seems to be quite serious. I called BigSky, and they are notifying his family. I have no news yet, but that doesn't mean anything good or bad. No news is just no news. Questions?"

Several participants raised their hands. Miranda pointed to Carol.

"Where's Rowena?"

Miranda looked down for a moment, considering the best way to answer. "She's still at Natural Bridge providing information to the Wolfe County sheriff. He's in charge of the investigation. She was at the scene and may know the circumstances that apparently ended up with an unconscious Mr. Burns. I don't have word yet when she'll return."

She pointed to Jeffrey's raised hand.

"Are you going to cancel the workshop? I mean, we

don't have a supervisor or an administrator. This seems like a real disaster to me. I don't think the company leadership has the same kind of vision for this workshop that you do."

"That's a good observation." Miranda smiled. "However, there are contractual issues involved here. You all know that money drives most decisions for a company. A small company like mine has fewer reserves than an established manufacturer like BigSky."

"In other words, you can't afford to cancel." Jeffrey glanced at his team.

"Before we go any further, I'm going to get in touch with Mr. Tobin and ask him to make the call on continuing or canceling. But just for my own information, let me have a show of hands of those in favor of continuing."

With a few looks at one another, all the participants raised their hands.

Miranda did a double take. "Really? I'm surprised. Do you mind telling me why?"

Carol spoke up at once. "We all want to get into the company's Fast Track Program. Don't we?" Heads bobbed up and down. "It guarantees immediate attention from upper management. That extra qualification will make the difference in being considered for the next round of promotions. It's called Fast Track for a particularly good reason."

"Good to know," said Miranda. "Continue with your drawings. I'll be back once I've reached Mr. Tobin." She pointed at Carol, then at Jeffrey. "I expect you two to keep control of your teams. Any disturbance will be reflected in your assessment rating."

She stepped out of the lodge and stood at the railing, looking down at the view of the winterized swimming pool. Everything had been stored away, and a large cover had been spread over the pool to protect it from the debris of the anticipated winter storms.

Miranda dialed Mr. Tobin's number, but it went straight to voice mail. She waited for the beep, but something went wrong. She was disconnected. Frustrated, she tried again with the same result.

This is ridiculous. Who else can I call? Rowena's not here to ask. Duh, I'll try the main number.

"BigSky Corporation. Your best sportswear supplier. How can I direct your call?"

"Hello, I'm Miranda Trent. I'm the owner of Paint & Shine, the provider of this weekend's management training course. I'm trying to reach Mr. Frank Tobin. Can you connect me?"

"Mr. Tobin isn't in the office today, but I can put you through to his voice mail if you want to leave a message."

"I tried that, but it shut me off. Do you have another number?"

"I'll check into the voice-mail problem for you, Miss Trent. Hold one moment."

"I don't need—" She heard that horrible elevator music.

She waited for a long five minutes and was just about ready to end the call when the voice returned.

"Miss Trent, I'm so sorry. We're having a company-wide issue with voice mail. I have issued a service call, and it should be up and running in no time."

That had never been Miranda's experience when reporting a phone problem.

"If Mr. Tobin calls in for any reason, please tell him to get in touch with me as soon as possible. Tell him that I would like to discuss canceling the management workshop. Would you do that for me?"

"Yes, certainly. If I see him, I'll let him know."

Miranda ended the call with absolutely no confidence that Mr. Tobin would ever get a message from her. She returned to the conference room to a scene of complete serenity. Everyone was drawing their recollections of the scene of the incident.

She smiled at Carol and Jeffrey in turn. "Thank you, team leaders. Well done." She waited a moment until she had everyone's attention. "Thank you for your patience. Unfortunately, I wasn't able to reach Mr. Tobin, so in the absence of any other direction, and because you have indicated that you're willing, we will continue the workshop."

"I changed my mind." John stood and threw down his drawing pencil. "This is a huge waste of time and all I'm getting out of this nonsense is a cramp in my hand."

Victor also stood. "I agree completely. All the artsy-fartsy exercises in the world won't demonstrate how you work under pressure. I'm going to pack up my stuff and get out of here. I canceled a trip to see my family because I thought this would be a better use of my time. It isn't."

"Calm down," said Miranda. "BigSky is having phone issues. I'm sure I'll hear something before long. You need to give this a little more time to work through your company's processes."

She felt the irritating presence of a looming authority.

"I hope you don't think Terry's little accident is going to stop us?" Mr. Tobin said while standing at the entrance of the conference room with his arms crossed. "This is an excellent example of how a good manager takes a bad situation and turns it into an opportunity." He looked straight at Miranda. "We're definitely continuing with the workshop."

Miranda snapped her head in the direction of the entrance. "I've been trying to reach you. It would have been helpful to your employees to know you were here."

He nodded. "I'm here now."

"Fine." Miranda pressed her lips together to keep back a sharp comment.

Mr. Tobin planted his hands on his hips and stared at Victor, then at John. "I'm going to give considerable thought to those last few comments. If this is your response to a difficult situation, you're going to have a tough time in a leadership role. In fact—" He looked at Victor's teammates. "You might want to make time for extra credit for your attitudes if you don't want this defiance to bring your assessment score down."

"Fine," said Miranda. "We'll carry on with the exercise, then."

At that moment, Austin entered, followed by a visibly upset Rowena. Her eyes were red and puffy, and she held on to her large handbag with a grip so tight you could see the whitened skin around her knuckles.

Austin winked a hello to Miranda then pulled out his phone. He grimaced and left the room to get a better signal.

Rowena whispered thanks to Austin and went down to the other end of the conference room with her chin almost touching her chest.

Miranda followed right behind her and whispered, "Are you all right? You look ill."

"I'm fine. I can do my job," she said in a trembling voice that broadcast the exact opposite. "I'm perfectly capable of continuing with the scoring and assessments I've set up for this workshop."

"Coffee?" Miranda prepared her a cup with a little extra sugar. She heard a rustle of whispering chatter around the table.

"Settle down," Tobin said in a barking voice. "Rowena, good. I was afraid I was going to be forced to handle the bookkeeping myself." He frowned. "Where were you?"

Rowena stood up as though reciting a poem in grade school. "I gave a statement to the sheriff in the back of his patrol car."

"Were you questioned?" Miranda asked, then pressed her lips closed. It wasn't appropriate to have this conversation in front of everyone. "Sorry, I didn't mean to ask that."

Rowena looked directly at Mr. Tobin. "The sheriff saw me at the scene and wanted a first-person account of what happened. There was no rockfall. It wasn't an accident. He believes it was a deliberate attempt to hurt Mr. Burns."

You mean the bloody rock you were holding. I was hoping it would all be cleared up after she talked to the sheriff.

Jeffrey wiped his mouth to hide a smirk. "Was it?"

Rowena responded quickly. "I told the sheriff that he planned to fire every single one of you who ended up on the losing team."

Chapter 10

Mr. Tobin motioned for Rowena to sit down. "Never mind that. This workshop will continue. It's even more important now that Mr. Burns is incapacitated for who knows how long. We'll need to appoint an acting vice president of operations, and that will cause yet another vacancy within top management. Do you see now why this is so important?"

Miranda felt a sour wave hit her stomach. *Did everything he encountered become an issue to use for his advantage? I would never stay in a job like that. I'm grateful I'm not in a situation where I need to be one of his employees—or more like one of his minions, for heaven's sake. I love being an independent business owner.*

This isn't helping. Relax.

Miranda took in a deep breath and shook out her clenched hands. "Good point. Let's get on with it, shall we?"

She turned back to face the participants.

They were all in various stages of understanding the stakes. Jeffrey was smirking and exchanging a fist bump with each member of his team. They exuded supreme confidence that they were invincible.

Carol shook her head in dismay but offered soothing words of encouragement to her teammates.

"Okay, everyone, settle down. I sympathize with your challenge, but the way to succeed here is to keep going. The next thing to do is judge your sketches. Carol, Jeffrey, huddle up with your team and choose the best one from your group." She looked at her watch. "You have ten minutes. While I'm out getting the judge, tape your drawing on the whiteboard. There should be no indication of which team is represented. That would cause an automatic elimination."

She went out of the dining room, down the hallway, and stood in front of the reception desk. "Doris Ann, I need a big favor. I'm desperate."

"What kind of favor?" Doris Ann lowered her brows.

"Would you mind judging a sketching competition? I was going to do it myself, but I've trained and coached them, so I'm biased."

"You want me to be a judge for drawings? Are you out of your mind? I don't know anything about art."

Miranda tilted her head. "You know these trails, don't you?"

"Of course I do, child. I've been coming up here since I was knee-high to a grasshopper."

"Then you would be perfect. The sketches are views of the Balanced Rock Trail."

"I'm still not sure." Her eyes pinched together in uncertainty.

Miranda took Doris Ann's hand in both of hers. "Please, please, please. You don't have to say anything about your choice. All you have to do is pick one. You can whisper your choice in my ear if that makes you feel better. Please?"

"All right, all right." She placed a sign on the desk that said she was on break and visitors should check with the dining room staff. "I can only give you five minutes."

They walked into the conference room. It was as quiet as a tomb. Miranda brought Doris Ann into the room. They stood at the whiteboard.

Miranda cleared her throat. "This is Doris Ann Norris, our judge for your drawings. She was born not too far from here and has spent most of her life working here in Hemlock Lodge. No one knows the trails and views of Balanced Rock and Natural Bridge like she does. She carries all that wisdom as the best qualification to judge your drawings."

Miranda signaled to Doris Ann, then she stepped aside. *I think I oversold that. Ugh!*

Doris Ann lifted her head and stepped up to the whiteboard. The two drawings stuck up by magnetic disks were both excellent. The left one illustrated Balanced Rock in a few broad, powerful strokes in a practiced and effective, minimalist style. The drawing on the right was so detailed it could have been a tintype photograph of Balanced Rock from the angle that evoked the Sphinx similarity.

Doris Ann looked at each of them for about ten seconds.

She turned to Miranda and pointed to the one on the left. "This is the best one."

Doris Ann gave the participants a quick nod and escaped out of the conference room as quick as lightning.

"Thank you," Miranda said to the disappearing receptionist. She turned to the group. "I happen to agree with Doris Ann. This is an incredibly expressive drawing of Balanced Rock that captures the dramatic setting as well as the spirit of the Sphinx. Who is the artist?"

No one moved.

"Come on. Don't be shy. This is gorgeous."

Lisa Porter lifted her hand a few inches, not even above her head. "I drew it."

"This is yours? Wow. Congratulations," said Miranda. "The first point goes to the Firehawks." Miranda clapped, and everyone followed. "Our next challenge is out at my farmhouse. Everyone please gather your things, take a fifteen-minute break to go to your rooms, and prepare for an afternoon of food and moonshine."

Everyone began to pack up their things and make their way out of the room.

Mr. Tobin blocked the entrance. "Hold up. One more thing." He lifted his eyes from staring at his phone. "I've got word from the hospital." That stopped everybody in their tracks. "Mr. Burns has a serious brain injury and has not yet regained consciousness. They've assigned his condition as critical." He paused to look at them. "We'll definitely be looking for an acting vice president of operations."

There was a rumble of comments through the team members.

Miranda frowned. *What a callous thing to say. He must be looking for employees who think the same way.*

Mr. Tobin continued. "You can Google it, but I already have. The critical condition is defined as an uncertain prognosis, vital signs are unstable, there are major complications, and death may be imminent." He took a big breath. "Don't get too concerned about this. You're still obligated to finish this workshop. You can't get out of it unless you want to be fired."

Miranda heard several of them grumbling among themselves, but they were careful not to let Mr. Tobin overhear.

They've all agreed to continue, but for pity's sake, what a terrible work environment.

Austin appeared in the doorway and looked into the room. "Rowena, I'm sorry. The sheriff wants to talk with you further. He told me to bring you back to his office in Campton."

Rowena inhaled a deep breath, gathered her things, and followed him out as quiet as a mouse.

Chapter 11

Saturday Afternoon, Farmhouse

Miranda drove the fifteen-passenger Ford transit van she had rented for the four days of the workshop. It was a little pricy, but a better value than chartering a bus service. Mr. Tobin followed in his sleek, black corporate car.

She pulled off Highway 15 onto Hobbs Road. In a couple of miles, the blacktop gave way to packed gravel.

They passed through a heavy wood, and then the view opened out onto a grassy clearing with a cottage-style farmhouse that faced the road. It was painted pale yellow with turquoise and peach trim. At the familiar sight, her heart swelled with warm memories of carefree summer days. She smiled.

The old-fashioned wooden house needed to be repainted, but that wasn't urgent. It had to wait until she had her distillery business up and running at a profit. Not yet. Besides, it played into the cultural atmosphere she was trying to share. It was a simple Craftsman bungalow with a full-width front porch. A well-padded wooden swing hung on one end, and a long, handmade, pew-type bench sat against the house on the other end. Various chairs and tables were placed for easy comfort for visitors.

Her neighbors rang true to the typical Appalachian type. They were hardscrabble, caring, and clever people with big hearts that embraced an appetite for good food, country music, and home-brewed drink. She remembered many evenings filled with laughter, singing, and a little sipping on those long-ago summer evenings.

Miranda pulled into the graveled driveway with Mr. Tobin following close behind. Almost too close. Everyone piled out of the van. Miranda stood in the front yard and waited for the two teams to gather in front of her. Mr. Tobin hung behind the candidates.

"Our next event is lunch."

There were cheers from both teams.

"The plan is to serve a buffet from the dining room table and the sideboard. The dining room is just beyond the front room. It's a small house. You can't get lost. There are plenty of places to spread out, including two picnic tables on the side of the house. At least that was the plan when I left this morning. I'll check with the cooks and let you know when everything is ready."

The screen door opened a crack, and out burst an apricot flash of a curly puppy.

"Sandy!" Miranda scooped up her puppy, and he licked her face with little puppy whimpers. "Don't cry. I wasn't gone very long."

Some of the candidates gathered around. "Oh, he's so cute."

"What a little fluff ball."

"How old is he?"

Miranda snuggled him under her chin, then turned him for them to see. "This is Sandy. He's a ten-week-old rescue terrier mix."

"Can I hold him?" Carol begged. "He's so cute."

Miranda handed him over. "Pass him around. I'm planning to train him to be a comfort animal for future events. Just don't let him get out into the road. It seems quiet all the way out here, but then folks barrel down this road like it was the Indianapolis Speedway."

Mr. Tobin walked up from the back and held up his hand. "Before things go any further, I have an examination paper for everyone to fill out."

Although there was some eye-rolling and a little foot shuffling, no one dared protest this unplanned assignment. "I want each team to sit at one of those picnic tables over there in the side yard. I have some paperwork for each of you to complete before we have lunch."

Someone's stomach growled.

"It wasn't me," said Oliver. But, of course, it was.

Miranda took Sandy from Carol's arms and lightly patted her back. She whispered, "I sympathize. Everyone is starving, for Pete's sake."

Carol and the others settled at the picnic tables.

Miranda shrugged her shoulders and opened the screen door. "Iris, Lily," Miranda called. "How's lunch coming along?" She went through the front room into the dining room.

The Hobb sisters stepped through the door that opened

up from the kitchen into the dining room. The sisters looked identical. Their matching khaki embroidered Paint & Shine aprons reinforced that impression. They weren't twins, but because they were born exactly a year apart, they shared the same birthday and were locally called Irish twins.

"Hi, Miss Miranda," said Iris, who was wearing a van Gogh printed T-shirt of her namesake flower. "We've been keeping things hot."

"Just like you texted," said Lily in a matching Monet lily flowered T-shirt. They both wore dark jeans under the logo aprons. "We've been worried about you having so many clients to look out after. Have they given you any trouble?"

"Surprisingly, they're working well with their team leaders. But there was a horrible accident on the trail. Mr. Burns is in intensive care at Lexington General Hospital. He's in critical condition. So, it doesn't look good."

Iris frowned. "That's terrible. So, the workshop will break up after lunch?"

"No, Mr. Tobin arrived to take over for him. I'm more concerned about Rowena. She was taken to Sheriff Larson's office by Ranger Morgan. I suppose they're trying to figure out what happened.

"Oh my goodness, everything smells delicious." Miranda squinted for a moment. They had followed her menu exactly. There was a large kettle of homemade chicken noodle soup, a bowl of spicy coleslaw, and a large basket of homemade herb crackers. On the buffet sat a pitcher of water with glasses, along with a setup for coffee and tea with cups, sugar, cream, and sliced lemons. There was a temporary table set up with a bowl of fresh fruit, along with small plates prepared with individual servings of blackberry pie. A spoon was carefully aligned on each plate.

"Something's missing."

Lily tugged at her Paint & Shine apron. "Everything's here like you said. We've stuck to your menu exactly."

Miranda looked around the room again. "Oh, I get it. Where are the dining chairs?"

"We put them in the woodshed for now," said Iris.

"There just wasn't enough room to get to the food with the eight chairs around the table," said Lily.

"Don't worry. It'll be no trouble at all to put them back after lunch."

Miranda smiled. "I'm not worried one little bit." These young women could think on their feet. It was their most charming trait. "You ladies will be running your own café before too long. Everything looks as elegant as those bed-and-breakfast pictures in one of those Southern maga-zines." She hugged each of them in turn. "Thanks. I'll call everyone in."

Miranda stepped out onto the front porch. The com-fortable swing, rockers, and long bench were deserted. She walked around to the side of the farmhouse and stood off to the side. The team members had apparently been listening to a lecture about the examination. Mr. Tobin still held the packet of individual booklets and a fistful of BigSky logo pens. He turned and held them out towards her. "Here. Pass these around. Rowena's not available."

"Certainly. My pleasure," she said in a voice dripping with Southern honey.

Mr. Tobin didn't skip a beat and didn't catch the irony. "Make sure you fill out the questions accurately. They will be used as evaluation material in addition to your performances here." Mr. Tobin put his hands on his hips and rocked back and forth on his heels. He waited until Miranda had given everyone a booklet and a pen.

"You have fifteen minutes to finish. When I call time, put down your pens. Time starts now."

All ten heads bent down to concentrate on filling out the exam.

Miranda motioned for Mr. Tobin to come over to speak with her away from the participants.

He frowned but complied. They walked over to stand at the end of the front porch.

"Why are you doing this now? I've got a hot lunch ready to serve. It's been delayed over two hours because of the accident. These people are hungry. They're not going to do their best."

"This has nothing to do with you. It's a stress test. The meal can wait." He turned and walked back over to hover over the shoulders of the participants.

You would think he was selling life support systems instead of overpriced sportswear. I wouldn't last working for him for more than ten minutes.

Miranda went back inside to tell the Hobb sisters to hold off again.

"What?" said Iris. "We just uncovered everything."

"Are you sure it's only going to be fifteen minutes? That man doesn't sound like he knows how long that is when he's doing the timing."

"You're right. Wrap and cover things up for at least twenty minutes." She looked at the big pile of herb crackers. "I'm going to eat some of these before I chew off my own arm." She slathered a couple with butter and drizzled it with local honey.

She didn't like to see the sisters' disappointed faces,

but they took most things in stride with a grounded sense of practical goodness.

After feeding Sandy in the kitchen, she went out to the front porch and polished off another handful of crackers just in time to see the official ranger truck pull into her driveway.

She smiled as Austin got out, put on his hat, and walked up to the front porch. "Hey, gorgeous," he said. "I could smell the chicken noodle soup from Roy and Elsie's house."

Rowena jumped out of the passenger side, then bolted straight into the house. Miranda heard her pounding up the stairs to the attic bedroom.

"What happened?" Miranda asked. "Why is she so upset?"

"She was interviewed by both the sheriff and the coroner. It was a mess. Rowena says she doesn't remember anything after taking a few pictures of Balanced Rock."

Miranda shook her head from side to side. "But I spoke to her right there on the trail. That seems suspiciously convenient. Last night Rowena seemed normal and balanced, but she mentioned a relationship gone bad. Now she's flipping out a little more than one would expect. Do you believe her?"

Austin shrugged his shoulders. "I don't understand any of this. She's your friend. You must know."

"High school was a while back. We grew apart."

"Hmm. From high school. Were you close?"

"Yes, at that time we were the best of friends. We were both shy and introverted, which is why we got on so well. But her behavior since we found Mr. Burns on the trail is more than weird. She's acting like she's had some sort of mental shock."

Austin said nothing for several long seconds. Then he leaned in and kissed her on the cheek. "Let me know how I can help." He raised his eyebrows. "Has everyone already eaten?"

Miranda chuckled. "You are always hungry. We haven't eaten yet because Mr. Tobin had a pop exam he couldn't wait to give the team members." She recognized a look of concern on Austin's face. "Don't fret. Let me sneak you a handful of Lily's homemade crackers to hold you over. They're wonderful." She gave him a quick kiss. "Thanks for bringing Rowena back. Do you have time to have lunch with us?"

"Always. What's with the groups out there on the picnic tables?"

Miranda peeked around the porch to look at the candidates scribbling away in their booklets. It was as quiet as a graveyard. She tiptoed back and motioned for Austin to join her on the porch swing at the other end of the porch. "Some sort of self-assessment exam. I had no idea he was going to do that. Obviously, I'm not happy with the delay in serving lunch."

"Try not to worry. BigSky is paying you a sizable amount to produce this, right?"

Miranda nodded. "Yes, they accepted my quote after a lot of negotiation. Sadly, I haven't received my deposit yet."

"What?" Austin raised his voice and nearly tipped them out of the swing.

Miranda clamped her hand over his mouth. "Hush, now. Rowena said that a little delay is perfectly normal, but she is checking with accounts payable to figure out what's wrong. I should have gotten the money by now."

"You trust her to check up on that?"

"Good question." She paused for a moment. "I don't have a single reason not to trust her, but there are always secrets."

Austin lifted her hand and kissed her fingers. "Mm-hmm. You taste like butter and honey." He slipped an arm around her waist and drew her closer.

Miranda stared into his eyes. "I had a sample. The Hobb sisters will soon be the best Southern cooks in the Daniel Boone National Forest." She smiled and removed his hand. "Don't distract me."

Austin lifted his hat and scratched the back of his head. "I'm not sure if I would extend that much trust to a friend I hadn't seen since high school. Do you want me to tell you about the interview with Felicia and the sheriff?"

"Yes, of course I want to know all about it. I was hoping we could find a little time together after lunch, but that doesn't look good now. Let me grab those crackers." She ran into the dining room and grabbed a handful. "Now, munch and talk at the same time. I don't know when this pop-up examination will be finished."

"Rowena doesn't remember that she was holding the bloody rock when we found them in the trail."

"She told you that?"

"Yep. At first Rowena didn't say anything at all to either the sheriff or me, claiming she couldn't remember what happened, but she wouldn't say anything beyond that. Then she got the hiccups again. Sheriff Larson asked if she would rather speak to a woman. That was a brilliant idea. She seemed relieved to speak to Felicia. It was Felicia who found out about the apparent memory loss."

"What's her situation? I mean, she's here, right? Not in custody or anything."

"There's just not enough to go further."

"Have you heard anything about how Mr. Burns is doing?"

Austin pulled out his phone. "Thanks for the reminder. I'll ask."

Sheriff Larson answered and barked a few curse words.

Austin ended the call and slipped the phone back into his pocket. "He's also trying to get some information out of the hospital in Lexington. No luck yet. It's a wait-and-see game with head injuries."

Just then, Miranda heard Mr. Tobin call out to the participants, "Time's up. Put your pens down. Carol, Jeffrey, gather up those papers, pass them across to the other team, and get them scored before we head out on the next challenge." He handed the answer sheets to the team leaders. "I'm going to need up-to-the-minute information on each of our candidates."

Miranda ran off the porch to stand next to Mr. Tobin.

"Hang on here a minute," said Miranda. "Don't forget we're having lunch before the next event. By the time they finish scoring, we'll have everything warmed up again. The delay was a little longer than I expected." She turned and glowered at Mr. Tobin.

His face tightened. "Fine. Get lunch, then."

Miranda darted into the farmhouse and back to the kitchen, where Iris and Lily were sitting at the enamel worktable having coffee. "We're back on!"

"Finally," said Iris. She took hers and Lily's cups over to the sink, and they went into overdrive to ready the lunch again. With three sets of hands making work light, the buffet was ready in a flash.

Miranda looked everything over one last time and

turned to the sisters. "Thanks for your great attitude. I appreciate it."

She went out into the living room and held open the screen door to yell, "Come and get it!" As they arrived on the porch, she continued in a welcoming voice, "We're serving a chicken noodle soup with homemade herb crackers, and a spicy coleslaw, followed by blackberry pie. I hope you enjoy it."

They filed in with barely concealed excitement. It had been a long time since breakfast.

After the candidates loaded up their plates and made their way back to the picnic tables, she saw Rowena filling up a plate for Mr. Tobin. She came up to Miranda with tension in her voice. "Do you have anywhere private for His Majesty to eat? He claims he needs to make a few important calls away from prying ears."

"Private? This is a farmhouse. There's nowhere private." Miranda was irritated.

"Shh," Rowena whispered. "He'll hear you. Please don't make things even worse for me."

"Oh, right. Sorry." She sighed. This was probably something she needed to learn to accommodate. Her future clients would be making all sorts of outlandish demands, and she might as well get used to it now. "How about the barn? There are a couple of tasting tables out there with a few barstools. Will that do?"

Rowena's face lit up with relief. "Yes, perfect."

"I'll get Lily or Iris—"

"Nope, they're busy, and this is my deal to handle." Rowena sounded resolved. "I'll take care of it."

"If that's what will work best for you," said Miranda. "But I don't think it's good for you."

Miranda filled up a plate and joined Austin and the Hobb sisters at the table in the kitchen. She thought about asking Austin to join her and eat with Mr. Tobin out in the barn. But she ditched that thought in a flash. If the man wanted to be alone and aloof, she could easily respect his wishes. It was better for her digestion.

Austin bolted down his food and put his empty bowl, plate, and glass on the counter beside the farmhouse sink. "Sorry to eat and run, but I've got to get back to work. I'll also drop into Campton later to see if there's anything new with the sheriff. He's not happy about the evidence."

Miranda expelled a deep sigh. "I'm not happy either."

Chapter 12

Saturday Afternoon, Farmhouse

As Miranda watched Austin's truck disappear down the dirt road, Mr. Tobin came out of the barn and walked over to her. He was on his cell and empty-handed. Not even remotely aware that someone would have to clear up his lunch things.

He ended his call. "What's next? We can't have everyone just standing around twiddling their thumbs. I'm paying good money for this."

"Speaking of paying good money—what's the status of my deposit?"

Mr. Tobin turtled his head and frowned. "I don't handle accounts payable. You'll have to ask Rowena about that." He attempted to walk around her.

Miranda held up her hand in a stop gesture. "Just a moment, please. I've already asked Rowena about the late deposit. She said you hadn't approved the purchase order for the workshop. Accounting can't send me a check unless you give them your approval."

A dark flush of red crept up from Mr. Tobin's collar and ended at the lobes of his ears. "I'm sure I approved that. There must be a mistake."

"Well, now is an excellent time to fix it. Rowena says all you have to do is make one call and I'll get my deposit."

He stood there in silence.

Miranda pulled her last card. "If you don't make that call, I have every right to cancel this workshop due to lack of the down payment. If you really want us to continue, prove it by making that call right now."

He gritted his teeth and actually growled out loud, then punched his phone so hard, Miranda thought he might shatter the screen. "This is Mr. Tobin. I am giving you verbal approval to pay the deposit for the Paint & Shine workshop. Got that?" He paused to listen. "Fine."

Miranda smiled, but she could feel the cold, steely look he gave her down to her boots. "If that deposit isn't in my account tomorrow morning, we're done."

Mr. Tobin spoke in a clipped voice. "It will be there. Now, tell me, what's the next event?"

"The next event is a tour of the distillery in the barn, as well as an art project in the hayloft studio. I'll gather everyone together as soon as they finish helping the cooks square away the dishes."

"Got it. I'll be at one of the picnic tables making calls." He started to go around to the side of the farmhouse. "Let me know when you're done with the tour and starting the next challenge."

Not likely. I'm not going to track you down like one of your badgered employees.

Miranda said nothing and went inside. She was proud of herself for handling that tricky negotiation. Maybe this business would boost her courage in tackling other problems.

The members of Team Sweatsocks were in the dining room, putting the chairs back in place. Team Firehawks were helping Lily and Iris put away the last of the dishes.

Miranda admired the ability of Lily and Iris to take full advantage of both teams to make their chores disappear. Even with all the delays, they were nearly back on track.

"When everything is done, come back out onto the front porch. We're going to tour the rest of my property. Then we start the next challenge."

There were comments from among the participants.

"I could use a nap."

"I need a bottle of that super caffeinated ginger ale."

"Me too. An Ale-8 would be perfect."

Miranda laughed. "Don't worry, I've got some out in the barn. I could use one myself. This next bit will be fun. Also, thanks for pitching in. You guys are great for helping Lily and Iris clear up."

She led both teams around to the back, and they stood in front of the rustic barn. "This is my grandfather's original tobacco barn. It was used for the main cash crop up until this year. My uncle finally stopped growing it and switched to organic heritage tomatoes just this past summer."

She pulled one of the large barn doors on its wheels to reveal a bright, industrial manufacturing space for her moonshine. "Here's my pride and joy." She waved her hand for them to enter. They huddled in the entrance next to a large, open space packed with shiny new distilling tanks, tubes, pumps, and spigots. She motioned for the groups to move up to a small area separated from the equipment by a barrier cord.

Carol led her group to the right and looked over her team to make sure that they had a good view of Miranda. Jeffrey followed his group to the left side of the barn, making eye contact with Carol's team and then with his own.

Miranda was struck by Carol's natural leadership skills and wondered again why the Sweatsocks had chosen Jeffrey. He seemed to be a puppet.

She cleared her throat to get their attention.

"My distillery brews corn whiskey or moonshine in a microbrewery quantity of about fifty gallons per production run. I'm recreating my uncle Buchanan's famous shine to sell in small quantities."

"Really, why do we care about your business?" Jeffrey whined. "We're here to win a management position with BigSky."

"'Patience and foresight are the two most important qualities in business.' Henry Ford said that."

Jeffrey flushed from the collar of his shirt to the tips of his ears. "We don't really seem to be getting anywhere."

Miranda hit him with a laser-focused stare that silenced the restlessness of the entire group. "We're getting there. You're going to need to understand this process because your ultimate competition will be for each team to brew a successful batch of moonshine."

"Awesome," said Carol. "I'd love me some shine!"

"Cool," said Victor.

Miranda led them back around to the front section of the barn. "Stand over there by the serving tables. I've got one table for each team."

Everyone shuffled over to stand in front of one of the

tasting tables. Some wandered over with interest. Some obviously were bored. A large concrete slab formed the top of the tasting bars, and simple bentwood barstools allowed everyone to sit.

On each table stood a five-gallon, stainless-steel soup pot sitting on a hot plate, a grain grinder bolted onto the edge, a bag of kernel corn, a jar of molasses, a package of malt extract, a packet of dry ale yeast, a nesting of mixing bowls, a selection of wooden spoons, and two gallons of distilled water.

Miranda stood between the two tables. "As you might guess, this is a multiday competition in the art of making moonshine."

"Real moonshine?" asked Janice. When Miranda nodded yes, Janice clapped her hands together. "Oh, I love this!"

"We're going to make the mash and then let it ferment until Monday evening. At that point I'll distill the mash in my sampler, one-gallon stills. I'll need to supervise the distilling very closely. Each team is going to compare the resulting shine from the micro stills head to head. This will take me a few hours."

"How do we win?" Jeffrey questioned in a clipped voice. "If everything is equal, they should taste the same."

"That is absolutely correct." Miranda faced towards the barn door and called out, "Ladies, bring out the cocktail samples."

On cue, Iris and Lily came into the barn carrying large serving trays. Each tray held ten mini mason jars.

"Here we go," said Miranda. "These are examples of moonshine cocktails you're very welcome to sample. One of them is a traditional mixture of moonshine and our local ginger-based soda pop, Ale-8, garnished with a lemon curl. The other is a cranberry moonshine cocktail garnished with a sprig of fresh rosemary. Give them each a try."

Everyone took both cocktails and sampled them.

"Iris and Lily are handing out both the cocktail recipes and also the instructions for making your moonshine mash. I'll show you step-by-step, just to make sure there are no misunderstandings."

"Thanks, I'm better at hearing instructions rather than reading them." Oliver sounded relieved. "Really. Thanks."

"That's good to know. Anyway, the instructions written on the card are a very common recipe for corn whiskey. In a nutshell, you heat the water to 120 Fahrenheit. Grind the corn and stir it in hot water until dissolved. Add the molasses and stir until the mixture is 145 Fahrenheit—about thirty minutes. Turn off the heat."

"Wait," said Eileen. "You said it was a common recipe. Are you saying this isn't your uncle's recipe?"

"Good observation." Miranda looked directly at the candidate. "No, it's not the secret recipe. I intend to keep that a secret for as long as my uncle managed—my whole life. It's a good business practice, especially if it puts you well ahead of your competition."

"That's something you had better learn and learn well," Mr. Tobin called out from behind the candidates. "A good marketing technique would be something we want to hide from our competitors."

Well, that was stating the obvious. I wonder why he felt that needed to be emphasized. Like maybe a Facebook ad campaign would be more important than the secret Coke recipe? Nope.

"Okay, let me finish describing the process for creating your mash. Next, you dissolve the yeast cake in a cup of warm water, then add both the malt extract and the yeast to the cornmeal and molasses. Pour everything into the copper pot and wrap it with cheesecloth and twine. It will stay out here until I'm ready to distill it on Monday night. Questions?"

"What's the scoring criteria for the competition?"

"There are three elements," said Miranda. "The first will be the quality of your corn whisky without adding any mixers—straight up—no ice."

Several of them shuddered.

"But I don't like straight liquor," said Sheila.

"Bleh!" Oliver put out his tongue and made a face.

"No problem, I'll taste that!" Xavier puffed up his chest.

Miranda disregarded their comments. "The second challenge will be to create a moonshine aperitif before our meal on Tuesday. Then the third is the post-dinner cocktail."

"But if we lose the corn whisky event," asked Eileen, "won't that mean we'll lose all three?"

"Not necessarily. I've used some pretty bad whiskey to make some excellent cocktails." She tapped her forehead. "Sorry, I forgot to add that part of the post-dinner cocktail must be an organic material gathered from my farm. It could be used as a garnish. There are some beautiful wildflowers at the borders of the road and along the edges of my fields. It could be used as a flavoring of the drink. There's also both mint and rosemary out there. It must be served in some way on or in the cocktail."

Miranda held up her index finger for emphasis. "Take care, however. There is this little white flower everywhere around here, and it's called Queen Anne's lace. It is poisonous to most animals and has a bitter taste. But the real issue is that it has a deadly look-alike cousin, hemlock. It also has small white flowers and fine, tiny leaves. The best bet is to avoid both of them."

She rubbed her palms together. "Now, let's make us some good moonshine."

Her phone pinged the tone she had assigned as a text from Austin.

"Excuse me one second. I asked Ranger Morgan to let me know if he had news about Mr. Burns."

She took her cell out of her back pocket and thumbed her way to the message. She read it to herself.

Bad news. Terry Burns died.

Chapter 13

Saturday Afternoon, Farmhouse

Miranda raised her hand to get the group's attention, then read out Austin's text. She looked at her clients, and they all appeared in various stages of shock. Some were wide-eyed and pale. Some were weeping and flushed. "I am so sorry for your loss." A stunned silence followed. The quiet hum of the distillery's commercial refrigerators could be heard inside Miranda's barn. But lively birdsong and rustling, wind-driven leaves sound drifted in from outside.

Miranda's phone pinged with another text from Austin. **I'll be right over along with Sheriff Larson.**

She noticed a shape silhouetted in the barn door. Mr. Tobin had just walked out on his way to either the house or his car.

"Lily. Iris. I'm sorry to put you on the spot. But please take over and explain to the teams how you made these cocktails. Mr. Tobin and I are going to have a chat outside."

Eyes wide, the sisters moved over to stand behind the tasting bar Miranda had just left. Before she got out the barn door, she could hear the twang of their voices explaining, in turn, their step-by-step recipe.

She glanced at Mr. Tobin, who had flushed red, his lips in a thin line and his fists clenched. He followed her, stomping like a prize bull.

"What do you mean, giving me orders? You're the subcontractor. I'm the customer here."

Miranda turned to face him with her arms folded. "But you don't own my business. I do." She paused until he acknowledged that with a slow blink. "I'm concerned about the sensibility of continuing this workshop. Death of a principle is usually more than sufficient cause for cancellation."

Mr. Tobin opened his mouth and then shut it with a plop. He frowned and looked down at the sparse gravel in the barn's driveway.

He's never had anyone challenge him. This must be a new experience.

Miranda waited another long moment. "I think there will be an investigation that will disrupt the flow of the workshop. Given the serious consequences of winning or losing, I think we should stop scoring for the day."

"We need to press forward. This is important to their careers."

"Let me explain my logic. Making the moonshine mash will take several hours, and there are no points awarded until the last day. If I know Sheriff Larson, all the questioning will occur within the next few hours. It will give the teams a bit of relief and will cause less stress for everyone without actually changing anything."

Mr. Tobin rubbed the back of his neck. "That's actually not a terrible idea."

Miranda inhaled a deep breath in relief that he was actually listening for a change.

Miranda smiled. "That works for me." This was the first reasonable conversation she'd had with him. Maybe there could be more.

She heard the gravel crunching as the sheriff's cruiser pulled into her driveway.

Sheriff Larson got out, tipped his hat to Miranda, then held out his hand to Mr. Tobin. "Good afternoon, I'm Sheriff Larson of Wolfe County. My condolences to you on the death of your fellow executive at BigSky. It must be quite a shock."

Mr. Tobin shook hands and bent his head in acknowledgment of his expressions of sympathy.

Sheriff Larson continued. "Do you know where we might find his wife?"

Mr. Tobin began tapping his foot. "I'm not sure, but she's probably with family. I will get our personnel office on that right away. There are some insurance and benefits matters that will have to be addressed with the widow. I'll get that rolling."

Wow, that was a bit cold.

Sheriff Larson quickly took control. "We have some routine questions for her. I'm sure we'll be able to find her, but your assistance is appreciated."

"What happens next?" asked Mr. Tobin.

Sheriff Larson waited for a beat. Taking his time to emphasize his answer. "I need to ask some questions of your employees to get a clear picture of what happened up on the trail. I'll start with you and then work through the rest of your employees. Except for Rowena Gardner. I've already gotten a statement from her."

Austin's truck spun into Miranda's driveway so sharply that gravel shot in all directions. He got out, put on his hat, and said, "I'm sorry about that. I saw the sheriff's cruiser, and I need to be here as well. The park is my patch. Our jurisdictions overlap, so we'll both be investigating the death of Mr. Burns."

Mr. Tobin switched his gaze from the sheriff to the ranger and back again. "This is a lot of manpower for an accident."

Miranda looked over to Mr. Tobin. "Obviously the sheriff doesn't think it was an accident."

"Now, Miranda. There's no need for you to be making assumptions about what I might think," Sheriff Larson chided her. "This way, Mr. Tobin."

Miranda smoothed down her hair and tucked in her logo shirt. Sometimes her quick mouth got her in such trouble. When would she ever learn to think before talking? Hopefully soon.

The three men made their way up to the farmhouse. Miranda was glad that everything from their lunch buffet had been cleared. They would probably take over the dining room. She sighed and went back into the barn.

The sisters were finished answering questions about the cocktails and had moved on to explain the local history of making moonshine. Fast driving through the backroads was a necessary skill if you wanted to stay out of trouble with the law.

"It was a cash crop for the things we couldn't grow or barter," said Iris.

"Like shoes and school supplies," added Lily.

Miranda stood behind the sisters. "Let's give Lily and Iris a hand for their impromptu presentation. I'm sure they gave you lots of helpful instruction for your cocktails."

The participants clapped, and the sisters ran out of the barn.

Everyone burst into excited chatter about the arrival of the sheriff's cruiser. It rose up as if they had been pent up, awaiting a chance to compare notes with one another.

Miranda took a deep breath and rapped on the table. "Attention. Attention. We still have a lot of work to do to get this mash going. If I'm going to distill this on Monday evening, you have to be done within the next couple of hours."

There were grumbles, but everyone focused on what she needed to tell them.

"Before you get started. Be aware that Sheriff Larson and Ranger Morgan are here to interview each of you about what happened to Mr. Burns up on the trail this morning. I imagine you'll go up to the farmhouse one by one."

"What about the fact that each team will be missing members throughout this process?" asked Carol. She looked over to Jeffrey's team. "That could make a critical difference."

"It could cause an unfair advantage," said Jeffrey.

Miranda shook her head. "Sorry, no dice. One of your most powerful and useful skills as a manager is to accommodate changing circumstances. Since there is no predicting who will be away, it's nice that each team has five members. I'll be either outside or in the kitchen, if you have questions. Taking advantage of all available resources is also an important management skill."

"But—" blurted Jeffery.

"No buts. Carry on." Miranda went outside and stood for a moment with her hands on her hips. She reflected that this workshop was more management stress than most of them would experience in a week, or maybe a month. Well, unless they came in contact with Mr. Tobin.

Austin came out of the house. She smiled as he approached. He looked towards the barn and also to the house, then gave her a passionate kiss. "How're you holding up?"

She snuggled deeper into his arms, and he held her tight. "I'm hanging in there, but this is not one bit like how I thought this workshop would go."

He chuckled. "That's two of us."

They held each other for a long moment, then Austin broke away. "I need to get a participant for Sheriff Larson. How do you want me to start?"

Miranda slumped her shoulders. "Start with the team leaders and then let them tell you how they want to send in witnesses. If you alternate between the teams, that won't give either of them an advantage and adds some randomness in doing without team members."

"Good idea. I'll bet Sheriff Larson will also want another crack at Rowena before the teams leave the farm. Oh, and he wants to interview you at the very end."

"Sure, that makes sense. I'll send in a team leader. Go on back," she said, then lifted her face for another kiss.

Miranda enjoyed watching him walk back up to the farmhouse. She turned back to the barn and told Carol and Jeffrey how the interviewees would be selected.

"Ladies before gentlemen?" said Carol.

"Age before beauty?" said Jeffrey.

They bantered back and forth on who should go first.

Miranda huffed her impatience, then gave Jeffrey a coin. He flipped to determine that Carol would be the first one to be interviewed.

It took longer to interview the participants than it did to prepare the mash. Quite a bit longer, in fact. The final interviewee was Sheila Collins. She came back to the barn, wiping away tears with a crumpled tissue.

"He was horrible. He was impatient. He was irritated. He even yelled."

Miranda frowned. "That doesn't sound like the sheriff at all. He's usually pretty even-tempered even when he's annoyed."

"Oh, I'm not talking about the sheriff," Sheila continued. "Mr. Tobin was waiting for me after my interview. He wanted to know what questions I was asked and how I answered them."

"He's going to get in trouble with the sheriff."

"Yes, the sheriff is talking to him now. Before he went in, he said he wanted to talk to you. Oh, I forgot, he wanted to talk to Rowena first and then you."

"Perfect." Miranda looked at the two groups seated in front of the tasting benches. "In order to keep to our schedule, I need to start the next competition." She tapped her knuckles on the surface of the tasting table. "Attention, everyone."

Miranda went over to a cupboard and pulled out two bags. Each bag contained five cameras. She held one up so everyone could see. "These are Polaroid cameras. Each camera pack contains eight film packets. The photography competition will be guided by each team leader, but every film must be taken and displayed on your table."

Xavier held up his hand. "What kind of photographs?"

"I was getting to that." Miranda looked outside the barn door. "Your snaps must be nature photos. Nothing man-made should be in the view. The theme for both teams is how nature inspires you and your vision of promoting yourself at BigSky."

"How long do we have?" asked Carol.

"I would like to say we had an hour, but this day has been a bit off. To be safe, at the end of thirty minutes, both teams should be back at this table with everyone's photographs ready for evaluation. Each team is to select the best shot from each candidate to be judged."

Jeffrey cleared his throat. "A lot depends on the outcome of these contests. Who will be choosing the winner?"

"I have a local artist coming over from the arts center who will act as our impartial judge."

Miranda left the barn with everyone else. They split up into the four directions of her little truck farm. Then she looked out over the farmhouse with a deep sense of satisfaction. It was a lovely farm.

She saw Austin waving at her from the porch. Probably to take her turn in the sheriff's fish barrel.

She trudged up to the house.

Chapter 14

Saturday Afternoon, Farmhouse

Miranda reached for the handle on the screen door, but Mr. Tobin flew out and darned near knocked her down. "Hey! Watch out."

He turned to glance at her. His face was the color of raw liver. He huffed, then blew past her, got in his car, started it up, and sped down the road, spewing gravel behind him.

Austin joined her on the front porch. "I take it he didn't react kindly to the sheriff's comments."

"That's the understatement of the day." Miranda leaned into him and put her arm around his waist.

Austin put an arm around her. "I have to admit, the sheriff handled him like a seasoned battlefield commander. He gave Mr. Tobin a dressing down that would have demoralized an ordinary man."

"But of course, Mr. Tobin isn't ordinary."

"Still, I felt kind of sorry for him."

"Don't waste your time. He wouldn't give any of us the time of day."

Austin tilted his head towards the house. "Go on in. The sheriff's taken over the dining room."

Miranda walked in to be questioned by Sheriff Larson. He was seated at the round oak table her grandfather made in 1929, the same year the farmhouse was built. Sheriff Larson sat tall, with an official police department notepad in front of him. He was clicking the top of a retractable ballpoint pen.

He looked up. "Sit down, Miranda. I hope you can help me untangle this mess. It might be a deliberate case of foul play. Or it could be horseplay gone tragically wrong. I need you to explain the movements of your clients this morning."

Miranda sat in the ladderback chair across from him, momentarily distracted by wondering why her grandfather hadn't made them as well. The matching set of eight had been ordered from the Sears catalog right along with the house itself.

She gave herself a mental shake. *Be alert now. Just because you know Sheriff Larson well doesn't mean he won't have serious suspicions.*

Austin arrived in the room but remained standing, his arms folded, leaning against the living room doorjamb.

"Well?" asked Sheriff Larson.

"Sorry, I was trying to sort out my thoughts. This is the biggest and most complicated workshop I've ever organized, and I'm finding it a challenge."

Sheriff Larson smiled. "I only ask that you do your best. You have an artist's eye, and you always pick up on things the rest of us ordinary folks don't appear to see."

A compliment? From Sheriff Larson? This is remarkable. He's never given me a compliment before. I must be winning him over.

She swallowed hard and blinked several times. "Where should I start?"

"Everyone was accounted for at breakfast and in the conference room, so start at the beginning of the hike."

"I've been dreading this all day." Miranda took a deep breath. "We headed out with everyone behaving nicely and excited, even though Mr. Burns had thrown a huge monkey wrench into the whole premise of the workshop."

"What monkey wrench?"

"The workshop was originally designed as a team-building exercise where everyone would learn more about one another. Because the participants were about the same age and had been with the company for about the same amount of time, BigSky would benefit from this group making strong connections. I would think improved interdepartmental communications would be excellent for an ambitious company."

Austin nodded his head. "That's actually a very smart idea."

"I thought so, too, but as soon as I started working with Mr. Tobin, it was clear that he wanted to add some self-serving layers to the workshop."

"How is that relevant?"

"I'm sorry." Miranda shook her head. "It isn't. I don't think. When Mr. Burns turned up as the designated substitute, he began changing the primary nature of the workshop. I wasn't that surprised by a different tack at the last minute, but I was highly irritated."

"Got it," said Sheriff Larson. "Keep going."

"Mr. Burns changed the structure of the workshop by assigning everyone to one of two groups. Then he announced, to everyone's surprise, that there would be winners and losers for each event."

"That doesn't sound so bad," said Austin.

"Right, but actually, the winners got a valuable reward. They would be inducted into the company's fast-track management program. That would give the winning team management support and recognition. This would be over and above the opportunities of their peers. However, it was rumored, but not confirmed, that the members of the losing team would be fired from their jobs when they returned from the Thanksgiving weekend. I thought that was harsh. But I also thought it pointed to a dangerous situation."

"Why?" said Sheriff Larson.

"People take their careers very seriously. It affects their entire lives. To leave it up to the results of a series of game competitions seemed frivolous and possibly damaging."

"Okay, I got it." Sheriff Larson waved his pen for her to keep going.

"Everyone took to the trail in great spirits, and I thought it might turn out all right even with the changes. Every participant in this workshop is an athlete. I would expect that from a sportswear organization, but it was nice to have a fit group to lead up to the shelter just past Balanced Rock. I demonstrated the basics of charcoal drawing at the shelter and handed out their materials packets. They spread out to find a view that represented the goals of their career at BigSky. Each participant was to make a drawing and bring them back to the shelter."

Sheriff Larson lifted his head from his notepad. "Why

meet back at the shelter? They could have gone back down the trail."

"They would have ruined their drawings. I brought a spray fixative to treat each sketch before they went back. Actually, it's just hair spray, but it was fast drying, so we were all able to roll them up and put them in my backpack for the trip down."

"Clever. You have a lot of details to juggle." Austin shook his head.

Miranda looked around the dining room. The Hobb sisters had left a pitcher of water and some glasses on the sideboard. "Just a second, I'm parched for a drink. I've been talking all day. Austin? Sheriff Larson?"

"No, I'm fine."

"No thanks."

She poured herself a glass and downed it where she stood, then refilled the glass, which she put on the table in front of her and sat again.

"Goodness, that's better. Where was I?"

"You put the drawings in your backpack."

"Yes, then I led everyone on down the trail so I could stay at the back and make sure we didn't have any stragglers. Austin stayed back."

The sheriff looked at them both. Austin folded his arms in front of his chest. Miranda flushed pink to her ears but didn't say anything else.

"Well?" Sheriff Larson prompted.

"We hadn't gotten far down the trail, and I began to catch up to the members in front of me. They were stopped because something blocked the trail. I turned the next bend, and there was Mr. Burns lying across the trail, bleeding from his head. Rowena knelt beside him, holding a bloody rock. She was crying."

"Did she say anything?"

"No, she was just bawling like a child."

"Hang on a second." Sheriff Larson scribbled in his notepad for a few long minutes, then looked up at Miranda. "Was anyone else that upset?"

Miranda chewed on the nail of her little finger. "Let's see. Carol Hampton wasn't so much upset as irritated."

"Why?"

"Mr. Burns was substituting for another senior staff member of BigSky. It had been a very disruptive opening session with the missing supervisor. Carol doesn't like inefficiency. Jeffrey Nelson seemed calm but distant, as if he were already calculating how this would affect his chances for being part of the winning team."

"You mean Nelson assumed the workshop would continue? Was that a certainty?"

"Not in my mind, but it turned out he was right. I wanted to cancel, but Mr. Tobin said we needed to continue. To be blunt, I really need the income. It did seem callous, but then, I don't know much about big business."

Sheriff Larson clicked his pen a few times. "BigSky is not known for the depth of their compassion in these parts. Go on. Any other reactions?"

Miranda closed her eyes tight. "I think Lisa Porter began to shake. Carol took charge and led her away. I told everyone to get back up on the trail and stay out of the way of the rescue team. By the time they got Mr. Burns off the trail, Lisa seemed fine."

"Anyone else?"

Miranda tapped her fingers on the table. "Let's see if I can remember." She closed her eyes again. "I remember Oliver using his cell phone." She pursed her lips. "There's something else I can't quite get." She closed her eyes yet again. "Got it." She sucked a breath through her teeth. "Eileen was filing her nails. I was furious at such insensitivity. Ugh! That's all I can remember."

"Yep, that's fine. Go on."

"The next thing was Austin calling 911. The dispatcher said that the mountain rescue team would be up to help us. Then I took care of getting Rowena settled on a nearby rock so I could keep an eye on her. Austin administered first aid, and then we waited."

"How long was that?"

"Those guys were very fast. They arrived with a litter in about ten to fifteen minutes. They must have been even closer than the dispatcher knew."

"What exactly happened while you were waiting for the rescue team?"

"Like I said, I got Rowena up from the dirt and led her out of the way. Austin pressed a compress on the wound and tried to wake Mr. Burns. He was completely unresponsive. Austin checked his breathing, pulse rate. Then he took off his jacket and used it to cover Mr. Burns's chest and legs. He also wrapped him in an emergency blanket. Austin kept yelling for Mr. Burns to wake up."

"Did he?" Sheriff Larson glanced at Austin.

Austin frowned and tipped his head towards Miranda.

She cleared her throat. "Mr. Burns didn't move a muscle. He was completely nonresponsive."

"Yep, all that tracks with what Austin said." Sheriff Larson flipped the pages of his notebook. "I'll have to check in with the rescue team, but all of that sounds like pretty near what happened. What I really need to know right now is who left the challenge during the event."

"I wasn't really watching out for that. Why would I? It's not like they were on a day trip for schoolchildren."

Miranda changed her tone. "Sorry, I didn't mean to sound brash. I just meant to say they're all adults."

"As I've said, you're observant. You might have taken notice of who left during the time they were supposed to be drawing."

"Yes, you're right. I did have a few wanderers. It was a little irritating. Especially because they all knew the stakes were high." She propped her chin on her hand. "I can't be one hundred percent accurate."

"Go on. Just tell me the ones you noticed."

"Both Carol Hampton and Jeffrey Nelson left their teams while I was walking around giving instruction to some of the less artistic participants. Also, Sheila Collins and Xavier Johnson claimed to have gotten distracted by the views from the trail. Oliver signaled to me that he needed a bio break, and I lost track of Eileen for a while. Oh, and at the end of the time, Rowena went down to meet Mr. Burns on the trail. She said he had texted her with more ideas about the workshop."

Sheriff Larson continued to make notes for a couple of minutes. "That's great, Miranda. If I need clarifications, I'll let you know."

"Sure."

Miranda and Austin escorted Sheriff Larson to his car and stood on the front yard to wave as expected by neighborly tradition as he drove down the dirt road.

Austin put his hands on his hips. "That didn't go too badly."

"Except for the miserable fact that," said Miranda, so softly that Austin had to lean in, "I've thrown Rowena under the bus. She had plenty of time on the trail to cause that injury."

Chapter 15

Saturday Afternoon, Farmhouse

Miranda went back into the barn. No one had returned from the photography challenge, so she checked the two mash formulas to make sure fermentation was beginning to happen. Each team's concoction had started producing tiny little foam bubbles at the edges of the stainless-steel pots.

Good. At least the mash was working the way it should. All the laws of nature hadn't stopped working just to torment her.

Miranda picked up the landline extension and called her friend, Felicia. She wondered how her job as coroner of Wolfe County affected her marriage to Sheriff Larson. From the outside, it looked like they thrived even when their roles were in direct conflict. Looks could be deceiving. She made a mental note to ask Felicia how she managed their two-career life. Just in case her relationship with Austin took a more serious direction.

"Hi, Miranda, are you calling to see if I'm doing the autopsy for Terry Burns?"

"You know me so well."

There was a belly laugh on the line. "I don't have to be Sherlock Holmes to figure out that if an incident involves one of your tours, you're going to be neck-deep in the investigation."

"All right. I surrender to your flawless logic. I find solving mysteries strangely addictive, and also satisfying."

"You appear to have the right intuitive skills, and I'm not ashamed to take advantage of them even if"—she faked a cough—"some of my family members think you are a pain in the backside."

"You're absolutely correct. Sheriff Larson and I have butted heads in the past, but I plan to win him over with this case."

"You may find your path pretty clear. He is softening up a little bit."

"Thanks, I appreciate that. About this case—are you performing an autopsy on Mr. Burns? It's not in your jurisdiction."

"I'm helping out because the local organization is grappling with staff shortages. It makes more sense for us to handle every aspect of the case over here."

"Anything yet?"

"Honestly, Miranda. You're so impatient. I haven't received the body yet, but it could happen at any moment."

"Will you let me know what you find?"

"You know I have to follow protocol for formal reports."

"Yes." Miranda ran a hand through her hair. "I know that, but I also know that you are as anxious about resolving mysteries as I am."

"No promises. If Sheriff Larson says I can share the results, I'll share. Otherwise, you'll have to ask him. Okay, I've got to get going. The transport vehicle with the body has just arrived."

Miranda replaced the handset and heard someone pull into her gravel driveway. She saw a lean man get out of an old blue Chevy pickup. He reached into the passenger seat and slipped a large camera over his shoulder. He waved to Miranda. "Hi, y'all. Is this the Buchanan Farm?"

"Welcome. You must be Dean Hill from West Liberty. I'm Miranda Trent." She walked out to shake his hand. "You're just in time for the photography contest, but it's going to be a little while before we have the images ready for you to judge. I love your work. I've practically been stalking you online. I'm so glad you could be our judge."

Dean ducked his head a tad and smiled. "I wanted to get out here a little early. I was hoping you would give me permission to take some shots of your property. I'm always on the lookout for new Appalachian images for my calendars. Would that be okay with you, ma'am?"

"Of course, I'd be delighted. Maybe I can use some of them for my promotional materials."

"Perfect." Dean reached into the front seat of his pickup and brought out another large camera with an enormous telescopic lens. He slipped that over his other shoulder. He noticed her notice that. "I use both old-fashioned black-and-white film along with the best digital camera I can afford. It looks a bit silly, but it works for me. When do you want me back here for the judging?"

Miranda looked at her watch. "The contestants are due

back in about thirty minutes, and then they'll need another thirty minutes to display their Polaroid shots on the long tables in the barn. The theme for both teams is how nature inspires you and your vision of promoting yourself at BigSky." She noticed his blank look. "It's an internationally famous sportswear manufacturer."

"Oh. That's perfect, then. Love the old barn." He snapped a few shots. "Originally used for tobacco?"

"Yep, from the 1930s right up until this last summer." She walked with him around to the side where the last crop had been harvested. "This was the last bed my uncle planted. No more after that, and I haven't decided if I'll plant anything yet. Probably not."

"Well, it's a long time until spring. You might change your mind by then."

"Well, I'm gonna need a kitchen garden to supplement my business. So, I'll probably take over the tobacco bed. I could do with some farm-to-table fresh vegetables, and I would especially like to grow some heritage tomatoes."

Dean smiled. "How long has this place been here?"

"My grandpa built the house in 1929 from a Sears catalog kit."

"Yeah, I thought I recognized it. That's fairly common. Nice paint. Anyway, I'll be back in an hour."

Miranda looked out over her property and saw little groups of two and three clients using their Polaroid cameras. While she had a few spare moments, she let Sandy out of the house for a potty break. Then, as a reward for them both, she treated him to a short game of fetch the stick.

After tucking Sandy back into the house, she used a cowbell to call in the contestants. "Everybody back in the barn."

In short order they arranged themselves at each tasting table, and everyone was spreading out their shots.

"You need to select the five best shots from your team."

"Does that mean we get one from each member?" asked Jeffrey.

Miranda thought about that for a second. She realized that her instructions had been unclear. An obvious sign of stress with this too-long, emotional day. "Put aside the five best ones from your team. It doesn't matter who took the image. There will also be points awarded for the best overall team, regardless of who has the winning shot. You have ten more minutes before the judging begins."

Miranda scanned the images and could see a wide range of quality. Some were macro images of plant and insect parts. Some were long-range images of the rolling hills as viewed from the gravel road. Everything was creative, at least. She was impressed.

Each table should have held forty photographs. The Firehawks team had only thirty-two.

"Carol, what happened? You're short a pack of images."

She made quick fists and then released and shook them out. "Yeah, somehow a pack got contaminated, and Sheila's photographs wouldn't process properly. So, each of us let her use our cameras for two shots each." She smiled at her team. "Strange coincidence that we had a faulty pack, but we made it work."

Miranda thought about the "somehow" defective film pack and concluded that Carol thought it had been tampered with. She was impressed with Carol's approach and made a mental note to ensure that workaround got incorporated into the Firehawk team's overall score.

She stepped across to the Sweatsocks table, where Victor and Oliver were standing chest-to-chest and yelling about copycats. The volume was growing louder, and the discussion was about to become heated.

Miranda wedged her way between them. "There's no yelling in this workshop." She placed a hand on each team member's chest and pushed slightly. "Take yourselves outside in opposite directions until you cool down."

"He started it by following me and replicating every shot," said Victor.

"There's no reserving an image out here. You're just mad because mine is better than yours while I was standing in the same spot."

Miranda took Victor and Oliver each by the arm and led them out the barn door. "Calm down. I said in opposite directions. Take a five-minute time-out and return to the event. If you don't control yourselves, I will report it to Mr. Tobin." She looked Victor square in the eyes, then did the same to Oliver. "You'll be out of here in a flash— without a job." She turned her back on them and returned to the tasting tables.

"Jeffrey." She motioned for him to follow her to the other end of the barn. "You've got to get your team under better control. You know what Rowena said about the consequences of a bad result in the workshop. You could all be fired."

"Yes, I know that. You don't have to remind me."

"Well, apparently I do. Talk to her. You need to be reminded of the full impact of your team's behavior."

Dean appeared around the corner to the entrance of the

barn. He seemed completely distracted by a butterfly that had landed on a stray wildflower lucky enough to escape the vicious mowing of Miranda's handyman. Ron loved using the gas-powered weed whacker to the point that she was afraid one of her young poplar trees might be permanently disfigured and at risk of dying this winter.

"Hi, Dean," Miranda called. "We're ready for the judging."

He looked up with eyes that seemed to have been in another world. He blinked several times. "Of course." He capped his lens and slung the camera back on his shoulder.

He advanced on the Sweatsocks table with a purposeful stride and scanned the images for no more than three seconds. Then he crossed over to the Firehawks display and again scanned not just the five images but the entire table. Again, he was done in seconds.

Dean went back to the Sweatsocks table, plucked up a photograph from the masses that were scattered on the other end. "Here's the winner." He placed it in Miranda's hand. "Do you mind if I take off now? I've got a long evening ahead of me developing these photographs." He nodded his head toward his film camera.

"Not at all." Miranda shrugged her shoulders. "You've done your part."

"Thanks. You have a really great farmhouse and barn here. If my images are as good as I think, I'll need your permission to put the barn in next year's calendar."

"Would you give my Paint & Shine business credit?"

"Absolutely."

"That would be wonderful." Miranda looked down at

the photograph in her hand. Dean's commercial aesthetic definitely drove his choice. The image was taken in a bower formed by arched. leafy branches. The arch framed a vaguely familiar silhouette of a tall man and a slender young woman looking into each other's eyes.

Miranda looked up. This was completely wrong for the theme. Now what?

Chapter 16

Saturday afternoon, Farmhouse

Miranda stood for a moment, trying to decide what to do. This image clearly didn't represent the requested inspiration for the challenge. Dean was the judge. But Dean was wrong. The theme was how nature inspires you. His selection was more appropriate for a Valentine's Day image. What was she going to do?

Dammit, I'm going to do the right thing. I'm going to make him pick another winner.

She looked out towards Dean's truck. He was still stowing his gear.

Miranda ran out, waving the selected photograph. "Hey, Dean. Wait up."

He looked over at her and frowned. "What?"

Miranda tapped the photo against her other hand.

"This photograph doesn't meet the rules of the contest.

This one wasn't in the group you were supposed to choose from."

"Oh? I thought I was supposed to choose the best one. That's what you paid me to do, and that's what I did." He finished stowing his cameras and got in the truck. "I've got another appointment. If you don't like it, fine, but that's still my choice."

He pulled out of the driveway and left.

Miranda walked slowly down to the barn and stood in front of the teams.

"Well, our judge has given me his choice and, unfortunately, although it's a fantastic photo, it has absolutely nothing to do with our theme."

A ripple of mumbling ran through the group.

Carol asked, "What does that mean?"

A voice came from the entrance to the barn. "It means that I decide who will win this contest." Mr. Tobin marched into the barn and plucked the selected photograph from Miranda's hand. He tilted his head back and stretched out his arm to study the image. He huffed. "This is ridiculous. This looks like the cover of a romance novel. We can't even use it for promotional materials."

Miranda grinned. "I absolutely agree with you. However, it is a photograph of merit."

"You didn't brief the judge correctly."

"I agree that he didn't understand your particular criteria, but he's a world-class artist with excellent judgment."

Mr. Tobin clenched his jaw. "Maybe so, but in this case, not at all useful."

"If you'll let me continue, I have a solution. I suggest that we award that photograph with points for artistic beauty, but you should select another one as representative of the theme that you can use on promotional material."

Jeffrey said, "That is fair. We need those points."

Mr. Tobin turned to Miranda. "You need to resolve this now."

Miranda completely ignored him. "Here's what I'm going to do. Pay attention." She looked at each team member. "I want each of you to select your best commercial image, and I'll choose the one that best matches the theme. An equal number of points will be given to the winner of the theme photograph. You have five minutes to hand me your chosen image. Mr. Tobin and I will agree on the winning shot. I'm sure we'll be able to pick something that can appear in your advertising media."

Carol snatched a photograph from the table and handed it to Miranda. That was quickly followed by the entire group doing the same. In minutes, Miranda was standing there with ten Polaroid snaps in her hands. The smell of those fresh snapshots reminded her of the first time she used a Polaroid at a family reunion. She'd loved the delight of her elders with the instant photos.

"Hang on just a moment." She motioned for Mr. Tobin to follow her a few steps from the tables and turned her back. They flipped through them, and one stood far above the rest in nailing the theme. She held it up to Mr. Tobin. "I think this is it, don't you?"

He reared back his head so he could focus, then nodded yes.

Miranda turned around and displayed her choice. "Who took this?"

John raised his hand. "I did."

"You are the winner. This photograph of Oliver, Victor, Jeffrey, and Sheila standing knee-deep in wildflowers examining each other's photographs says everything about how nature can influence your approach to your work. Congratulations."

Jeffrey puffed out his chest. "That means we get both contest points. Wonderful."

"This is only the first day," said Carol. "We have a long way to go."

"Exactly," said Miranda. "Meanwhile, let's not waste all the creative energy that went into these images. Let's all thumbtack them onto the wall so they can continue to inspire us."

As soon as everyone stepped back from the wall, Mr. Tobin picked up the romantic photograph and waved it in the air. "Who took this photo?" Mr. Tobin asked. "That looks like behavior that would be against company policy."

There was a thick silence from the participants.

He put his hands on his hips. "No one is going anywhere until I know who these two are."

"Does this mean the workshop is canceled?" Miranda said with a hopeful lift to her voice. "Stopping an event is effectively stopping the competition. Is that what you mean to do?"

Mr. Tobin pressed his lips together in a thin, pale line. He practically spat, "No. It's not canceled. Get on with the next event."

Miranda started towards the barn door. "It doesn't matter. It was probably posed for the dramatic effect. I'll let the Hobb sisters know that we're about to start the next competition."

She left them and went up to the house to alert Lily and Iris.

The sisters met her at the door. "We've got everything set up for cooking the venison stew over an open fire."

Miranda created two fire rings in her side yard near each of the picnic tables. She supplied each site with iron tripods, cast-iron stew pots, mixing bowls, and a bare minimum of cooking tools to prepare their evening meal.

Lily and Iris had filled coolers with identical cuts of meat. There was also a wooden box filled with olive oil, balsamic vinegar, fresh rosemary, dried sage, condiments, flour, sugar, and an assortment of spices.

"Everything looks perfect." Miranda put her hands on her hips. "You two are going to be the judges for the stew."

"What do you mean?" Iris said in a high shrill. "We can't do that."

Lily put her hands in a stop position. "We can't. We're not trained cooks. We just can't."

"I disagree," said Miranda. "You were brought up by one of the best cooks in the area. You have more experience in the kitchen than any of the participants. No one has prepared as many pots of venison stew as you two. Am I right?"

They looked at each other, and they both took a deep breath. Iris looked over to the side yard. "But I thought we were going to help each team. We're good at seasoning venison with whatever is on hand. They don't know how."

Miranda nodded. "Maybe not, but they will have detailed instructions, and you are permitted to answer any direct questions. I'm betting these teams will surprise you."

"Fine." Lily smoothed her apron. "We can do this."

"Thanks. I'm ever so grateful for your support." Miranda looked over to see Mr. Tobin coming over to the side yard. *You have no idea.*

"What's the next thing?" asked Mr. Tobin.

"I sent you an agenda for the remaining events." Miranda tried to keep her voice calm but was pretty sure she'd failed.

"I don't have time to look it up." He snapped his fingers. "What is it?"

"The participants are cooking a venison stew for their supper. Are you going to stay and oversee how they handle the challenge of cooking over an open fire?"

He looked at his watch. "No, I've got to get back to the plant for a few hours. There's an emergency board meeting I have to attend. It's mandatory because of Terry Burns. I have to be there." He looked around. "Where's Rowena?"

"I'm right here." Rowena walked out from the front porch with Sandy in her arms. "I'm sorry to be unavailable. I needed a little snuggling time from the puppy." Sandy was licking her face so quickly he was panting in puppy whimpers. "I feel better now." She put him down in the yard, but instead of tending to his business, Sandy ran over to Mr. Tobin, grabbed a pant cuff, and growled, then wrestled it into a wet knot.

"Sandy!" Miranda grabbed him, but his tiny teeth were caught in the fabric, and she had to release each tooth one by one. She cringed each time a tooth ripped the material. Sandy was growling deep from his belly. "I'm sorry. I don't know what has gotten into him." *Well, that's not true. Sandy feels the same way I do about you. You lousy piece of management slime.*

Mr. Tobin's jaw tensed and he cursed under his breath through gritted teeth. "I don't have time to get home and change." He pulled a set of keys out of his pocket. "Keep that little devil under control."

"He's just a puppy," Rowena said as she stepped forward in front of Mr. Tobin.

"He shouldn't be allowed loose." Mr. Tobin brushed his trouser leg with one hand. "Never mind about that. Make sure you compile the scores of today's competitions and give me an assessment of each candidate's written essay. I'll need that emailed to me before the start of tomorrow's event. Understood?"

Rowena looked down. "Yes, sir."

"Keep him away from me." He got in his car, backed out of the driveway, and drove down the dirt road with a plume of dust rising after him.

Miranda took Sandy back into her arms. "Sandy isn't the real devil around here."

Chapter 17

Saturday Evening, Farmhouse

Beyond all expectations, the venison stew was wonderful. The sisters took little bowls of both versions. They walked over to stand on the front porch while they deliberated. It was taking a long time. Finally, Miranda approached them.

"What's the verdict?"

Iris turned her eyes to the ceiling. "The problem is that they're both delicious."

"Delicious, yes," said Lily, "but in different ways. One is perfectly seasoned to bring out the gamy flavors. The other is very tender, with a creamy sauce."

"What do you think?" asked Iris.

"Oh no, you don't." Miranda grinned. "You won't get out of this that easily. This is your event. I agree with you. I thought they were both remarkable. We really should have figured out that as sportswear employees, they would be experts in all things outdoors, but I didn't think they would be such great cooks over an open fire." She folded her arms. "Well, almost all of them. Eileen seems like a fish out of water."

Iris and Lily folded their arms and stared at Miranda.

After a few moments, they burst into giggles. "We've chosen our winner," said Lily.

"We were just pulling your chain." Iris pointed to the Firehawks. "They're the winners. Not by a lot, but their venison stew was definitely more tender, with a richer, meatier flavor."

Miranda palmed her face and sighed. "Don't do that. I'm having a tough time with this workshop as it is."

"Well, it was fun to catch you out." Lily smirked. "We'll get the cornbread and collard greens and join you and Rowena at their tables."

"Great, I'll mix up the moonshine cocktail and be right behind you." Miranda fed Sandy, then whipped up a cocktail with a sprig of mint as a garnish.

After all the food and drinks were on the table, Miranda tapped her mason jar with a spoon. "Our judges have spoken, and the winner of the venison stew competition is . . ." She paused for dramatic effect. "Team Firehawks."

That was followed by hoots and jeers.

"Team Sweatsocks is still ahead, but these events are by no means easy for anyone." She raised her cocktail. "Congratulations on a very challenging first day. Enjoy your stew, and I encourage each of you to try a sample of the other team's stew. You'll understand why Iris and Lily had such a difficult time choosing a winner. Cheers!"

Everyone seemed to enjoy the meal and the fact that there were no more events for the day. Both teams helped the sisters clean up the kitchen and store everything in the cupboards. They also cleaned up the side yard and put out the fires.

Rowena walked among everyone, taking notes. When everything was finally finished, she told Miranda that she would be upstairs typing up her assessment of today's activities.

Miranda drove the competitors up to the lodge. When she returned to the farmhouse, Austin was lounging on the porch swing with Sandy on his chest.

"You two look comfy."

Austin smiled. "Lily and Iris handed him over to me when they left. They think he's been upset by all the comings and goings here today. I do, too." He patted the quilt next to him. "Come on in."

Miranda snuggled in, and Austin folded the quilt over her and put his arm around her. They swayed gently to the peaceful snuffling of puppy snoring for quite some time.

Sandy jerked up as if poked with a stick. He wanted to get down on the grass. Miranda took him down, and Austin followed. "How are you doing?"

"Well, it was both fantastic and an awfully long first day." She scooped up Sandy and motioned for Austin to follow her inside. "This requires an extra-strength moonshine cocktail. I have a new recipe using local wild lavender. Do you want to try one?"

"Absolutely. The lavender will be relaxing as well."

"Could you stoke up the fire for me? I'm feeling a bit chilly."

In a few minutes, they were sipping their drinks on the couch in the front room. Sandy was in his cage with the door open, snoring in a sound asleep. "These are unusual but satisfying." Austin sipped his drink again. "I'm not sure if I'll ever be able to sip straight shine again."

Miranda felt a double layer of warmth spread from her chest to her toes. It wasn't just the shine that caused it.

"I'll be right back." She popped into her bedroom and returned to the couch with a fist full of drawing pencils, colored markers, and a brand-new composition notebook still in its plastic wrapper. "I'm starting a new murder notebook to get us better organized for this investigation."

"Us?"

"Yes, I wouldn't think of investigating without you. Even though you are dangerously close to being on the wrong team."

"What do you mean?" Austin straightened up on the couch.

"Relax." She pushed him back onto the couch with her hand in the middle of his chest. "I just want to make sure that Rowena gets the best we can give. Sometimes that means going down a different trail from Sheriff Larson."

"That's a lot to take on for a friend you haven't seen since high school."

Miranda tore open the wrapper of the sketchbook. "Sometimes you don't know how much a friend has affected you until you think back. She was a good friend and deserves a brand-new murder notebook."

"Yes."

She wrote "Murder Notebook" on the cover, and underneath she wrote "Mr. Terry Burns."

She continued, "I've at least got a pretty short list of suspects because I've already told everything I know to Sheriff Larson."

She made a quick sketch of Terry Burns on the first page and underneath that made a list of those who had an opportunity to attack Mr. Burns.

The list included Carol, Jeffrey, Lisa, Oliver, Mr. Tobin, and, finally, Rowena. She made a thumbnail sketch for each of them. Then she added a few words about their background and what kind of relationship they had with Terry Burns.

After she finished with Rowena's page, she dropped the notebook and pencils onto the floor and collapsed onto the back of the couch.

"What's wrong?"

"I feel a bit overwhelmed."

"Lordy, lordy, lordy. That's how you feel at the start of each of these cases," said Austin. He gathered up the notebook and picked up all the pencils and pens. "You question yourself constantly about whether you should meddle in a death investigation."

"I don't have the qualifications."

"But you have a unique set of skills. You've done it before. The truth is that every time you rise to the challenge, you make a difference and help deliver justice."

"That's important to me."

Austin fell completely silent, and they let the silence grow into a comfortable, cozy companionship. He drew her into a warm embrace and held her against his chest.

"I know you're going to go ahead with your investigation, but I want a promise from you this time."

Miranda stiffened. Was he going to ask her to stop meddling? Stay in her own lane? Behave like a lady? "What promise?" She heard the strain in her voice.

"I want you to promise that we'll go on a real date. A

grown-up date at that fancy inn in Lexington. What was the name of that place? Oh, the Merrick Inn."

"A date?"

"Yes, it's time we set things straight with the rumor mill around here. We're seen together here at your farmhouse almost every day. But you're still publicly insisting that we're just business partners. I would like that to change."

"You're right. I'm more established now as a serious businesswoman. I agree that it's time to be more open."

"Good. I want some time set aside for just us. Promise?"

Miranda nestled back into his arms. "Mm. That's going to be an easy promise to keep. But only after I've done everything I can do to clear Rowena. That's important, too."

"Important enough to risk putting yourself out for ridicule and even arrest?"

Miranda inhaled deeply. She looked at the notebook and pencils in her lap. "It's because I know deep down that Rowena wouldn't harm anyone—ever."

"Are you talking about me?" Rowena said from the bottom of the stairs. "I felt my ears burning." She plopped down in one of the rocking chairs. "What are you guys doing?"

Miranda shrugged her shoulders. "She knows these people. It would be silly not to use her to help."

Austin nodded. "Of course she's been working with them at BigSky for the limited time they've been with the company. She's been an employee for years. She should know how things work from the inside of the corporate culture point of view."

Miranda held up the Murder Book. "I'm a bit of an amateur sleuth around here. I collect my thoughts in these sketchbooks. Would you mind helping?"

"Heck no," Rowena said. "I'd jump at the chance. I'm the one who is the chief suspect in the sheriff's mind. What do you want to know?"

Miranda smiled. "Perfect." She flipped through the sketchbook pages. "Let's start with Carol. What can you tell me about her?"

Rowena leaned back in the rocker. "Oh, I like Carol, but she has a nose for opportunity. She wants to advance into the top levels of management. You've noticed that there's a distinct lack of diversity. I think she's planning to take full advantage of this adventure to prove her leadership skills. She's already convinced her team to elect her as leader."

Miranda wrote that in her sketchbook. "But that's not a strong enough motive."

"I agree, but she's been working in HR. An administrative assistant can gather a lot of information that most people wouldn't want others to know. She has access to everyone's personnel files."

"You could have something there." Miranda scrunched her brow. "Is anything obvious?"

Rowena shook her head. "Oh, wait. There were some rumors that Terry tried to force her to date him—or worse—when she first started with the company."

"What happened?"

"I'm not sure, but he came into work one morning with his cheek all scratched, which he claimed was from a girlfriend's cat. After that, Carol avoided him."

"Okay, let's move on to Jeffrey."

"Jeffrey is a complicated fellow." Rowena squinted

her eyes. "He has had a very difficult time finding his way in this good old country boys' environment."

"But he's a sports star," said Austin. "That should be an absolute gold ticket to the top."

"You would think so." Rowena shook her head. "He and Xavier are the first two black men in management. It hasn't gone very well."

Miranda widened her eyes. "In this day and time? Who gave him trouble?"

"It was Mr. Burns, of course. He's a racist. Oh, I mean, he was a racist. This is not exactly a progressive company, and it's headquartered in an area that still calls the Civil War the War of Northern Aggression." She paused for a moment. "Eventually, Jeffrey's expertise and social skills won everyone else over to accepting and actually respecting him."

Looking up from her sketchbook, Miranda leaned toward Rowena. "I don't really see a motive there since Jeffrey has won over the executives."

"Maybe not everyone," Austin said.

"Okay." Miranda flipped a page. "Next is Lisa Porter. She seems so mild. I mean, she works in accounting and collects rare teacup sets. You couldn't hope to find a milder personality. It's so mild, I'm not sure I would say she had one."

Rowena tilted her head. "Still waters run deep. There have been some whisperings about the many private meetings between her and Mr. Burns—in his office—after office hours."

"Okay, okay," said Miranda. "Maybe they're having an affair, and she's threatened to what? Tell his wife? Or the other way, he's threatened to tell her husband? That's a fairly good motive."

Sandy yipped from her bedroom doorway, and Austin picked him up. "The more likely scenario is that Mr. Burns promised to leave his wife and then got bored with her. A jilted Lisa might be capable of violence. Maybe he threatened to fire her to get rid of the problem and she took her revenge."

"That could be the reasoning behind the team assignments. He wanted to make it a plausible dismissal." Rowena sighed. "I couldn't really figure out why a mere accountant got invited." She frowned. "Company policy prohibits relationships. They both risk getting fired."

"The more I learn about the participants, the more suspicious I get." Miranda flipped to the next page. "Then there is Oliver Young. Now, to my mind, he seems the most aligned to the company's mission. He was a surfer and now he's a rock climber."

"Right," said Rowena, "but he's new in the legal department. Apparently, he specializes in international copyright and patent law."

"Is he part of the new global expansion initiative?" Austin struggled to keep Sandy from chewing on one of his shirt buttons.

"Right," said Rowena. "Quite the bright new star as far as upper management is concerned."

"No motive?" Miranda asked.

"There were some rumors about his overseas connections. That they might be very political."

"You're talking China?"

"Wow, that's a big leap in logic. But maybe. Yes. There was an initial negotiation trip to Beijing and he asked to go, but because of the high cost, they said no."

"That doesn't sound that ominous," said Austin.

"Well, here's the thing. On the day before the flight, and in barely enough time for the visa to be processed, Oliver took the place of the vice president of the legal department."

"Why?"

"A couple of days before the flight, the VP got food poisoning so bad he had to be taken to the emergency room. They quickly put Oliver's details on the visitor list, and he went on the trip."

"That still doesn't sound like a motive," Austin said.

"There was a lot of tension in the office between Mr. Burns and Oliver after they returned from the China trip." Rowena sighed. "But I don't know what caused it. It's all I have about Oliver."

Austin plopped down on the couch again, and Sandy curled up in his lap. "This is exhausting. It feels a lot like high school gossip. How many more are in that little sketchbook?"

Miranda smiled and flipped the page. "Only one more. That's Frank Tobin. What have you got to tell us about him?"

"Other than that he's an utter and complete slime bucket?"

"I've come to that conclusion myself, but you must have more on him than just an aggressive personality."

"Nothing concrete, but he's the most aggressive executive at BigSky. He's heartless and has no empathy. When we had a large layoff last year, he held the meetings and processed all the unemployment paperwork like every payout was coming out of his own pocket."

"What about the working relationship between him and Mr. Burns?"

"I never heard anything that could be turned into a motive for killing Terry. They were sort of two birds of a feather. In fact, they were holding a lot of meetings together over the last few months. I don't know why."

Miranda finished scribbling in her sketchbook and snapped it shut. "I have to say that given your information, I wouldn't hire any of these people. How on earth do you know so much?"

Rowena stood and stretched, then started toward the stairs. "It's my superpower. No one looks twice at an admin. I'm practically invisible."

Chapter 18

Sunday Morning, Rock Bridge

The second day of the competition took the group to another beautiful, scenic overlook. The weather was crisp, along with a crunch of frost amplifying everyone's footsteps. The trail wasn't anywhere near civilization. The rarely used path wiggled through woody hillsides and crossed babbling streams using narrow log bridges. They arrived at Rock Bridge sandstone arch by passing over a rippling stream.

They stopped at a wide clearing with several moss-covered picnic tables, a rusted charcoal grill, and a bashed-up, metal trash can with bear-safe fastenings that chained it to a post.

By the time everyone arrived, most were overheated in spite of the crisp temperature. Their packs contained everything they'd need for today's events. In addition,

Miranda had split up the ingredients for lunch and stowed them among the candidates.

As soon as everyone caught their breath, Miranda found a little, cleared-off spot to stand on. She waved a hand for the group to gather around.

"I know you're all anxious to learn about today's first challenge. Let me tell you that it is an exciting one. That's why it's the first event of our awfully long second day of team building."

Jeffrey frowned, removed his hat, and wiped the sweat from his brow with his arm. "Just get on with it. We're ready."

"As you say, but we're going to rest here for a few minutes while I explain things. The physical challenge is for each team to build a rope bridge using a simple braiding technique. After the rope bridges are complete, you'll need to transport a five-pound sack of confectioners' sugar to the other side. The sacks are one hundred percent cotton and will not protect the sugar inside." She grinned. "I originally planned for it to be a fifty-pound sack, but I thought that was a real downer."

"Thanks for considering my back," said Xavier.

"Finishing up here. The first team to get everyone to the other side with the most sugar is the winner." Then she held up her finger. "The sugar must be carried by the last person across. Just so you know, confectioners' sugar dissolves like cotton candy, so any moisture at all will reduce the amount of sugar in the sack."

"Couldn't we just wade?" asked Oliver. "It doesn't look very deep."

"You could, but your team would be disqualified. That's one of the primary conditions for the win. The driest team wins the event. I'll be watching."

"Any little bitty hints?" asked Carol.

Miranda nodded. "What you want to do is make sure your bridge is high enough to stay above the surface of the stream under the weight of your heaviest team member."

As one, the whole Sweatsocks group looked at Jeffrey.

He raised both hands in a yield position. "I'm muscular, not fat. Muscular."

Carol laughed. "So for once, the Firehawks have a physical advantage? Priceless."

"In addition to that, here are the heaviest lunch packets for you to transport across the creek. I will give you your packet when your bridge is complete and proven to be strong enough to carry the largest member of your team. We'll be having our lunch over there, so be careful, or we'll starve." She handed out several booklets to Carol and Jeffrey. "Here are some guidelines on traversing streams that I've extracted from a few guidebooks. You will have thirty minutes to study those and form a strategy before you begin. A plan will make all the difference in this challenge."

"What if neither team finishes in time?"

"I'll make a judgment call for who has come closest to meeting the challenge. Your time limit is ninety minutes altogether. Thirty to plan your strategy and then an hour to create your rope crossing, transfer each member individually to the other side with your packet completely dry. No more than one person can be on the ropes at any time. If two people are on the bridge at the same time, that's an automatic disqualification.

"There are four trees of fairly equal size and distance across the creek. I've marked them with a ring of red yarn." Miranda pointed out the four trees. "Your team captains will flip for the chance to choose their crossing."

Carol won the toss and chose the upstream crossing.

The teams each gathered around their crossing site and started to plan out their rope bridges.

In thirty minutes, Miranda called out, "Planning time is up. Build your bridges."

Team Sweatsocks managed to throw a line into their tree and anchor it. Jeffrey performed a chest-beating ritual that inspired his teammates to join in.

Miranda frowned her disapproval.

Rowena began jotting down comments in her notebook, and the hooting abruptly stopped. Jeffrey turned pale and mouthed an *I'm sorry* to Miranda.

Team Firehawks climbed up their sturdy tree and affixed one end of their support rope. Then they used strategically stacked rocks to cross the stream, where they fastened the other end of their support rope securely to another large tree trunk. By tossing the ends of the balance lines to team members on each side, their support line was ready within the first ten minutes.

The teams called for their cargo at the same time. Miranda handed a package to Jeffrey and Carol, and they began the transfer of cargo and team members.

Jeffrey went over first and supplied a constant stream of yelling at his team to move faster and faster. The effect was to hinder their progress.

Just as Team Firehawks was transferring the last team member over the stream, there was a loud twang, and their support rope broke. Carol grabbed the safety guide ropes and avoided a face-first fall into the stream, but she and her cargo got drenched.

Miranda yelled, "Stop! Stop the contest. Team Sweatsocks has won by default because Team Firehawks has gotten their cargo wet. Congratulations, Jeffrey." The words hadn't left her mouth before there was another loud twang and the Sweatsocks rope bridge fell into the stream, with Sheila getting herself and their cargo sopping wet.

The candidates crossed the stream by way of the Firehawks' stepping stones.

"The next thing we need to do here is to collect our supplies and put everything back where it was. We want to leave nothing and take only memories."

She waved Rowena over. "Please help me by having everyone put all their rope in this trash bag. I want every single piece collected and then returned to me. Don't leave a single scrap lying around."

"What do you suspect?" Rowena narrowed her eyes, squinting.

Miranda said in a low, flat tone, "I'm suspicious. Two breaks in a perfectly good rope are too convenient."

It didn't take long to police the area. Then Rowena handed over the trash bag to Miranda and began updating her notes.

Miranda built a fire in the grill to dry everyone out. Luckily, no one was very wet because it was a little stream, and no one had been wearing their backpacks.

"That water is cold." Sheila slapped her arms and jumped up and down in front of the fire. "Luckily, we're wearing the best sportswear money can buy from BigSky. This will dry in a couple of minutes in the heat of this fire."

"That's one of the perks of this workshop. New sportswear for all." Carol looked at Miranda's clothes. "The company didn't send you a promotional package?"

"Nope." Miranda added more wood to the fire and checked the pot of coffee she had brought. "Rowena didn't get one either, and she works for BigSky."

"I wonder why." Sheila rubbed her chin. "I don't think they're in financial trouble." She smiled. "It could be just an oversight. Most likely it's because she was added to the program so late. Also, mistakes happen."

In fifteen minutes everyone was warm, dry, and had a cup of coffee.

Miranda stood. "I'd like to let you warm up longer, but I need to keep to our schedule." She smiled broadly. "I love this next part. It's one of my favorite painting approaches on the trail. We're going to try ultrafast watercolor painting."

There were groans throughout the group.

"I hate painting," said Janice. "Everything I try turns to absolute mud."

"A complete lack of any talent is my problem," said Oliver. "I'm fairly good with computer graphics most of the time. Real actual painting gives me the shakes."

Miranda smiled. "Then this is a chance to try something quick and new." She handed out lightweight bamboo boards and pads of already sized watercolor paper. "You'll have to share the masking tape. I only brought two rolls. Go ahead and tape a sheet of paper to your fiberboard, and I'll show you how we're going to get some amazing watercolors."

After the taping was done, the next things Miranda handed around were drawing pencils and erasers, along with small packets of watercolor pens with brush tips.

She held up her board, which had been prepared with a sketch of the rock bridge already on the paper. She demonstrated a quick, spare, delicate approach to painting the scene with the sketch showing through and limited patches of color that only occasionally blended into one another.

"Okay, Janice, pay close attention. This is how you avoid mud in your watercolor painting. Follow this simple basic rule. You simply don't allow colors to bleed unless they are next to each other on the color wheel. Contrasting colors need white-space separation."

Janice smiled. "Brilliant. I can do that."

Sheila raised her hand. "What's a color wheel?"

Miranda reached into her pack and brought out a sheet of paper. "I have one for everyone to share around. It's a circle based on the primary colors of red, blue, and yellow. Adjacent colors are those you can permit to bleed. Colors that are opposite on the wheel are contrasting. For example, purple and yellow are contrasting. Does that help?"

Sheila's eyes lit up, and she smiled like she'd had a light bulb moment. "Yes, absolutely."

"That's your demonstration, and now you will be judged on both your drawing and painting techniques, as well as your creative use of color. We'll have an hour to paint. I will be happy to give you advice. You will select your best effort, and Ranger Morgan will choose the winner."

Miranda looked at her watch. "He's supposed to show up in about an hour. As soon as he arrives, you must put down your brushes. On your mark, get set, paint!"

Over the next hour, Miranda was able to give pointers to most of the candidates. Jeffrey shrugged her away. Surprisingly for such a gruff character, he had a real gift for bare-bones sketches. In only a few strokes, he completely captured the timelessness of the dark, moss-covered rock bridge.

The drawings were fair, and most of the watercolors were pretty good.

Victor had wandered over to stand in a spot right in front of Eileen. He took a step back and stepped on her foot.

Eileen yelped, and Victor fell backward over onto her. Paints, brushes, and paper went flying. She shoved him away, and he landed on his backside beside her.

"You've completely ruined my painting."

Victor backed away from Eileen. "Don't get your dander up. I was only trying to get a better view to paint."

"How does knocking me to Sunday and back help you get a better view?" Her drawing was planted face down in the mud.

Miranda ran up to stand between them before they began to throw punches. "Don't worry, Eileen. I have an extra set of painting tools." She glared at Victor. "If you need it. I'll give you extra time."

Then she pointed her finger right at the spot between Victor's eyes. "If you get a so-called case of clumsy one more time, I'm removing you from this event."

Miranda turned to address the whole workshop. "Let me make this clear. If anyone deliberately tries to impede the work of another member, I'll make sure Rowena documents that in her assessment forms." She paused and looked at each member. "Clear? Good."

The group was quiet as a graveyard. The only sounds were the running stream and the birdsong in the beautiful trees.

Austin arrived on time and stood next to Miranda. He leaned over to whisper, "How is everyone?"

She whispered in return. "There's a saboteur in the group. We had two ropes snap during our crossing challenge. I've collected the empty film cartridges, but I haven't had time to examine the ropes. I'll do that while you're giving your lecture."

"Perfect," Austin whispered. "I'll turn everyone's attention towards the rock bridge for at least fifteen minutes."

"Thanks," said Miranda. He turned back towards the candidates. "Hey, campers," Austin hollered, then waited for everyone to pay attention. "I understand that your painting time ends at this point. Right, Miranda?"

"Absolutely. So, if each of you will place your best painting on this table over here, Ranger Morgan has some interesting history about this arch to tell you."

There was a scramble of candidates selecting and placing their drawings on the table beside Austin. After they all submitted one, he waited until everyone was seated again and stood in front of the arch.

"Welcome to one of the most tranquil settings in the Red River Gorge. Officially, this is Rock Bridge Trail number 207. There are more than a hundred arches in this area. The largest concentration east of the Mississippi River."

Austin passed his hand to follow the length of the bridge. "Of all the sandstone arches, this is the only natural bridge over water. The small waterfall upstream is called Creation Falls. I have no idea where the name came from. I've asked countless old-timers in the area, but obviously not the right one. Yet. The waterfall, this arch, and the scenic trail make this the most popular out-and-back trail in Daniel Boone National Forest.

"The multiple cliff lines have established this as one of the world's top rock-climbing destinations." He paused. "That and the fabulous Miguel's Pizza out on Natural Bridge Road."

Everyone laughed.

"This is the home to the Red River Gorge Climbers' Coalition. The area is nicknamed 'the Red' by climbers."

John raised his hand. "Why do we call this Red River Gorge?"

"Basically, it names the canyon system formed by the Red River. It's a unique natural area that attracts thousands of visitors each year. A portion of the Red River Gorge is also designated as Clifty Wilderness. It covers more than twelve thousand acres of rugged forest. Can you name the reasons why?"

"Rock climbing."

"Sandstone arches."

"Hiking."

"Canoeing."

"Hunting."

"Wildlife."

"Because there are a lot of cliffs?" said Miranda.

Everyone laughed at that.

"Everyone is right. This is a beautiful sight," said Austin.

While everyone, including Rowena, was listening to Austin, Miranda grabbed the bag of collected rope. She examined the ends and came across an end that had a sharp cut halfway through. Continuing to search, she found one more cut that had caused the rope to fail. More worrying, she found several more cuts that had been made but hadn't been used for the weight-bearing part of the bridge.

"Excuse me, Ranger Morgan," said Miranda, "but we're running a bit late. Could you please select the painting you believe reflects the spirit of Rock Bridge?"

"Certainly." Austin walked over to the table where the ten paintings were placed. He clasped his hands behind his back and leaned over to examine each painting. He selected three of them and wedged them in the picnic table cracks so he could step back and view them from a distance. After several minutes of walking up and back, he picked out a winner.

"This is the one that best captures the spirit of Rock Bridge. You can almost smell the peaty clay coolness that is peculiar to this spot."

Miranda took the picture and held it high. "Who is the winner here?"

No one spoke. Sheila poked Jeffrey in the ribs and whispered, "Speak up. It's yours."

The whispering drew a sharp glance from Carol, then she quickly looked away.

Miranda noticed that Carol and Jeffrey were definitely behaving like they were more than coworkers. Maybe they were even more than friends. That would complicate things. Carol seemed decidedly uncomfortable.

Jeffrey raised his hand. "It's mine." Then his eyebrows raised. "I won?"

"The winning team is the Sweatsocks," announced Miranda. "Congratulations."

Rowena handed out box lunches to everyone. "These are from Lily and Iris back at the farmhouse. They send their good luck along with country fried chicken, an ear of corn, some coleslaw, and a slice of apple cobbler.

You'll have to rough it with your water bottles for a beverage."

"Don't worry, there'll be another moonshine tasting after our dinner tonight," Miranda promised.

While the candidates were eating, Miranda motioned for Austin to join her. They stepped behind some thick brush and dumped out all the rope. Miranda showed him the cuts she had found.

He looked through each piece and paid particular attention to the broken segments. "No mystery here. This has been partially cut so that it would break when stressed."

She quickly showed him that the other ropes had been damaged as well.

"Just as I suspected."

"What?" asked Austin.

"Someone has begun to sabotage the workshop."

"I would have expected a more focused attempt against the opposite team." Austin stuffed the rope back into the trash bag.

"I know. This is worse. This was sabotage against the whole workshop because no one could know which bit of rope was used in what part of either team's bridge."

Austin stood and checked his watch. "I've got to hightail it to another talk in the lodge. I'll stop by tonight."

Miranda shook her head sadly. "We're going to have to be vigilant in looking over all the equipment for an event before someone actually gets hurt."

Austin huffed his frustration. "This is what happens when the stakes get high."

He gave Miranda a peck on the cheek and hustled.

In the back of her mind, Miranda knew that Rowena had access to the equipment, and also knew the exact sequence of challenges.

Chapter 19

Sunday Afternoon, Hemlock Lodge

The group returned to the lodge to change out of their creek-spattered clothes. Everyone regrouped in the makeshift conference room for a series of business-focused challenges. Rowena led them through the mechanics of how to format and present the monthly status report. Each department head was responsible for not only supplying their financial numbers but supporting data must be available as well.

Mr. Tobin arrived shortly after Rowena's session started. "Now, this is a competition that will be useful. These monthly status meetings are the lifeblood of BigSky. We make all our important decisions based on the current numbers presented in that meeting." He settled into a chair at the back of the room and gave Rowena a wave to continue.

Rowena looked up at the ceiling with her jaw clenched.

Mr. Tobin was completely oblivious to her irritation at the interruption. She inhaled and continued, as if nothing were wrong at all. "Mr. Tobin is right. You may not think you'll be contributing much to the meeting right now, but after this training, you can be a substitute for your boss when they're unable to be there."

Carol raised her hand. "With this, you're hinting that we will be valued by upper management." She glared at Mr. Tobin. "Right?"

He stuttered. "Well, s-sure. Yes. Right." Then he waggled a hand for Rowena to continue.

"Thank you for clarifying that, Mr. Tobin. Oh, by the way, are you planning to conduct the trivia quiz on the history of the BigSky chain?" She paused. "That's scheduled to start right after everyone turns in a slide deck."

"Oh, no," said Mr. Tobin. "I wouldn't think of taking that away from you. You're doing an excellent job. You can carry on with the trivia competition. This is going great."

Miranda's phone pinged. It was a text message from Felicia. The gist of it was that Burns's death indicated foul play.

Her next event wasn't until the dinner challenge at the farmhouse. She waved a little goodbye to Rowena and slipped out of her chair in preparation for leaving, but Doris Ann blocked the exit.

"Is Mr. Frank Tobin here?" she called in her strongest back hills accent. "I've got a bone to pick with him." She slowly scanned each man in the room until her gaze rested on Mr. Tobin. "Your credit card is denied for your room charges."

Rowena and Miranda exchanged looks. He was staying here but wouldn't let Rowena have a room?

"That's impossible," huffed Mr. Tobin. "Try it again."

Doris Ann drew herself up to her full petite presence. "Do you think I'm addle-brained? Of course I've tried it several times." She handed him the card. "Not only that, I've called the credit card company directly. They want you to give them a call."

He grabbed the card from her. "Fine. I'll handle this."

Doris Ann held on to it for a few seconds. "I'll need another card to finish checking you into the suite."

Miranda had an alarming thought about the rather large balance BigSky owed her for this four-day workshop. Was the company in financial trouble or just Mr. Tobin?

Mr. Tobin growled under his breath and reached for his billfold. It was twice the size of an ordinary wallet. He had to sort through a dozen different charge cards before he handed one to Doris Ann. "That one will work."

Doris Ann raised her eyebrows. "Yep, I've never heard that little tale before." She took the card, turned on her heel, and marched out of the conference room. Miranda followed right behind her.

"Doris Ann, wait up."

Doris Ann slowed her pace but kept going. "Let me get this to the front desk cashier. She's very young, and I don't want to see her cry in public."

Miranda watched as Doris Ann handed over Mr. Tobin's credit card to a young woman who didn't look more than twelve. Doris Ann bent over and whispered a lot of instructions. Given the young looks of many of the locals, she could have been in her twenties as easily as in her teens.

Doris Ann turned to Miranda. "What's with that idiot? Did he think we would just let him use a bad card?" She shook her head from side to side. "No siree! Not while

I'm a workin' here." Doris Ann settled back into her reception desk. "Now, what is it?"

"Doris Ann, have you noticed anything unusual with this group?"

"Don't tell me you're going to investigate that Mr. Burns feller's accident?"

Miranda leaned over closer to use a softer voice. "I just heard from Felicia. She going to stop by to talk. That probably means that Rowena is still in trouble."

Doris Ann's eyebrows raised. "That nice school girlfriend of yours?"

"Yes. She was holding a bloody rock when we found her and Mr. Burns."

Doris Ann folded her arms. "You've got your work cut out for you this time. She doesn't look like the type to bash someone over the head without a darned good reason."

"She's not the type." Miranda rubbed the back of her neck. It was holding a lot of tension. "So, I need to know anything unusual about this group. Anything that might strike you as odd or out of the ordinary." Miranda frowned. "Speaking of out of the ordinary. What are you doing here on a Sunday? I'm shocked you aren't at church."

"You hush your mouth," Doris Ann protested. "You haven't been living in these here parts long enough for you to know what's what."

Miranda shrank back. "Sorry, sorry. I didn't mean to pry."

Doris Ann smirked. "Gotcha. You're right, I'm not usually here on Sunday, but I just couldn't leave this young girl here alone with this ornery gang from the sportswear company. She would be completely ruined."

"Ruined?"

"I mean, she might get powerful discouraged about the hospitality business if she were left to deal with these ya-hoos all by herself. I'm not about to let that happen. These folks are all out of the ordinary."

Miranda smiled. "You're absolutely right. You've got a nose for bad behavior."

"Are you mocking me? That's not how your mama raised you."

"Doris Ann, I'm merely pointing out what everyone knows. You can smell trouble ten miles away."

Doris Ann tilted her head, and her focus floated, as if she were looking into the past. "There is the fact that the two group leaders have been visiting each other's rooms after hours."

"What?" said Miranda loudly. She clamped her hand over her mouth. "Sorry, I didn't see that one coming. They act like mortal enemies during the day."

Doris Ann widened her eyes.

Miranda sighed. "Of course you know everything. Still, can you keep an eye out for me? This company seems to have the moral compass of a groundhog."

"I'd be most happy to do that, child."

Miranda looked at the floor. *Would she be called a child until she was eighty? For pity's sake, she was a grown woman with a farm, a business, and a distillery.* She relaxed her shoulders. It was the country way, and she actually wouldn't change that for anything.

The cashier trotted down the hallway to wave the credit card at Doris Ann. "It worked. I'm not in trouble anymore."

"That's good, sweetie. Now return it to Mr. Tobin for me, please."

The youngster nodded slowly. "Of course. I'm sorry

for the trouble. I'll keep on studying the employee manual as soon as I get back." She scurried down the hall.

"You almost expect her to start skipping, don't you?" said Doris Ann.

Miranda thought for a second. "She's related to you, isn't she?"

Doris Ann smiled. "She's my niece. But everybody in these parts is related to everybody else in one way or another."

Miranda thought she should know that by now, but her New York City experience had dimmed some of those basic facts.

The entryway door opened, and Austin strolled into the lobby. Miranda waved him over to join her on the sofa in front of the stone fireplace.

"What's the mood with your contestants?"

"That sounds so weird. It's beginning to feel more and more like a reality show gone wrong." Miranda plopped down on the sofa. "Only the drama isn't scripted, It's real."

"Your Mr. Tobin seems to be taking that role to heart."

"He's not my Mr. Tobin. I would never put up with his antics."

Austin leaned back. "Just from the little time I've spent with him, he appears to be instigating conflict between the employees of his company. Even worse, he appears to be enjoying causing such distress and chaos. What does he have to gain by that?"

"I think this is his way of doing business. You're probably right. He gets his kicks by tormenting underlings. I have the emotional scars to prove it. Actually, I think he has informed them one by one that the losing team will have no future at BigSky." She looked at her watch. "The end of the workshop will be the end of their job."

"How long is this session going to take?"

"It's scheduled to last until about five. Then we'll go to the farmhouse and prepare a dinner there and check on the moonshine mash." Miranda smiled. "That means we have a little time to do some investigating. What's the news from Sheriff Larson?"

"He hasn't updated me since late yesterday. I'll give him a call right now."

Miranda put her hand on his arm. "Do you think we have time to go to his office? He won't be able to put us off as easily."

"Perfect," said Austin. "Let's take my truck. We should be back in plenty of time for you to take your group to the farmhouse."

"Better yet, I'll drive the van to the farmhouse and check up on things. You can pick me up and drop me off there. That'll save you a bit of mileage. The distances between everything here adds up."

After checking on the Hobb sisters and giving Sandy a snuggle and walkie, Miranda climbed into Austin's truck. On the road to Campton, Miranda turned off his radio. "Sorry, I can't talk and listen at the same time."

"You don't like talk radio, do you?"

"Nope. What gave me away?" asked Miranda.

"Maybe the fact that you turn it off every time you get in the truck?"

"Right, but I don't have to spend as many hours traveling in the truck as you do. I think some of them are interesting while some are merely provoking."

"Looks like we have a difference."

Miranda smiled. "It won't be the only difference in taste." She looked at his kind face, and it made her feel good. "Stop distracting me. I want to tell you that while you were giving your ranger talk about Rock Bridge, I noticed some odd exchanges between the two team leaders. Did you pick up on that?"

Austin squinted against the bright fall sunshine. "Now that you mention it, it did appear that they were trying to communicate with each other. What do you think?"

"I think they might be involved."

"You mean like in a relationship? Lovers?"

"Yes. Remember, Rowena said it would be against company personnel policy and would get them both fired."

"Is that still legal here in Kentucky?"

Miranda splayed out her hand towards the passing countryside. "We are living in a state that still has a law on the books that says a woman cannot buy a hat without her husband's permission. That's only in Owensboro, though, by the way."

"Okay, I get your point. That would be a difficult situation, but could it cause either of them to attack Mr. Burns to cover up their relationship? That seems extreme, but then, I don't know how hard it is to find another job in sportswear manufacturing."

Miranda shrugged her shoulders. "We need to confirm their situation. We don't know how getting fired might affect either one of them. There could be extenuating circumstances—a dependent parent, a medical situation, a debt problem, a thousand reasons."

"You can ask Rowena, can't you?"

"Right, I'll do that tonight, after I take everyone back to the lodge for the night."

"I'll stop by. You'll have some dessert left, won't you?"

Miranda huffed. "Of course. There'll be plenty. Ice cream, too."

"That clinches it."

Austin drove into Campton, turned onto Court Street, and parked a few doors down from the sheriff's office. The new courthouse was quite a change for the sheriff and the coroner. They had been located in a very tired building on Main Street.

The sheriff's office still smelled of new drywall and even newer fresh paint. He still had his old wooden desk, table, and file cabinets because the moving budget had been cut in half—twice. Miranda wondered if perhaps he didn't want to give up some familiar things. He was hunched over a laptop on the table beside his desk.

Miranda motioned for Austin to hurry. They slipped into the sheriff's office, and she gently shut the door. "We haven't heard anything about the case, so we're here to find out what's going on."

Sheriff Larson leaned back in his chair and stood up with his hands massaging the small of his back. "Ugh! I just finished my report. I hate reports. I particularly hate typing reports. I especially hate typing reports that Felicia promised she would type out for me."

Felicia stood in the doorway. "You should have taken a typing class in high school like I did. There were several boys in the class." Felicia walked into Sheriff Larson's office and sat in one of the guest chairs.

"No way. I was the captain of the basketball team. I would have been run out of town on a rail."

Felicia waved at the two remaining guest chairs. "Sit, sit. I have some news."

Miranda and Austin sat and looked at Felicia.

"Terry Burns died of a blunt force trauma." She looked at her husband and then at Miranda. "It was no trail accident. He was struck by the rock Rowena was holding."

Miranda bowed her head. "That's what I was expecting." She turned her attention to Sheriff Larson. "What are you going to do?"

"I'm going to hit up the judge for a warrant for her arrest."

Chapter 20

Sunday Afternoon, Farmhouse

"He's crazy," said Miranda.

"No he's not. He has solid evidence that ties her to the murder. He's going to arrest Rowena." Austin parked the truck in the farmhouse driveway. "Where's your van?"

"The girls probably parked it around behind the barn. It leaves the driveway free for all the deliveries I'm getting from local farmers. Most of them just leave things on the porch with a slip of paper for an invoice. I love that."

"The community is finally coming around to seeing how this cultural business is good for them."

"They are. Yesterday, when I took Sandy for his first walk, there was a basket of eggs and a pone of fresh cornbread. The note said they were extras at no charge."

"That's right neighborly. They must have heard about the new workshop."

"There are no secrets."

Austin paused. "That's the exact opposite from the truth. There are only secrets."

Miranda also paused, then squinted towards the farmhouse. "I think I agree. Secrets are the real truth here."

Iris and Lily came out of the house loaded with the ingredients and utensils needed for the cooking competition.

"Hey, Miranda," said Iris. "We're getting everything set up for the chicken pot pie competition."

"What happens if a team's pie is a complete mess? I mean—" Lily paused.

"Yucky?" finished Iris with a giggle.

"Revolting?"

"Repulsive?"

"Horrendous?"

"Disgusting?"

"All right, all right, that's enough." Miranda frowned until her forehead wrinkled. "You wouldn't want to be any of them trying to survive this workshop." She shook her head from side to side. "I still think I need to cancel it."

"You still need the money," said Iris.

"We still need the money," said Lily.

"Right."

Miranda felt the heavy burden of being the sole source of income for these young women. If she closed, they would find work somewhere. It would take time, and they might have to move to Lexington, Louisville, or Cincinnati. She knew they wanted to stay with their grandmother. One of her middle-of-the-night brainstorms was to set up a bakery counter in the distillery gift shop. Something to let them earn a little cash in the off-season.

It would go over well with the locals, in general, to be able to sell homemade goods. It might not be much, but every bit helped. She'd have to work out the numbers. One more thing on the list.

Miranda smiled. "We could make them go without supper as a just reward for wasting good ingredients." She saw the look of horror on their faces. She waved a hand back at the farmhouse. "Don't worry. We have plenty of leftover venison stew to serve up as a last-minute dinner."

Austin motioned for Miranda to follow him back to his truck. "I don't think we can possibly clear Rowena before he serves that warrant. How are you going to keep running the workshop and still investigate?"

She sighed again, acknowledging to herself that she was doing more sighing than anything else lately. "I've been thinking about that since Mr. Tobin will likely want me to continue anyway."

"Well?"

"I'll scale back on the remaining challenges. My excuse will be that I can only manage the events that don't require Rowena's evaluation assessments. We'll concentrate on pass/fail contests that lead us up to the Thanksgiving dinner."

"What if he insists that you continue with the assessments anyway?"

"I'll insist that he perform the evaluations himself because he would be the benefactor of the results. I can also assert that I don't have the qualifications, and his fellow executives would object. He certainly would want to avoid that."

"Perfect. I'll be back after you've taken everyone back to the lodge."

She watched him drive down the dirt road. Thoughts of their date night began to play in her mind. Why would he suggest a fancy restaurant? He despised them. Did he even have a dress shirt and tie? Of course he would. Every grown man out here had a funeral suit.

Miranda drove back up to the lodge, and the participants were waiting under the shelter of the entry porch. They were somber and subdued to the point that Miranda considered calling the evening off herself. But the thought of the ensuing argument with Mr. Tobin put that wish right out of her head.

"Let's take the scenic route back to the farmhouse this time. I can tell you a bit about the geology of the area. We usually see a few birds and animals as well. With the trees bare, you can see so much more."

Miranda drove a little below the rated speed limit to reduce the effect of the switchback curves and to allow her passengers time to view the rocky cliffs and deep ravines. She recited her normal patter to a very quiet van. They finally turned off Highway 15 onto the small road that led to the farmhouse.

"Let me out! I'm going to be sick."

Miranda pulled over as quickly as she could without tipping the van over into the deep drainage ditch on the side of the road. She hopped out and slid open the side panel door. Out jumped Lisa. She ran to the drainage ditch, dropped to her hands and knees, then retched.

Miranda grabbed a bottle of water and shouted to the passengers, "Anyone got a clean handkerchief or something?"

"I have some paper towels I took from the bathroom."

Miranda rolled her eyes but grabbed the stack from Victor.

Lisa was sitting back on her heels.

Miranda wet a paper towel and gave it to her. "Use this to wipe your face."

"Thanks. I don't know what came over me."

Miranda moistened the rest of the towels. Then she pressed them to the back of Lisa's neck.

"I'm sorry," said Lisa. "I'm holding everyone up for the next competition."

"There's no rush. I'm in charge of the next event." Miranda saw the look of relief on Lisa's face. "Mr. Tobin won't be coming out to the farmhouse until later this evening—if he shows up at all."

Lisa sat flat on her bottom and moved the wet towels from the back of her neck to her forehead. "I'm feeling much better now." She started to get up, then sat right back down.

"Don't rush it. You're going to be fine. We're going to sit here until you feel like you can make it to the farmhouse. It's only a mile and a half up this road. See if you can drink a little water. If you can keep it down, we'll get going again." Miranda recalled that Lisa had allergies to pollen. Why on earth would she be working for a sportswear company? Of course, she didn't usually work outdoors.

Lisa drank a few swallows and sat still for a few more minutes. Then Miranda watched the color slowly return to her pale face. At that point, Lisa straightened her shoulders and stood. "Wow, thanks, I feel so much better."

"Good, but let's put you up front with me."

Miranda held her steady by one arm and helped her climb into the passenger seat. She started up the van, turned the air down, and adjusted the vents to blow on Lisa.

They were in the driveway in less than five minutes.

"I'm fine now. I'm convinced I was carsick. It hasn't happened since I was a kid, but those twisty roads did it."

"I won't take the scenic route again. It's highway all the way for this group from here on."

The Hobb sisters had everything ready on the picnic tables in the side yard. Each table had precisely the same ingredients, utensils, and identical recipe instruction cards.

"Gather around your tables while I go over the ground rules."

The group quietly gathered and looked at Miranda. Everyone was dull and lethargic. This was no way to compete. They needed to snap out of it.

"Come on, guys. What's the matter? You've never been so quiet."

Carol replied immediately. "Knowing that one of your coworkers might get arrested for killing one of your bosses is quite the experience."

Miranda pressed her lips together.

Jeffrey spread his hands out wide. "Why is this farce continuing? We should all walk out and . . ."

Miranda shrugged. "If that's what you want to do, I'll drive you back to the lodge and I'll take my lumps."

"What do you mean?" asked Carol.

"I will lose a pile of money by not completing the contract." She pointed to the ingredients on the tables. "I had to pay cash money for these ingredients. Small farmers don't deal in credit. The down payment has cleared the bank, but that won't cover what I've spent so far."

Oliver blurted out, "It doesn't look promising that Mr. Tobin's corporate credit card was declined up at Hemlock Lodge."

Everyone looked down at the ground and at one another. Carol looked at Jeffrey and shrugged her shoulders.

Miranda softened her voice. "There's no one here but us, so I can tell you that this event results in a tie."

"A tie?" said Jeffrey. "But we haven't even made them yet."

"No, you haven't, but I think you deserve a night of relaxation and a chance to do some honest team-building with your peers."

"So no scoring?" asked Carol.

"No scoring. You have all the ingredients you need. Relax and enjoy making a meal with people you're going to work with for a long, long time. I hope."

The mood lifted immediately, with smiles and a few high fives spreading among the group.

Miranda put her hands on her hips. "Now, that's the kind of attitude I thought would be developing in this workshop." She smiled broadly. "Give your pies to either Iris or Lily for baking, and then we'll go out and look at our mash."

She turned to leave them to assemble their pies. "Oh, I have a bit of my uncle's finest for a little sampling for our time out in the barn. It's a new cocktail I'm trying out. It's called a Shinetini."

Chapter 21

As soon as the chicken pot pies were in the oven, Miranda gathered everyone in the barn. She continued instructing the candidates about the state of their mash and helped them make any flavoring adjustments they needed. Team Firehawks had decided to add a cinnamon spice with ginseng flavoring while Team Sweatsocks went with jalapeño and lime.

Sandy was on his best behavior around the crowd, begging for pets, cuddles, and belly rubs. He lightened the mood just by being curious, cautious, and especially lovable. Miranda thought he would be a great addition to her future cultural experiences. Especially when he had outgrown his shoestring-pulling, ankle-attacking, boot-chewing phase.

"Now, as your reward, and as a training example,

here's how I mix my latest concoction using a rare jar of my late uncle Gene's famous moonshine. Don't forget, each team will create a cocktail that will be served with our Thanksgiving meal on Tuesday."

Miranda packed a large copper cocktail shaker with ice from a copper ice bucket. She added about six ounces of her uncle Gene's moonshine and topped it with a generous splash of vermouth. She shook the mixture for about a minute and strained it into miniature mason jars.

Then she garnished each jar with a spear of rosemary and passed the drinks around to every candidate.

Lifting her jar, she said, "Let's toast to a good life, good friends, and the joys of food, drink, and the creative arts."

Everyone clinked jars and sipped the unusual cocktail.

As Miranda expected, the reactions were all over the map. Two pulled sour faces and put down their mason jars.

Xavier coughed like a barking seal and grabbed his throat. "I have an intolerance for rosemary. I didn't think a garnish would trigger it, but I was wrong."

Carol's eyes widened. "Do you have an EpiPen?"

"No, it's not that kind of reaction. I just need to take a maximum dose of Excedrin and lie down in a dark room for about an hour." He started wobbling. "Soon. Soon would be good."

"Great." Miranda came over and slipped Xavier's arm over her shoulders. "Can you get the other side, Carol? He can use my bed in the front room. I have plenty of Excedrin."

They frog-marched Xavier out of the barn and into Miranda's bedroom. Carol helped him get off his shoes while Miranda grabbed the Excedrin along with a glass of water. They soon had him tucked in under a heavy quilt, with Miranda's new blackout blinds pulled down.

"I'll check on him in a few minutes," whispered Carol as they backed out of the room and returned to the barn.

"Hey, everyone." Miranda noticed all the jars were empty. "Those pies are smelling very close to done, and I see the cocktails are gone. Let's get your pies and dig in."

The pies were shared and eaten with a green salad wilted with bacon grease.

Meanwhile, Miranda ate leftover venison stew in the kitchen with Sandy and the sisters.

Afterward, Lily and Iris passed out blondies with a scoop of homemade vanilla ice cream. Everyone enjoyed at least one serving, and some begged the sisters for a second helping.

Cleanup had started and appeared to be going well. Everyone was in a great mood. The candidates were wandering all over the place, but things were winding down. Miranda was delighted with the way the group interacted with one another during this noncompete event.

Miranda was about to clear the final place setting from one of the picnic tables when Xavier appeared in the side yard. "Hey, why didn't you wake me up? I'm hungry."

Carol pointed to a vacant space with a serving of chicken pot pie and salad covered with a kitchen towel. "We didn't forget you. I would have saved some pie for you."

Xavier lifted the towel and inhaled the aroma. "Wow, I'm starved."

After everyone helped the sisters clear off the picnic tables, wash, dry, and put away the dishes, Miranda began telling everyone to assemble on the front porch so she could make some announcements and then take them back to the lodge for the night.

A long black car drove up, and Mr. Tobin got out and slammed the door. He was looking at his cell phone. "Hey, there's no signal." He looked at Miranda, back at his phone, then back at Miranda, as if the world had turned into a foreign planet and she knew its customs. "I need to make an urgent call."

Miranda didn't roll her eyes, but it took a massive amount of control, and she probably revealed her irritation anyway.

"Use my landline. There's a handset in the front room."

He bolted into the house, letting the screen door slam behind him.

She went ahead and rolled her eyes this time, and then her shoulders slumped. He had parked his BMW right behind her rental van. She couldn't take the candidates back to the lodge. They were stuck until he finished his conference call and moved it.

Miranda was about to open the screen door to go back into the house when Lisa barged in front of her. "Look out. I'm going to be sick." Lisa ran through the house into the bathroom just off the kitchen.

Janice had stepped onto the porch but turned back and fell onto all fours and retched into the grass.

Carol stood up from the picnic table and clutched her stomach. "My stomach hurts."

Miranda yelled into the house. "Iris and Lily. Quick. I need wet towels out here. People are getting sick. It looks like food poisoning."

Lily was first out with two wet towels. Miranda pointed to Janice, and Lily bent down to comfort Janice with soothing words and cool towels.

Iris soon followed, and Miranda pointed to Carol, who was sitting in the grass, holding her stomach and rocking back and forth.

Miranda dashed into the house. She knocked on the bathroom door. "Lisa, are you all right?"

The bathroom door opened and a very pale Lisa stepped into the kitchen. Miranda grabbed her arm and helped her sit on one of the kitchen chairs.

"Are you okay?" Miranda grabbed a clean towel from the bathroom, wet it, wrung it out, and placed it on the back of Lisa's neck. "Do you feel better now?"

Lisa took the towel, leaned back, and put it on her forehead. "Just shaky."

Mr. Tobin was sitting at the dining table, still on his conference call. "But that won't get up the market share we're after. You have to come up with a better plan."

Miranda went into the bathroom and foraged in the medicine cabinet. Nothing. She returned to Lisa with a cold bottle of Ale-8 from the refrigerator. "Here. I know this is the last thing you want to take, but it's full of ginger. I promise it will make you feel better within fifteen minutes." She looked into Lisa's doubtful eyes. "I promise."

Lisa took a large swig, then shuddered from her head to her shoulders, then down to her hips.

"You need to lie down." Miranda helped Lisa get up. "Let's get you onto the couch."

Lisa moved like a newly walking toddler, but she made it to the living room with Miranda supporting her around the waist. "Lie down here for a few minutes. I'll be back with a stronger ginger tea."

Miranda covered Lisa with the quilt that was folded over the back of the couch, then replaced the wet cloth on her forehead. "Stay quiet."

She ran outside to help Lily with Janice. They got her into the house and put her in Miranda's bed. Lily raced back into the kitchen and rolled some ice into the towel while Miranda tucked Janice into the quilt.

This bed has seen more occupants in the last hour than in the last decade.

Miranda dosed Janice with the ginger ale and then asked Iris to stay with her. Then she checked on Lisa, who was breathing easily and holding the cloth on her head.

"How are you doing?"

"Better. You were right about that ginger ale."

"Uh-huh," Miranda went into the dining room. Mr. Tobin was still on his conference call. She stood there, wondering if it was worth the trouble to get him off the phone. He would only make the situation worse. It was better to get everything under control before she interrupted him.

Shaking her head in frustration, she ran outside to see if she could help Iris with Carol.

In a demonstration of real teamwork, the candidates had taken off their jackets and fashioned a comfortable space on one of the bench seats for Carol. Miranda gave her a dose of the Ale-8. She had a good supply on hand because it was a great mixer with her moonshine. It was also her favorite pop. "How are you doing?"

Carol was pale around the lips and was shivering, even though everyone's jackets were piled on her. "It's awful."

"Take this." Miranda offered her a dose of the ginger ale.

"No, no, no." She struggled to push away the pink bottle. "I can't. It only makes me worse. There's something about ginger ale that turns my stomach. I don't know what it is, but I've always been this way."

"No problem. What about a sports drink? I've got some Gatorade."

Carol made a face.

"How about a little baking soda in warm water? Can you take that?"

Carol lay back down. "Yes, that's no problem."

Miranda ran back into the house and mixed a tiny bit of baking soda into a glass of warm water. Carol was able to sit up and drink that down, but she groaned and waggled her head from side to side. Carol turned her head to the side and retched up the baking soda mixture into the grass.

"Not much help, then. Hang in there. I've got one more thing to try. If that doesn't work, we'll be taking you down to Doc Watson's clinic in Campton."

Carol groaned with the pain, then snuggled deeper into the pile of jackets.

Miranda looked around at the completely unaffected Sweatsocks team. That meant that someone had slipped something into the Firehawks' chicken pot pie.

"Okay, fellows, let's get her inside. It's too chilly to be out here to be without jackets. We may have to take her to the Campton clinic. I've got one last old-timer's remedy. We'll know what we have to do in a few minutes."

On her way to the kitchen, Miranda thought Lisa was looking much better, and she checked on Janice as well. They were both on the way to recovery. She put her hands on her hips. "What kind of person would do this?"

In the kitchen she pulled down the bottle of apple cider

vinegar from her spice cupboard and poured a half cup into a glass, then added an equal measure of water.

Was it time to interrupt the elephant in the dining room, who was still on his conference call? She hesitated. What could he do to help? Nothing. He would only make things worse. She felt like a coward but was convinced that it was better for everyone if she waited until he finished up with his teleconference.

As an extra measure of general hospitality, Miranda made a supper tray for Mr. Tobin that included a bowl of venison stew, some homemade crackers, and a cup of mint herbal tea that always tasted great with her stew. She placed the tray next to Mr. Tobin on the dining table. He grunted thanks and continued with the conference call. *At least he can't say we aren't taking care of everything in reasonable order.*

She checked each of the sick participants several times over in the next quarter hour, with Mr. Tobin absolutely oblivious to the activities happening around him. Cool cloths were refreshed. An additional dose of ginger ale was given to Lisa. Carol had finally begun to recover and was able to keep the apple cider vinegar mixture down.

At the end of another fifteen minutes, thankfully, everyone was sitting up, talking, sipping water and/or juice to rehydrate themselves. Things were looking better.

Miranda inhaled a huge sigh of relief. Everyone was going to recover.

She heard Mr. Tobin sign off his conference call. He walked out into the living room and replaced the handset in its charging stand, then looked around at the activity. "What's going on here?"

Miranda turned to stand directly in front of him. "Three of the candidates got food poisoning."

"What? How could you let that happen? Don't you know the basics of simple food care?"

Miranda folded her arms tight across her chest to ensure that she wouldn't hit him right smack in the nose. "It wasn't the food *I* served. I believe that a member of Team Sweatsocks sabotaged the chicken pot pie made by the Firehawks team." She gave him a fierce look. "This is in response to your horrible competition."

"That's ridiculous." He folded his arms to mirror hers and stared. "You're trying to cover up the incompetence of your staff. Are they old enough to work? Are they legal?"

Miranda pressed her lips together to avoid cursing up a blue streak. She mentally counted to five, slowed her breathing, then counted to five again. "You can be sure that I will get to the bottom of the food poisoning, but I strongly suggest that we stop the team-to-team scoring and get back to the original team-building concept."

"That simply will not support my goals." Mr. Tobin stared at her, daring her to protest his decision. "Now, I need to make a few announcements. Have everyone gather on the front porch."

Furious at being ordered around like a lackey, Miranda stood mute.

This won't help, she realized. *He'll just pick one of the candidates to do it. They've been through enough today.*

"Fine." She turned on her heel and went outside. She cupped her hands around her mouth. "Hey, everyone, Mr. Tobin has some announcements. Gather all your personal items and assemble in the front yard."

There was a general grumbling and griping, but soon everyone, including the recently sick, stood on the front porch with their backpacks, jackets, and water bottles.

The temperature had begun to drop and darkness had fallen. Miranda flicked on the porch light.

She stood beside Mr. Tobin on the porch while Iris and Lily began the cleanup of today's less-than-successful final event.

Mr. Tobin cleared his throat. "Your attention, everyone." He glared at each of the candidates one by one. It was a small-minded technique to emphasize his status and power.

"I've been told that there have been some disturbing incidents regarding the competition." He paused until the silence was suffocating. "I want to reinforce that the stakes are high. Your career is at risk if you don't perform well in this workshop. That will also be the result if I find out that any one of you has resorted to sabotage to gain an advantage."

Absolute silence from the candidates.

Mr. Tobin put his hands in his pockets and began to rock back and forth on his heels. "Now would be the perfect time for you to withdraw if you feel this isn't the way you want to work."

Again, nothing but silence.

"Good. If that is your decision, I want to make this perfectly clear that you can, of course, stop participating at any time." He glanced sideways at Miranda.

There was a rustling of whispers that swept through the group.

"However, there will be consequences. If anyone wants to drop out, he or she can expect a severance package waiting for them back in the Human Resources department." He grinned and waited a moment. "Anyone?" Another pause. No one moved. "Very well. I'll see you tomorrow."

He stomped down the porch steps, got in his corporate car, and drove off.

Everyone stood there for a moment, not sure of what was expected of them.

"Okay, everybody. Let's get back in the van. I need to get you back to the lodge for a good night's rest. Tomorrow is another challenging day, and I'm adding extra precautions about food safety from this moment on." Miranda stepped down from the porch, helped them pack up, and then drove them to the lodge. Just before they arrived, she asked the group, "What do you think? Should I call my new cocktail a Shinetini or a Moontini?"

Jeffrey grimaced. "In tribute to your unfortunate participants, it should be called a Doomtini."

Chapter 22

Sunday Evening, Farmhouse

As soon as she returned from Hemlock Lodge, Miranda collapsed onto the couch and patted the cushion beside her for Sandy. She didn't ordinarily encourage him to hop onto the furniture, but it had been an awful day. It took six tries, but his short little legs made it and he wobbled his way up onto her lap. Miranda loved his lickity kisses. She felt like she had been rode hard and put away wet.

"I think we need these," said Rowena. She stood in the doorway to the dining room with an opened bottle of red wine and two glasses.

Miranda sighed. "Are you feeling well enough? I'm worried about your memory."

"Would you rather have chamomile tea? I've opened the bottle, but I can put the cork back in and shove it back into the fridge. It would be no problem."

"No, no. Actually, the wine's perfect. Just what I need."

Rowena filled the wineglasses, handed one to Miranda, then cozied down into the other end of the couch. "This has been beyond horrible, and I'm glad I'm staying here with you."

"I'm so glad. I know we haven't seen each other in such a long time, but actually, it feels like it was only yesterday."

Blinking rapidly, Rowena sipped her wine. "That makes me feel so special." She looked around the room from one end to the other.

"What do you need?" asked Miranda.

"A tissue. I'm really emotional."

Miranda bolted into her bedroom for the tissue box she kept beside her bed. She pulled out two and gave them to Rowena. "Here you go. You know, it's completely understandable to be emotional after a traumatic event. Have you ever been a witness to a car accident?"

Rowena took the tissues and blew her nose. "No. I've never even been to a funeral. My family is quite long-lived." She snuffled into the tissues. "My mee-maw is over ninety, some aunts are in their late eighties, and I have a great-uncle who is one hundred and three."

"Take some long, slow, really deep breaths. That calms me sometimes."

Rowena just stared at her.

"Really," said Miranda. "Try it. What have you got to lose? A bunch of tense muscles heading for a headache, that's what." She paused again. "I'm telling you, do it."

Rowena pressed her lips into a straight line, then put her wineglass on the end table. "Fine." She closed her eyes, inhaled a deep breath, held it for a count of four, then exhaled for a count of eight.

"You've taken yoga, haven't you?" Miranda noted the changed posture and the practiced belly expansion on the inhale.

Rowena said with her eyes still closed. "Uh-huh, so have you. Either join me or stop talking."

They continued with deep belly breathing for more than ten minutes.

Miranda stopped first to check on how Rowena was doing. That broke the spell, and Rowena opened her eyes and smiled brightly for the first time since the incident.

"Thanks, that feels so much better." Rowena picked up her wineglass again. "It gives me enough courage to ask you for a giant favor."

"What do you need?"

"I think I'm in over my head here. I've always been able to handle whatever problems came my way. That's the way I was raised. You know the drill. Don't be a bother. Don't make waves. Go along to get along. I've done that my whole life."

"That's what my folks taught me as well." Miranda rolled her eyes. "It didn't work with me."

Rowena choked back a loud cough. She said *sorry* with her eyes.

"I think that's why they sent me down here so much," said Miranda. "It gave them a rest from my misbehaving ways and my relentless curiosity. I was always getting into mischief. Nothing bad really, but I'm sure they appreciated the rest."

Rowena sniffed and wiped at her eyes. "I would like

your help. I don't think I hit Terry. Unfortunately, I can't say for sure that I didn't. I'm asking you to investigate for me, and I'm praying that you may be able to save my life."

"That's a giant favor, all right."

"I know it is, but I don't have the money for an attorney. I don't think I did it, and you've done this before. That's what the sheriff's wife said. She said you had a talent for investigation. The kind of attention to detail and picking up on things other missed."

"I'm not going to promise anything, but I will do my best to find out what happened. Be aware that you might not like the answer."

"I understand, but that's all I want." Rowena sighed and stood. "Time for me to get to sleep. I'm still feeling disoriented and a little fuzzy. Something's in there that is tickling my mind about something important, particularly important, but I can't remember. The harder I try, the farther away it fades."

"Try not to think about it. It might return if you stop torturing yourself about it."

Rowena nodded, then stood. "I'm exhausted. If you don't mind, I'll take this wine upstairs and read for a bit. I need to escape."

"Did you bring a book? My uncle's library is in the second bedroom. He was a big fan of Michael Connelly, Stephen King, Lee Goldberg, and Jeffrey Deaver."

"No thanks. I need a book that gives me comfort, not nightmares. I have my two favorites with me, *Little Women* and *Pride and Prejudice*. I know them practically by heart. I can start anywhere and be asleep in minutes. Good night."

"See you in the morning." Miranda heard the door to the upstairs attic close and tracked Rowena's footsteps to the bedroom overhead.

She heard steps on the porch, and Sandy yipped a friendly yowl. That was followed by tapping on the screen door.

"Everybody has gone?" asked Austin.

"Finally," said Miranda. "Come on in and help me get my head around what we need to do to get Rowena cleared of this mess. Oh, and there's wine. Go get a glass."

Austin came in and picked up the bottle of wine. He examined the label. "Perfect. Anything from New Zealand is wonderful. I'll be right back, don't move." He returned from the kitchen with a wineglass and poured for himself. "What's the matter? You haven't moved an inch."

"I'm feeling like a failure. This team-building workshop looked so promising on paper. My planning was meticulous. I enjoyed setting out the challenges. Everything should have been such fun, but it's an awful disaster. I feel like giving it all up and telling Mr. Tobin to just go away."

"Wow. That's not like you at all." Austin put his glass on the end table and scooted over towards Miranda. "You need a hug."

She smiled. "Yes, I do." She met his embrace and shared a lingering kiss. It soon ended when Sandy protested his lack of participation. Miranda laughed and held Sandy up in front of her face. "Are you jealous, my little man?" She sat him on the floor, and he ran to the front door.

Miranda giggled her amusement. "Duty calls. Let's go out and look at the stars."

"Get your jacket. It's crisp out there." They stood at the

edge of the porch and gazed up at a starry sky while Sandy gave the front yard a thorough border patrol search.

"Did you notice any sign of a relationship between Carol and Jeffrey?"

Austin folded his arms and bent his head. "Nope. I noticed that Carol took a leadership role with her group more successfully than Jeffrey was able to manage. Do you think they might be in a relationship?"

"If they are, it's a serious violation of company policy."

"I wonder if there's any sign of it on social media."

"Good idea, let's check." She clapped her hands and rubbed them together. "Sandy, come on in."

They signed on to her computer and searched through the most popular sites until they found one where they both had accounts. Miranda looked back several years and discovered a few posts of them together about six months ago.

"There hasn't been anything at all in the last few months. That's no help."

"But it also supports the theory that they're actually a couple. If they're violating company policy, they won't post anything to give the personnel department reason to discipline them."

"Right. That's not normal. There should be family, outings, vacations, that sort of stuff." She sat there for a moment. "What about Tyler? She might be able to dig up some information about BigSky staff that have been in the *Lexington Herald*. More to the point, she could find stuff that didn't make it to print."

"Sure." Austin started typing into his smartphone. "I'll text her the names. Have you got a list to email me?"

Miranda sent the client list, and Austin forwarded it to his reporter sister. "How long do you think she'll take?"

"Depends on what she's working on. If she's busy, we might never hear. If she's bored, we might have a chance to interest her."

"I think it's wonderful that she takes the time to support her baby brother." She grinned up at him and watched his face growing dark. "You really don't like that, do you?"

"Sorry, but she really plays that up in public. I'm not very little anymore."

Miranda pressed her lips together to keep from saying something. She couldn't suppress a smirk, though. "I'll just give a quick look and see if anyone else has questionable social media interactions." She typed away while Austin looked over her shoulder. She thought it should bother her for him to hover—but it didn't.

Turning back to the keyboard, it was easy enough to find social media posts on the candidates. Most were athletic competitors and loved to share images of race finishes and photos of training diets.

"I haven't found anything at all on Oliver. Why would he be applying for a marketing job in a major sportswear company without some qualifications? That seems off."

Austin's phone pinged. He read out the message. "'Lisa is struggling with an ugly divorce. The custody of her three-year-old daughter hangs in the balance. She must provide proof that she is gainfully employed at a hearing next week. On deadline. Will send other results later.'"

"That could be a motive if Mr. Burns was going to use this workshop as justification to furlough Lisa."

Miranda heaved an explosive sigh and stood. "I'm exhausted. I need to get some sleep. Tomorrow is packed full of events, and we're getting nowhere."

"We need to give my sister some time to trawl the archives. She'll get more for us tomorrow, I'm sure."

Miranda shut down her computer and walked Austin out to the front porch.

He waved. "It will be better tomorrow."

Chapter 23

The first competition of the day was set at a local zip line attraction. Each team would complete an aerial obstacle course more than fifty feet above the ground. The early morning start was deliberate. The owner guaranteed Miranda that they would be the only customers. In fact, he confided that they would be his last customers. He was shutting down for the season after their visit.

The event was organized as a relay race, with the five members of each team completing a circuit on an obstacle course, then passing a token to the next player. The token was a simple whistle attached to a lanyard—a red one for the Firehawks and a blue one for the Sweatsocks. Miranda explained that each candidate had to hand the lanyard to the next person on the team. Anyone who threw the token would be disqualified, along with their team.

"Because we're not professional athletes, here, each team member can elect to skip one of the challenges."

Rowena tapped Miranda on the shoulder. "Can I say something?"

"Absolutely." Miranda stepped aside.

"There's a good reason for the tokens to be a whistle." She held up the red lanyard and blew a healthy blast. "If you get into trouble on one of the obstacles, your whistle will let us know. Give it a huge blast."

Miranda smiled. If she ever needed an assistant, Rowena was shaping up nicely. She resumed. "I'm going to give everyone fifteen minutes to examine the course and choose the running order for your team. Strategy is the key to winning this event, and placing your team in the right order will ensure that you perform at your best. Your time starts with the whistle." Miranda looked at her watch and waited until the second hand swept to the twelve, then blew her whistle.

The Sweatsocks scrambled towards the obstacle course. Carol huddled her team into a small group off to the side, and she began shuffling the order. Then they all practiced a round of transferring the token while they stood there.

Jeffrey's team tackled the obstacles in no particular order, and he yelled at them to pay attention to his instructions. They ignored him completely. He was furious. After some particularly nasty name-calling from Jeffrey, they gathered around him and appeared to take a few instructions in the brief time that was left.

At the end of a fast fifteen minutes, Miranda blew her whistle. "Time's up. Everyone, please return to your places at the starting line."

The teams were only six feet apart and lined up in race order, with both Carol and Jeffrey taking the anchor positions. Lisa was first for the Firehawks and Oliver was first for the Sweatsocks. Miranda stationed herself off to the right of the course and Rowena was positioned on the left in order to observe and document the state of fair play among the competitors.

Miranda waited until everyone was silent and ready for the race, then blew the whistle.

Lisa and Oliver exploded into action against the course. They finished with Oliver about ten feet ahead and passed off to Victor and Janice.

The next two runners were Eileen and John. The Firehawks fell a little farther behind. The competition flipped sides when Xavier overtook Sheila, so that Carol had a bare five-foot lead over Jeffrey.

At the second obstacle, Jeffrey overtook Carol, and it looked like a victory for the Sweatsocks was in the bag. Jeffrey leaped onto the balance beam but tumbled off into the chipped bark. Carol sped past him and crossed the finish line alone.

Team Firehawks jumped up and down with Carol in delight at the win. Then Carol looked at the Sweatsocks and discovered that they were huddled over at the beam. She sprinted back. "Jeffrey! What's wrong?"

Jeffrey was sitting up and holding his left ankle with both hands. "Ouch, I think it's broken."

Miranda knelt and slipped off Jeffrey's shoe and sock. She felt the joint and noticed the tightness and heat from the injury but couldn't immediately tell if anything was broken. "Sorry, Jeffrey. You've got to go to the clinic and get that looked at. You're out of the running for now. Pick a replacement leader."

Jeffrey looked up at Carol. "What do you think? Oliver?"

Carol nodded. "I think that's a good choice."

Jeffrey turned to John. "Okay. You're the new leader. Keep things going so that we win. I need to keep my job."

Rowena wriggled her way into the circle surrounding Jeffrey. "I'd better take him over to the clinic." She looked at Miranda. "It's logical. I'm the company representative, and I want to make sure this is documented properly. Everything should be covered as an injury at a company-sponsored event."

"I agree you need to be with him. But actually, we'll all have to go with you." Miranda stood. "We only have the van. I'll take you and Jeffrey directly to the clinic, and then I can transport everyone over to the farmhouse. Then I'll come back to pick you up, and then—" She caught a sense of overload from Rowena. "Don't worry. I'll see what we have to do at that point. Xavier and John, go help Jeffrey get to the van. Everybody, grab your stuff and let's get going."

Dr. Watson x-rayed Jeffrey's ankle and diagnosed it as a mild strain. He prescribed some pain medication and told Jeffrey to keep it elevated for the rest of the day. Given Jeffrey's excellent physical condition, Dr. Watson thought he would be as good as new tomorrow.

Back in the van, Rowena sat upfront. "I'm glad his injury is minor. The company isn't sympathetic to workers' compensation issues."

Miranda turned onto the Mountain Parkway to return to the farmhouse. "What do you mean?"

"There have been some issues against BigSky for ignoring legitimate claims when employees have been injured on the job. In fact, at one point they were fined for late payments to the company's policy in the state of Kentucky."

"When was this?"

"Only a few months ago. The chairman of the board called a special meeting to review current company financial statements, and they discovered nonpayment of quite a few of the employee benefit accounts."

"How did that happen?"

"I don't know. There were a lot of closed-door meetings." She tossed a worried look at the passengers and dropped her voice to a whisper. "Mr. Burns was included in all the meetings, and so was Mr. Tobin. The interesting part was that Lisa from accounting was in on a lot of those meetings, along with both Carol and Jeffrey."

"That's food for thought," said Miranda.

At the farmhouse, Miranda gave everyone fifteen minutes to take a break and told them to reassemble at their team's picnic tables in the side yard. She tucked Jeffrey onto the living room couch with a fluffy pillow beneath his injured ankle.

"Would you like a warm drink? Herb tea or hot chocolate?"

"No thanks." His eyes drooped, and his voice turned soft. "I'm going to take a nap."

Miranda started to reply, but he was already asleep.

She walked to the side yard and stood in front of the two picnic tables. At the Sweatsocks' table, Oliver was sitting in Jeffrey's spot.

These guys are all hyperaware of position and protocol. I'm so glad I work for myself. I wouldn't do well in such a political environment.

"Thanks for getting in place on time. Our next challenge is an artistic one. No more athletic challenges until tomorrow."

A ripple of relief went around the tables.

Miranda waved a hand around the surrounding farm-

land. "However, you'll still need to be on your toes. The
artistic event seems like a simple challenge, but you'll
need to pull from emotional depths to win this one. You'll
notice that the Hobb sisters have placed a clear vase filled
with water on each picnic table, along with a sharp pair of
pruning shears. Each team is to collect material from my
farm and create a centerpiece, but not just any centerpiece. The winning creation will have a theme and a reason for the elements selected. You have thirty minutes
starting now."

Oliver waved his whole arm at his team. "Come on.
Let's go!" He led the Sweatsocks out onto the field behind the barn. "Get some of that long stuff and try to find
something with a bit of color."

In contrast, Carol brought out a little notebook and
asked, "Let's choose a theme first. Then we'll gather materials that support our approach to the theme. Ideas?"

Lisa spoke first. "How about something that ties with
Firebird?"

"Great," said Janice. "We could gather branches with
red leaves. There are still a few around."

"Good," said Carol. "Eileen, what's your thinking?"

"Something that could represent flight. That would be
a good tie-in."

"Oh, I know," said Xavier. "I saw some milkweed
pods. We could include a sequence of several pods that
go from closed to releasing seeds and then to empty."

Carol's smile lit up her face. "That's awesome. Let's
say that our theme is rising fire, and keep that in mind as
we forage. Okay, let's gather for say"—she looked at her
watch—"ten minutes, and then we'll finish the arrangement."

Miranda watched in admiration. She would choose to

have Carol on any project that needed to get done quickly and meet the quality requirements as well. Hopefully, BigSky appreciated her skills. But given the nasty personalities at the top, Miranda hoped Carol would find employment with a company more aligned with her work ethic and substantial skills.

Miranda heard a car coming down the dirt road. She groaned. It was Mr. Tobin. He pulled into her driveway, and she walked over to meet him.

"Where is everyone?"

Why can't he keep up with the events? I gave him a schedule both as an email and a paper copy, too.

She quieted her thoughts before answering. "This event is to create a centerpiece for their lunch table, where each team's arrangement is expected to portray a chosen theme."

"Humph," said Mr. Tobin. "Not especially challenging."

Miranda raised her eyebrows. He obviously had never tried.

"Snake!" A screech came from behind the woodshed. "Help! There's a snake."

Miranda grabbed a hoe that was leaning against the house and ran around behind the woodshed.

Eileen was pale, rigid, and standing near the edge of what had been the tobacco patch that summer. "It's right there in that lump of grass."

Miranda walked over and stood next to Eileen. "Point out where you saw it."

Eileen pointed a trembling finger to a dried clod of thick grass. "It was right there."

Holding the hoe in front of her, Miranda stepped closer to the edge of the tobacco patch. She heard the movement in the dried vegetation before she saw it. It was a snake. She backed up a step and dropped the angle of the hoe and peered close. "You can relax. It's a black snake. They're beneficial, and we don't harm—"

"Here, I'll take care of this." Mr. Tobin grabbed the hoe from Miranda and quickly chopped down on the head of the snake. With two more mighty blows, the snake was dead. "There," he said. "That's a good job done." He handed the hoe to Miranda and turned back towards the side yard.

She stood holding the hoe for a few seconds. "Wait. You had no right to do that. That was a perfectly good black snake. They eat rodents and keep the ground aeriated." She stopped talking. He didn't hear a word she'd said.

Chapter 24

Monday Noon, Farmhouse

The centerpiece competition looked like it would be an easy win for the Firehawks. Carol's arrangement of their red, maple-leafed branches and milkweed pods floating in a flat bowl of water looked like it had been delivered by a florist. On the other table, the Sweatsocks had gathered random, unrelated bits of brush and bramble and jammed them into their vase with no hint of a theme.

"Are you ready for judging?" asked Miranda. She stood right next to the picnic tables and folded her arms.

Sheila huffed a great breath. "Could you give me just five minutes to straighten out this mess? It's terrible, and I don't want to go forward with this as our entry." She scowled at Oliver. "Some of us care about our jobs."

Miranda looked over at Carol, who shrugged her shoulders, indicating that she had no objection. "Fine.

Five minutes, and I'll be back with Mr. Tobin so he can judge."

Sheila smiled a grateful thanks. Then she grabbed the vase and pulled everything out of it and spread the collection across the surface of the table, sorting them by type as she worked. "While I'm rearranging, the rest of you see what kind of inspiring phrases you can generate around the theme of sports and community."

Victor and John stared at Sheila and then turned to Oliver for guidance. He put up his hands in a surrender position and pleaded, "She's right. This is rubbish, and we don't have a theme. Take over, Sheila."

She nodded. "Victor, write down this tagline and we'll brainstorm a campaign. A fit community supports a healthy environment. Ugh. We can do better than this. You guys start acting like we're in the office on a last-minute panic deadline. Think! Think! Think!"

Miranda left them to their challenge and went inside to fetch Mr. Tobin away from his work to choose the winner. As soon as she opened the front door, Sandy pounced at her shoelaces, tugged like a little badger, and untied her boot. She tripped and went down hard, but artfully avoided falling on him. Her hip took the brunt of the accident. Luckily, the fall was cushioned a little by the handmade rag rug in the center of the living room.

"Sandy, Sandy, Sandy." She scooped him up as he took advantage of her floor-bound posture to get in a dozen face licks before she scolded him. "No licking." She held up her index finger in front of his mouth. "Remember your training. No licking."

She struggled to stand up while carrying Sandy and rubbing the offended hip. "I'd better get some pain reliever for this, Sandikins. We still have a long day ahead of us." She hobbled into the dining room, where Mr. Tobin was on a conference call with someone who needed to be told something about a detailed financial process that meant nothing but gibberish to Miranda.

Do I need to be concerned about collecting the rest of my fee for this workshop?

After taking some pain pills, she checked with Iris and Lily on the progress of lunch. It was coming along quickly and would be ready in a few minutes. Still holding Sandy, she took a calming breath and went back into the dining room.

Mr. Tobin was typing away on his laptop with extraordinary focus, noisily pounding the keys as if they could emphasize the urgency of his message.

Miranda cleared her throat. "Sir, the teams are ready for you to judge the centerpiece and theme competition."

Mr. Tobin frowned, stopped typing, and looked up.

Sandy whined, and Miranda shushed him quietly.

Mr. Tobin looked at her with a distant focus and seemed to suddenly realize that he wasn't in his office. "What?"

"It's time to judge the centerpiece and theme competition. I think this particular challenge will highlight how each team would support new campaigns for BigSky. Are you ready? They've had a little additional time because I didn't want to interrupt you in the middle of a conference call."

He stood, flipped his laptop closed, and started out the door. "Fine. let's get this over with."

Miranda held the screen door open but wondered why Mr. Tobin didn't seem to be interested in the outcome of this event. Maybe he'd found out something from headquarters that had changed his hyperfocus on the workshop. She hoped that would make things easier for her.

Miranda followed Mr. Tobin outside to the side yard but put Sandy down for a potty break and a few passes of a fetch-the-stick game. Even though she tried, it was impossible to ignore the judging process. Mr. Tobin was standing tall just out in front of the two tables, with Rowena standing right next to him, taking notes in her stenographer's pad.

Mr. Tobin pointed to the Sweatsocks. "Let's hear your theme and its tagline."

Sheila stood up and gave an inspirational speech about the importance of sports play in the community and how BigSky uses its brand to inspire strong support for positive youth involvement in local charities.

Even though Miranda couldn't hear every word, she was impressed by Shelia's poise and sensed her spirited passion on the topic. She sat down, and the Sweatsocks gave her a round of applause.

Tobin looked over at Carol. "Your turn."

Carol stood. "Thank you, Sheila. That was an inspirational topic. We need to bring that up to the marketing department next week." Then she launched into her team's campaign.

Miranda didn't hear Carol's presentation because she accidentally threw Sandy's stick out too far and it landed on the road. Sandy tore down the little embankment like he was on fire. Miranda followed as quickly as her throbbing hip would allow. Locals tended to race down this road because there was hardly ever any traffic. There was a real danger that Sandy could get hit. She picked him up and then the stick and made it back to the front yard in time to hear Mr. Tobin say, "Sweatsocks win."

Rowena looked over and gave Miranda a silent signal for eating.

The Hobb sisters must have been watching because as soon as Rowena lowered her hand, the back porch screen door opened and then slammed. Lily and Iris brought out heaping trays of a local favorite. It was a filling lunch of fried bologna sandwiches on toasted, plain white bread with a good slathering of mayonnaise, accompanied by dill pickle slices and a coleslaw side salad. They also had a platter of double-fried French fries for each table and mugs of hot cider.

Rowena had her lunch with the Firehawks, and Mr. Tobin sat at the head of the Sweatsocks' table.

Miranda went back into the farmhouse and had the same lunch with Iris and Lily. She gave the teams plenty of time to clear their plates, then she walked back out to the picnic tables. "Now for our cooking challenge of the day. You will be preparing a trio of traditional Thanksgiving pies. The flavors are pumpkin, pecan, and chocolate cream."

She waved for the Hobb sisters to clear the tables. "While Lily and Iris are turning your tables into pie preparation areas, let's go into the farmhouse. I'll explain the rules."

The gathered in the living room. Jeffrey was awake. "I feel fine."

Miranda smiled. "Good. Oops, I almost forgot. Before starting the pies, you need to make a final check on the flavoring in your moonshine mash in preparation for the distillation process. I'll start distilling as soon as you approve your team's formula, so this is your last chance to make any adjustments.

"After that, each team will make their own pies, but the Hobb sisters will do the baking because there simply isn't enough room in my tiny kitchen. Then, you need to prepare your team's turkey for brining overnight. Next, you need to create a Jell-O salad to sit in the refrigerator overnight. Don't forget, before you start anything else, you need to check on your moonshine mash. I'll be starting the distillation process after I've dropped everyone off at the lodge for supper."

Jeffrey raised his hand, and Miranda pointed at him. "That's quite a long list of tasks. Are you certain we'll have time?"

"There's plenty of time if you split up your team to tackle the individual tasks. There are five of you."

"But my team is short one member." He pointed to his injured ankle. "I'm supposed to keep my leg elevated for the rest of the day—essentially, I'm still out of commission."

Miranda smiled. "The superior manager will allocate their limited resources according to current needs and capabilities. When they're under extreme pressure—that's when a great leader's skill is revealed." She tilted her head. "Go ahead and get your team organized. You can do your part from the living room couch. With another pillow or two at your back, you can sit up and we can keep that leg elevated. You can certainly mix ingredients quite handily from that position."

Carol stuck out her tongue at Jeffrey, and he returned the gesture.

Miranda turned back to the participants. "There is, of course, a ticking clock for these tasks. You all have until five o'clock this evening. At that time I'll take you all back to Hemlock Lodge for their buffet supper and, hopefully, a restful evening. I'll be picking everyone up at six o'clock tomorrow morning to start our Thanksgiving meal preparations. It's the final day of this workshop. Have fun, but keep your team focused."

Oliver raised his hand. "Can you see if Jeffrey is well enough to come back?"

"I'll check. He was supposed to keep that leg elevated for the rest of the day. But I don't see why he couldn't do that here at the picnic table. I'll be right back."

Miranda returned to the living room and found Jeffrey sound asleep with Sandy curled up in his arms, snoring softly. Sandy lifted his head and wiggled out to jump down and run to Miranda. She picked him up. "Jeffrey? How are you feeling? Your team is asking for your help."

He shook his head and stretched with both arms wide, along with a wide yawn. "Wow, I really conked out. I'm going to sleep well tonight." He wiggled his wrapped foot. "That feels much better."

"Good, you can move out to your team's picnic table if you feel up to it. I think Oliver would appreciate it. He seems a little lost."

Jeffrey huffed a great sigh. "Oliver has no confidence. He's good at nearly everything he attempts, but it defies logic that he thinks he's a clumsy idiot." Jeffrey stood and took a tentative step with his injured ankle. "I think I'm good to join them." He raised his eyebrows. "With a little help, of course."

"Perfect." Miranda grabbed a pillow and helped him with his jacket, and then took him outside. It only took a few minutes to get him settled at the leader's position at the Sweatsocks table.

Oliver smiled as bright as the summer sun. "Glad you're back."

Miranda left them to their delegation exercise. She went

back into the house to help the Hobb sisters clear up lunch. After everything had been put away, and all the kitchen surfaces had been wiped clean, Miranda said, "Go on out and help the teams with their pies. They should have gotten to the stage where they will be delighted to see you."

Miranda checked on Sandy and then went down to the barn. She stayed down there, working with each team's designated moonshiner. The Firehawks had sent their best cook, and Janice spent lots of time stirring the mash, adding a lot more cinnamon spice along with a little more ginseng flavoring.

Team Sweatsocks sent Oliver down to the barn. He stood in front of the mash, gave it a sniff, and shrugged his shoulders. "It's okay, I guess."

Miranda squinted her eyes. "Don't you think you might want a little more lime to cut the bite of the jalapeño?"

"Sure." He turned his back and escaped out the barn door.

Chapter 25

Miranda was exhausted after driving her clients back to the lodge and finally getting rid of Mr. Tobin. He treated her as if she was his personal aide. However, in all fairness, he treated all his employees that way, especially poor Rowena. Although Mr. Tobin wanted to keep working, Miranda insisted that she needed Rowena's help with all the preparation tasks for the big Thanksgiving dinner on Tuesday. He reluctantly agreed, but told Rowena she wouldn't be paid.

Miranda fed Sandy and was grateful that Lily and Iris had left the kitchen spotless. Those girls were worth their weight in ginseng. She stood in front of the opened refrigerator and asked Rowena, "Do you mind an omelet for supper? I'm barely on my feet, I'm so exhausted."

Rowena collapsed in one of the kitchen table chairs and propped her chin in her hands. "I'm almost too tired to eat, but as soon as you mentioned it, now I'm starved. An omelet will be just right."

"You're right about needing simple food. I've got mushrooms, spinach, and cheddar cheese. How's that?"

"That sounds exactly right."

Miranda chopped the onions, sliced the mushrooms, rinsed the spinach, and grated the cheese before she put the pan onto the burner with a large knob of fresh butter. In a separate bowl, she whipped four eggs and added a tiny bit of water. When the butter melted and the sizzling died down, she tossed in the onions for a quick caramelizing, then she added the mushrooms until they soaked up some butter. After that, she wilted the spinach. Finally, she poured in the egg mixture.

"Would you mind pouring us some prosecco? I'm in the mood for a little fizz."

"That sounds wonderful," said Rowena. "There's also a little coleslaw salad left over from lunch, along with a handful of purple grapes."

"Perfect."

Miranda waited for the liquid to firm up, then folded the omelet onto her plate. She cut it in half for Rowena's share, dusted each with salt and pepper, and threw on a pinch of fresh parsley.

They ate in silence, and by the time they finished their meal, Rowena's eyes were drooping at half-mast. She shook herself alert and started to clear the table, but Miranda stopped her. "Go on upstairs and get some rest. You've been more than helpful, but tomorrow is going to be busier than today."

"Thanks, but are you sure? I can help."

Miranda smiled. "No, you can't. Besides, I'm expecting Austin, and you'd be doing me a favor if I could actually spend a little time with him alone."

"In that case, good night."

Although it was only seven o'clock, Miranda was pretty sure Rowena would be asleep in minutes. The landline phone rang.

"Miranda, this is Sheriff Larson. I'm out by you on another call and would like to stop by for a chat about your workshop folks."

"Sure, anything I can do to help." That was what she said out loud. However, Miranda felt a cold rush down her arms to the point that she shivered. "I've got some prep work to do for tomorrow, but whatever you need to know, I'm glad to help."

She replaced the handset and put her hands on her hips. This was worrying her. Was the sheriff closing in on Rowena? Was he coming over to arrest her for Mr. Burns's murder? She brushed the negative thoughts aside. She would know soon enough.

Miranda cleaned up the kitchen and began checking that everything was ready for tomorrow's big Thanksgiving dinner. The turkeys were brining, the pies were ready to bake, and the last chore was to go out to the barn to make sure the distilling moonshine was bottled and secure.

She called out for Sandy and put on her jacket for a sniff-and-piddling walk down towards the barn. She got a flashlight, then put him on a leash because it was pitch-dark. His energetic puppy ways could get him into serious trouble, ranging from a skunk spray to porcupine quills or even a rattlesnake bite.

Sandy had led Miranda around the side of the house to

the front yard with his eager snuffling. He yipped when he saw Austin walking up the drive and pulled hard to drag Miranda towards the ranger.

Miranda laughed. "It's a beautiful evening."

"Yes," said Austin, giving Sandy a scratch behind his ears, then he kissed Miranda on the cheek. "Is everything ready for the big day tomorrow?"

"I think so, but I'm worried."

"Worried? That's silly. I'm sure you've got every detail under control as usual."

"I'm not worried about the Thanksgiving dinner. I'm worried that we haven't gotten close to helping Sheriff Larson find out who killed Mr. Burns. He's trusted me to help figure out what happened up there on the trail and I haven't gotten any further with the investigation than that first day."

"Nonsense. There's been no time. Don't worry. You're good at observing details that are obvious to you but invisible to the rest of us. You're organized about it, too."

"I don't feel like any of those things right now. Even worse, Sheriff Larson's coming over tonight to see if I have any additional information about my clients. Oh, before I forget—you're invited for our Thanksgiving dinner tomorrow."

"What time?"

"If everything goes to plan, one o'clock."

"Perfect, I'll stop in. Tell you what, though. Let's go inside and review your notebook. It might spark a situation we could throw to the sheriff." Austin scooped up Sandy, and they headed into the farmhouse. "I know he's committed to finding the truth, but sometimes he tramples all over everything else in his search for the solution."

"Have you heard anything back from your sister?" asked Miranda as she climbed the front porch steps.

"Nope." Austin pulled out his cell. "I'll give her a call. Maybe she has an update." He placed the call. "It went straight to voice mail. She must be on deadline. She'll call as soon as she's done." He put his cell away. "Remind me to make a trip over to Lexington to see her. I haven't taken her out to lunch for more than a month. She might be a little annoyed. How's Rowena holding up?"

"Not good. The strain is telling. I insisted that she go straight up to bed right after supper. She's being asked to fill in more and more of what should be Mr. Tobin's management role so that he can continue to hold long teleconferences with the BigSky executives. I wouldn't want to pay his phone bill for those. I haven't given him my internet access because he refused to pay for his usage. Mercy, but he's really aggressive.

"How about a cocktail? I've got a new one called Honeysuckle Fizz. Do you want to try it?"

"It sounds a little, well, fizzy."

"It is more like zingy. It has freshly squeezed lime juice. You don't have to finish it if you don't like it."

Miranda mixed the cocktails in the kitchen and used old-fashioned glasses instead of the champagne flutes called for in the recipe. She wanted Austin to like the drink, and he wasn't keen on fancy glasses.

She brought the drinks out on a tray, along with a few crackers topped with a bit of Wensleydale Cranberry cheese. "I know you like the cheese at least."

They clinked glasses, and Austin sipped. "Wow, you're right. It's zingy." He took a second sip. "That's your uncle's moonshine, isn't it? It goes down really smooth."

Miranda smiled wide behind her glass. "Nope, that's

mine. Thank you for the compliment. I've finally gotten as close to his secret recipe as I'm ever going to get. This is the formula I'm going to start distilling in small batches to sell."

Miranda got her workbook, and they settled down on the couch with Sandy between them. She opened it to the page that listed all her suspects. "Whoof, I haven't updated this since I created it, uh, when?"

"Saturday night, if I remember right."

"Wow, it seems so long ago, but it was only two nights. Anyway, I think we should eliminate the ones with, as the saying goes, ironclad alibis. Our list of suspects includes Carol Hampton, Jeffrey Nelson, Lisa Porter, Oliver Young, Mr. Tobin, and, finally, Rowena Gardner."

Austin shifted closer and disturbed Sandy, who let out a puppy growl and hopped off the couch. "Sorry, buddy." He peered at the list. "Okay, first, there's Carol. What do you think of her?"

"She's very competent and takes great care to make sure her team is doing well. She's the best manager in the whole group." She paused. "However, she's created some enemies by taking that kind of compassionate style and may have known that Mr. Burns would have been a major obstruction to her promotion path."

"What about her relationship with Jeffrey?" asked Austin. "According to Rowena, that's clearly against company policy, and she could be fired. Given the company culture, it would definitely be her who would get fired, not him."

"Even worse, Rowena said it would be typical of BigSky that Jeffrey would not only keep his job but get a secret nod of approval from some of the older members of the leadership team."

"Okay," said Austin. "That means Jeffrey had very little reason to kill Mr. Burns."

"Not necessarily. He might have appeared too competent to Mr. Burns, and maybe they had bad feelings about each other within the company. We need to ask one of the other team members." She took the notebook back from Austin. "Let me write that down before we discuss anyone else."

After she scribbled a few lines on both Carol's and Jeffrey's pages, then flipped a page and handed it back to Austin. "Let's keep going. Sheriff Larson will be here any minute."

"Next in line is Lisa. Isn't she the one with allergies? Not to food, I take it."

"No, just basically anything that grows outdoors. It's odd that she's up for a management slot."

"Do you think management even knew about her pollen issues before this workshop?"

Miranda lifted back her head to stare at the ceiling. "You know, that's a good point. She might have kept that under wraps for a long time if she hadn't attended the workshop. Of course, she's also a cost clerk. If anything is fishy about the books, she might know about it."

"That seems weak," said Austin.

"Well, there was an embarrassing issue with Mr. Tobin with the company credit card. It was denied, and he had to use a personal card to pay his room bill." She took the notebook back. "I'm going to make a note to find out about BigSky's credit rating with Standard and Poor's. That's what I used to do for the art galleries in New York City. You would be shocked to learn how many corporations are on a cash-only basis due to their poor financial standing."

Austin took the notebook back. "Okay, let's see who's next? It's Oliver Young. He's the cliff climber, isn't he?"

"Yes," said Miranda. "He also works in the legal department. That could be a useful source of information about any of the BigSky executive teams. He would be in a perfect position to look up any past or current lawsuits, harassment allegations, or just general hijinks going on with anyone in the company."

"Right," said Miranda. "But he seems like a very good fit for the company. He's athletic, amiable, calm. He took over the Sweatsocks after Jeffrey wrenched his ankle."

"How did that go?"

Miranda made a half-smile. "Not so good, really. Sheila basically led the group into a win for the centerpiece and theme competition. She took charge by asking for a little more time, directed a brainstorming session with the other members, and then told them what foliage to collect and reassembled the centerpiece in jig time. I was impressed with her leadership skills."

"So Oliver isn't such a great leader. Would that be motive enough to bash Mr. Burns's head in with a rock?"

Miranda sighed. "When you put it that way, no."

Sandy lifted his head from the rag rug and yipped.

"That must be Sheriff Larson."

Chapter 26

Monday Evening, Farmhouse

Miranda got off the couch, scooped up Sandy, then pulled open the front door.

Sheriff Larson walked in and shook hands with Austin, then took off his hat to Miranda. "Thanks for letting me visit so late. I've come to have a look at your little notebook. I'm at a complete stop in all the different threads of this investigation. Perhaps your thoughts will open up some new areas for me to investigate."

Miranda raised her eyebrows. "You wife suggested it, didn't she?"

He shifted his weight and circled the brim of his hat through both hands. "She might have mentioned it to me during supper."

Miranda laughed. "She's a smart woman. I always follow Felicia's advice. Let me have your hat and jacket.

We're going to be at this awhile. Let's move into the dining room. Do you want a beer or coffee?"

"Black coffee would be great if you've got some handy."

"I'll have some, too. Please," added Austin.

"Won't take a minute. You guys make yourselves comfortable in the dining room." Miranda put Sandy down, took the sheriff's coat and hat, and laid them on her bed. She made the coffee and, as an afterthought, gathered up a large plate of shortbread cookies.

When she returned to the dining room, Austin and Sheriff Larson had their heads huddled together over her notebook. She placed the tray on the table, poured the coffee, and sat down with her cup of chamomile.

They were so engrossed in the notebook they didn't notice her at all.

Miranda cleared her throat, and they both looked up at her like she was a stranger.

Austin recovered first. "Thanks for the coffee." He got a cookie and dunked it.

Miranda sat down and munched on a shortbread cookie. "Sorry. I've forgotten something." She stood up and ran into the second bedroom.

Miranda returned with a folder full of drawings. She watched Austin and Sheriff Larson exchange what-now looks. "I just remembered these. While we were up on the trail, I asked all the participants to sketch the section of the trail where Mr. Burns died just to document what they had seen. Maybe we can glean something new from them."

"That was quick thinking," said Sheriff Larson. "The whole area was disturbed by the paramedics, and we thought it was an accident, so we don't have any crime scene photos." He took the folder and slowly examined each of the ten sketches. As he finished with each sketch, he placed them into two piles.

"Most of them aren't helpful. The drawings are pretty bad, but these three may be useful. The drawings are clear enough to figure out what was seen." He spread them out across the table.

Austin leaned over the drawing nearest to him. "What's interesting about this one is that it shows so many people in the sketch."

"If you count them, there are only seven participants," said Miranda. "Both Carol and Jeffrey are missing."

"Who drew this one? There's no name on it."

"It was drawn by John O'Reilly. I remember looking at it when I collected them." Miranda grabbed another cookie.

Sheriff Larson tapped his finger on the next drawing. "This one is an image of the scene after the paramedics arrived, and it shows Rowena standing a little distance away with her hands covering her face."

Austin squinted at the right-hand lower corner. "This was drawn by Janice Utz. It looks like she drew everyone going down the trail after the paramedics left with Mr. Burns."

"Let me see that one," said Miranda.

Austin handed it over to her.

She squinted at the drawing. "This one has Carol and Jeffrey in view, but not Oliver Young or Lisa Porter." She handed it to Sheriff Larson. "Do you think any of this helps?"

"It at least confirms the statements that were given. Mainly, that at one time or another, the only ones who had an actual opportunity, other than Rowena, are Oliver, Lisa, Carol, and Jeffrey." He huffed in frustration. "That narrows the list for me. Let's see if I can get any hits from police records."

He drained the last of his coffee in a big gulp and got up. "I'm going to take these drawings with me. Also, I'd like to take your notebook for further study."

"With Felicia?"

The sheriff flushed beet red right up to the top of his large ears. "Yes, with Felicia."

"That makes sense. I'm not comfortable with giving the original to you." She saw the sheriff puff up to make a stronger demand. "Don't worry. I can copy it with my all-in-one printer in just a few minutes. If I do that, would you be willing to keep me in the loop on the investigation?"

"Felicia thought you might ask for that. I'm willing to share what I can, but criminal records are not always available to the general public. But I promise to do what I can."

Miranda grinned. "Thanks. That's all I expect."

"I'll have a good, long study of these yet tonight. Maybe Felicia can find something we've missed."

"I'll take another look as well and see if I've missed something." Miranda copied the notebook and then gave Sheriff Larson the copied pages as well as copies of the three drawings he'd singled out.

"Thanks," he said as he put on his jacket and hat.

"I'll keep an eye out for any awkward indicators tomorrow," Miranda said. "It's the last day of the workshop, and the last time I'll get a chance to notice any unusual behavior or interaction from any of the participants."

"Don't forget Frank and Rowena. They're still in the picture," Austin reminded her.

"I don't envy you that."

Miranda and Austin followed him outside with Sandy trailing behind. They watched the sheriff's car drive down the dirt road.

It was a cold, clear night with the piney smell on the wind to signal an approaching front. The stars were bright, and Sandy stood and pawed on Austin's pant leg, so he picked him up. "This looks hopeless."

"It always looks hopeless until we get a break."

Austin's cell rang to the tune of "Wonder Woman." "It's my sister. She must be off deadline now.

"Hey, Tyler. What? My cell phone is cutting out. Can you call Miranda's landline? It's the only reliable way to talk."

He had barely ended the call when Miranda's phone rang. Austin answered and punched the Speaker button. "Hey, sis, I've got you on speaker. Good news for me?"

"Hey, baby brother. I'm not sure if this is helpful, but Oliver has gotten himself in the news with a new manufacturing process that not only saves time but is environmentally friendly in that it's a weaving process that incorporates recycled water bottles."

Miranda spoke. "I've heard of something similar in ladies' shoes, but not in clothing."

"Yeah. It's something that could change the way we manufacture our leisurewear in a big way. I'm surprised BigSky doesn't just fire him. Don't they have a noncompete clause you have to sign? I would certainly expect they would have."

"Thanks, that's worth following up. I'll drive into Lexington next week for lunch. Good?"

"Perfect. Hey, wait. Am I going to see you for Thanksgiving? Even star reporters get the day off."

"Um." Austin rubbed a hand through his hair. "I don't think so. I'll let you know tomorrow. This mystery is causing a lot of disruption."

"Maybe so, but family is more important than a job. I shouldn't have to remind you about that. Okay? Bye."

"She didn't sound happy." Miranda picked up Sandy and headed towards the front door.

Austin set the phone back in the charger. His brow was wrinkled in thought. "Since our parents died, we've always gone out for the buffet lunch at Hemlock Lodge. With this murder still pending, I feel torn between keeping her safe and you safe. We really just need to bring this case to an end."

"Understandable." Miranda went outside and sat Sandy next to his favorite tree.

Austin followed and folded Miranda into a warm embrace.

"I'd like that, too." Miranda held on for a moment longer.

"The one with the strongest motive is Oliver. It's got to be him. Whoever hit Mr. Burns was strong enough for the blow to crack his skull. That could be all we need to focus on. Who was strong enough?"

"I'm not sure I agree with you there," Miranda countered. "The rock could have been thrown. So, it might have just been a lucky pitch. Can we find out if either Lisa or Carol had softball pitching experience? That would have been about the same size as the rock. I wonder how fast they get up to for an average pitcher."

"What is your physical challenge tomorrow morning?"

"Axe throwing down behind the barn." Miranda shrugged her shoulders. "I would think if you were a skilled softball pitcher, it would be child's play to throw an axe."

"We want to do more than just observe, don't we?"

"Yes," said Miranda. "We want a reveal that leads to a confession."

"Right. Do you want to make a bet on who killed Terry Burns?" Austin baited her. "I think I know."

"That's awful. This isn't a game, you know."

"Come on. What are you afraid of? Neither of us has enough information or they'd be in custody."

Miranda nodded. "That's certainly true."

"How about five dollars? We'll both write our choice on a piece of paper and put it here in the sugar bowl."

Miranda folded her arms and gave him an are-you-that-immature look right in the eye. "I'm not afraid to stand behind my guess. It's mostly a case of being insensitive to the seriousness of the situation. Instead of a five-dollar bet, the loser has to contribute to the animal rescue center. Not in money, but in actual, hands-on labor. Shall we put the figure at forty hours?"

Austin smiled. "The center is going to love you."

"Ha. We'll see."

Chapter 27

Tuesday Morning, Farmhouse

Miranda was up early with Rowena, checking the last-minute details. It was delightful to see the Hobb sisters arrive in their beat-up pickup truck. It was truly astonishing that the old relic still ran. Mostly because folks looked out for one another. Iris and Lily were very lucky to have a cousin who owned the Childers' Auto Repair & Tire Shop in downtown Campton. The sisters' ancient farm truck was a pet project. Their cousin used it to help train auto repair apprentices from the high school.

Miranda reviewed today's schedule with Lily and Iris, but as usual they were way ahead of the game and even improved upon her capstone challenge of a full Thanksgiving meal with pies for dessert, followed by the moonshine tasting. First, though, she needed to get up to the lodge to collect her group.

Rowena came downstairs. Her smile got wider with every step. "Good morning. I'm so glad this is the last day of the workshop. I don't believe I could stand another day of this madness. Starting tomorrow, I'm going to sleep for a week."

"How are you feeling?" Miranda looked at her closely. Her skin had color and her eyes were bright. "You look much better. Did you have a good night's sleep?"

"Absolutely fabulous." Rowena smiled wide. "I also feel like my memory is better. Like all that sleep knit together the problems around that blank space. Unfortunately, I don't remember anything about the critical time yet, but I feel like I might at any moment."

"That's wonderful." Miranda enfolded Rowena into a giant hug. "I'm so glad, but promise me, if your memory returns, you'll tell me right away—no matter what is going on. Promise?"

Rowena formed a cross over her heart. "Cross my heart and hope to die."

"Heavens. Don't say that. Tempting fate is never a good idea."

Miranda pulled into the covered entrance at the Hemlock Lodge at 6 am, right on the dot. The BigSky members were all waiting just inside the door, and they loaded up quickly. On their way to the farmhouse, Miranda briefed them on the day's activities.

"First, you need to choose a member of your team to work with the Hobb sisters to get your turkeys into the oven. They also need to help prepare the side dishes that will be served. No one else will be allowed in the kitchen. Not even me." She looked at her passengers in the rearview mirror. "I suggest you send someone who can cook. I'm sure you want our dinner to be fabulous."

"Did you hear that, Jeffrey?" asked Carol. "What she's really telling us is that all the food is going to be carefully monitored. No chance of anyone making us sick this time."

Miranda smiled. "Yep. You got that right. Then there's the axe throwing competition, followed by our Thanksgiving dinner, the tasting of the pies, and the final event will be the sampling of the moonshine. After all that, we'll give out the awards and certificates. How's that for a busy day?"

Carol yawned. "Couldn't we go back to bed instead? I'm tired just hearing the list."

"That won't get you the win." Jeffrey grinned a challenge.

Well, that needs a follow-up. They're not even pretending to be antagonistic. I need to talk to those two by themselves and confirm their relationship.

The teams chattered among themselves, and by the time Miranda arrived at the farmhouse, the Firehawks had chosen Janice to work in the kitchen and the Sweatsocks had chosen Sheila.

Miranda led the rest of the participants to the area she had marked off behind the barn for the axe throwing. She had mounted a four-by-four square of three-quarter-inch plywood to the back of the barn and painted a simple bull's-eye target with red, white, and blue rings for scoring.

"Everyone, please gather around and I'll explain the rules." Everyone moved in. "In general, I'm using World Axe Throwing League rules as a guideline. And by guideline, I mean a loose guide, but in case of dispute, what I say is final."

Chuckles rippled through the group.

Miranda continued. "The first bit is about safety. Do not touch the blade directly with your fingers to avoid stitches and a quick trip down to the clinic. It's sharp. It's really sharp. Second, make double sure the target is clear of people before attempting to throw the axe. That means you shouldn't throw an axe while anyone is near the target, behind the target, over the target, or walking towards it. The phrase at most events is 'throw together, retrieve together.' We only have one axe, so the bottom line is 'don't throw until you are absolutely positive no one is near the target.'"

Miranda stepped away from the target and positioned herself for a throw.

"Third, each thrower must not step over the throwing line before the axe hits or misses the target." She pointed to a tobacco stick she had anchored into the soft grass. "That's your line. It's twelve feet from the target, which is the recommended distance. One foot must be on the ground while the axe is thrown. Any thrower who steps over the line gets zero points. Before we start, everyone gets a lesson and a few practice throws."

"How many throws?" asked Oliver. "This is pretty nonstandard axe throwing."

"The scoring is five points for the bull's-eye, three points for the white inner circle, and, finally, one point for the outer blue circle. If the axe is in two rings simultaneously, the participant is awarded the points for the value of the ring where greater than fifty percent of the axe lies. Each player gets three throws. We only have the axe I use for chopping wood, so the teams will alternate."

Miranda stepped up to the throwing line and demonstrated both the one-handed and two-handed throws. She hit the red circle each time. "I prefer to use a two-handed throw. Before we start practicing, are there any questions?"

"What if the axe hits and falls?" Victor asked. "Can you catch it?"

Miranda smiled. "Obviously you've been to some competitions where you get to keep the points if you catch the axe before it hits the ground."

Victor nodded. "Yeah, it's loads of fun."

"Sorry, no such thing for us," said Miranda. "I'm keeping this simple. The axe needs to stay in the target until it is scored. Anything else?" She paused for a moment. "Well, let's start. I'll help each of you with your practice throws. While that's going on, Carol, you and Jeffrey need to select the order of your throwers."

She gave each player some pointers and suggestions, but they were all reasonably good. Finally, everyone had practiced and the real competition began. The Firehawks won the coin toss and decided to let the Sweatsocks go first.

John stepped up to the line and threw the axe into the red circle, followed by two throws into the white for a total of eleven points. He was followed by Xavier, who managed a perfect score of fifteen.

Victor stepped up to the team's line, and everyone backed up several feet. In practice, Miranda had advised him to take a two-handed throw and try to keep his eyes open. He gave a mighty pitch, but the axe hit flat and fell to the ground. On his second throw, the axe bounced back and nearly hit his foot.

Miranda took the axe from him. "I think in the interest

of safety for all, we're going to count that as an elimination total of zero."

Eileen was next, and she scored a neatly executed nine by hitting in the white three times. She was followed by Oliver, who threw the axe so strongly it bit deep into the target. Unfortunately, he was a bit wide of the mark, for a score of thirteen. Lisa stepped up to the mark. Although the axe stuck into the board, she didn't make a single point.

Miranda gave the axe to Jeffrey. "At this point, the score is tied at twenty-four each. The winning team will be chosen by their captains. Make every throw count."

Jeffrey landed two fives and a three. He stepped back and gave room to Carol with a bow. "See if you can beat that."

Carol took a deep, cleansing breath and threw the axe for a three. She rolled her eyes and glared at the target as though she could burn a new scoring circle on it. It kind of worked because her next two throws were in the center for a total of thirteen as well.

The Firehawks shouted with joy. "It's a tie! Sudden death!"

Miranda shook her head. "That's right. Carol and Jeffrey, you each get one more throw. We'll use the same order, but this time the winner will be the axe closest to the center of the target. Jeffrey, you first." She handed him the axe.

He stepped up to the line, settled into his form, and threw a picture-perfect bull's-eye. Everyone gasped. It was the only throw to make the exact center.

Jeffrey raised his arms high like an Olympic gymnast

landing a perfect ten. He softly punched Carol in the arm. "Beat that!"

Carol tilted her head and raised her eyebrows. "No problem."

Miranda handed her the axe. "Good luck!"

Carol touched the women's tobacco stick with her left toe, double-checked her grip, took careful aim, then threw the axe with a mighty grunt. It stuck with a loud thud in the center of the target. "Got it! We win."

Jeffrey ran up to the target, and his shoulders slumped. "It's a Robin Hood."

"What's a Robin Hood?" Miranda splayed her hands.

"That's from the vintage movies. It means that she hit the exact same spot I did." He walked up to Carol, and they exchanged high fives.

Miranda enjoyed the feeling of good sportsmanship but knew it was only because Mr. Tobin was nowhere in sight.

"That's not a legitimate win," said Mr. Tobin.

Miranda let out a startled yelp. *How does he manage to sneak up on us like that?*

He stood looking at the axe, which was clearly stuck in the same spot as Jeffrey's throw.

"Jeffrey's throw was first. His throw is the winner."

Miranda protested, "But that's not the way—"

"I have spoken, and I have the final say." Mr. Tobin folded his arms and stood, awaiting any challenges.

Everyone stood in silence for several beats.

"No problem," said Carol. "I'm good with that ruling. The Sweatsocks win."

Carol turned to her group. They had started to protest, but she stopped them with just her hands. The Firehawks stood in red-faced silence.

"Well, then," said Miranda. "That's over. Let's get this big meal on the table. Everyone back into the farmhouse." The participants trudged up to go into the back door to the kitchen. Miranda waited until they had gotten out of earshot. "Why did you do that? The competition was already finished."

Mr. Tobin grinned with obvious pleasure. "They need to have things overturned now and then. It keeps them lean and hungry."

Miranda shook her head in exasperation. "That might be what you think you're doing, but I think you're causing frustration and confusion. If none of your staff can predict your reactions, how do you expect them to act in support of your company goals? I just don't get it."

"Well, missy. It's not your job to get it. Right?"

Miranda stared at him with cold eyes. Finally, she said, "Right." Then she turned on her heel and went into the farmhouse back door.

The kitchen was buzzing with activity. Lily Hobb was monitoring the roasting turkeys while also rotating the competitors' pies in and out of the oven at the same time. Iris was in the dining room with the Sweatsocks, organizing side dishes, cutlery, condiments, and beverages. Her cheeky grin broadcast her pleasure at ordering these management types around like children.

Mr. Tobin had followed Miranda into the kitchen and on into the living room.

He tapped her on the shoulder. "I need a quiet place to work. I have a weekly teleconference in five minutes."

Miranda lost it. "Why didn't you tell me yesterday? Or any time before now? It's a regularly scheduled meeting." She sighed deeply and dropped her head to stare at her shoes. "Why must you be so annoying and selfish?

We are supposed to be preparing for a Thanksgiving dinner!" She clamped her mouth shut. Her words had been
heard by everyone, and there was a sudden stillness in the
whole house.

Sandy whimpered and pawed at her show of impatience. "Oh, I'm so sorry, Sandikins." She lifted him up to
her face and let him give her puppy licks. She snuggled
him into the crook of her arm and looked at a still stunned
Mr. Tobin. "Take my office and close the door. That will
have to be good enough." She turned without looking
back and went out the front door, snatching Sandy's leash
as she went. The screen door slammed behind her, and
that sound felt good.

Sandy wasn't all that good at leash walking, but he
hurried over to the nearest tree and lifted his leg. Miranda
scolded herself for her loss of patience. On the other
hand, she was unlikely to agree to another workshop
without first meeting with the company to gauge the cultural environment. She had learned a lot of lessons if she
decided to sign up for another group event again.

Good temper restored, Miranda returned Sandy to the
cage in her front bedroom and went into the kitchen to
help with the dinner preparations. With Mr. Tobin loudly
participating in a teleconference, everyone was quietly
getting on with the work at hand.

Miranda had to shoo participants away from hanging
around the door to her office several times. Oliver wasn't
even trying to pretend that he was doing anything but
eavesdropping on the occasionally loud exchanges that
would erupt between long bouts of silence.

Due to the frigid breeze coming down from the north,
Miranda decided that they should move their dinner tables from the side yard into the front room. Using the par-

ticipants as rough labor, it was a quick job to move the couch and chairs out onto the front porch, along with the coffee table. She pushed the end tables with their lamps still in place along the walls in case the approaching storm turned dark and overcast.

It only took a few more minutes for each team leader to move in their picnic tables and decorate them with not only their centerpieces but place settings as well.

"Howdy!" said Austin as he came into the living room and removed his hat. "This is a great solution. We're about to have a healthy dose of early winter weather. There's a big storm comin' in really fast."

Oliver frowned. "Does that mean we should get back to the lodge?"

Miranda splayed her hands. "We're safe until this evening. We'll be done here by no later than two o'clock."

Chapter 28

Tuesday Noon, Farmhouse

Miranda was so focused on meal preparations that she lost track of time and was surprised when she heard Austin's voice. She went into the living room to meet him.

"You know there's a storm coming, right?" Austin turned and waved a hand at the approaching front of storm clouds at the edge of the horizon.

"Hello to you, too. I didn't know about the storm prediction. It felt like it was getting too cold to eat outdoors. What's the forecast?" They both went out to the edge of the front porch and looked across the valley. She shivered in the cold wind. Austin put his arms out and tucked her into his jacket. They saw a dark gray bank of clouds moving across the skyline at an alarming speed. Snow was beginning to stick.

Austin pointed to the north. "This front started in

Canada but appears to be dropping down here faster than they expected. Are you prepared for a blizzard? It will probably arrive sometime during the night."

"I've got coal, wood, water, plenty of staples, and a ton of puppy food. Hopefully, the snow won't get too high." She sighed. "The last thing I was thinking about this morning was that we might be snowed in with this group. This will be my first winter in the farmhouse. I was hoping for a mild one." She looked over to the north again. "Do you think I should abandon the workshop and get everybody up to Hemlock Lodge?"

"The road up to the lodge is still open, and so is the lodge. I'm afraid you're not going to get saved by bad weather." Austin turned and held open the front door. "In you go to battle with the sportswear superstars."

She displayed a weak smile and went back inside.

The living room was a noisy, raucous, overheated, heavenly smelling whirl of holiday chaos. The picnic tables were augmented by four of her dining room chairs, so there was room for eight at each table. The Hobb sisters had added salt, pepper, and a tub of butter as well.

The dining room served as a staging area for the side dishes. Lily and Iris placed huge platters of mashed potatoes, green beans, candied sweet potatoes, fruit salad, gravy, and a giant basket of dinner rolls on the round dining table. They were adding the final touches with serving spoons.

Miranda walked back to the kitchen, where both turkeys were resting on the counter. Each looked magnificent. Next to them were the baked pies. Also awaiting judging were the Jell-O salads. She had set up a little table in front of her bedroom door to act as the judging station.

The problem of who to choose as the judge had given her quite a little headache, but she finally solved it. It couldn't be either herself or Rowena because they had helped the participants create their dishes and moonshine. Mr. Tobin was completely out of the question for judging. He couldn't be trusted to make objective decisions. She hoped Austin would take the role of the judge in good form. He was her only hope for a fair contest. His integrity was beyond reproach. He was a forest ranger, for pity's sake.

Miranda raised her voice over the happy din. "Settle down, everybody. Find your seats." There was a bit of hustle and bustle to get into their places. The Sweatsocks' table had Mr. Tobin down against the wall at the head. He immediately pulled out his phone and started reading his email. The Firehawks hosted Rowena at the head of their table. Austin found his place at the last seat with the Firehawks, and Miranda knew her seat was at the end of the Sweatsocks' table, facing Mr. Tobin.

Miranda tapped a fork against her water glass and waited for silence to fall. "Lily. Iris. Bring in the roast turkeys and the Jell-O salads." She stepped to the side while they placed the turkeys on the small table. The turkeys had been beautifully sliced yet still held their general shape. Then they arrived with the two studded, milk glass molds in the shape of a chicken. The Hobb sisters also put a small saucer with a fork and spoon in front of each turkey, ready to be used for tasting.

She smiled. *Those girls are wonderful. They've really gotten into the swing of the competition.* "Before we go further, please join me in a moment of grateful silence for the blessings we enjoy."

Miranda closed her eyes and lowered her head. She

was grateful for so many wonderful things in her new Kentucky home. She mentally listed friends, family, her new business, and the natural beauty of the Daniel Boone National Forest. She lifted her head. "Everyone, please give Lily and Iris a big thank you for providing for us over the last few days."

They both covered their blushes with the tail ends of their aprons and darted back into the kitchen.

After they left, Miranda stared directly at Austin. "Now, all we need is a judge." She paused and looked all over the room and then stared at him again. "Ranger Morgan, would you be willing?"

His shoulders sagged, then he lifted his head. "That's fearsome kind of you, but I'm not a chef."

"Maybe not, but you're an enthusiastic eater."

Everyone laughed, and Austin flushed. "That's mighty true."

Miranda lowered her voice. "Please, Austin. You're our only impartial guest." He didn't move. "You also get to taste all the pies."

Austin tipped his head and stood up. "In that case, I'd be delighted."

"Thanks. The first tasting is the gelatin salads, then you do the turkeys. No one knows which one is which, so tell us what you think and then choose the one you like best."

Austin picked up the spoon on the first saucer and scooped out a little taste of the first Jell-O salad. "This is a traditional lime pear gelatin in two layers. The top has pear slices with walnuts in a well-set form, and the bottom layer is the cream cheese with lime, I think." He took another bite. "Yes, it tastes like lime."

He took the second spoon and tried the next gelatin

mold. "This is different. The pear, the gelatin, and the lime are in one layer, and it looks a bit like a dump cake." He tasted it again. "I don't taste any lime at all."

"What's your verdict?" asked Miranda.

"Definitely the two-layer salad. It is tasty and looks great."

The Firehawks clapped and hooted. "Yay!"

"Obviously, that gelatin belongs to the Firehawks. Well done." She turned back to Austin. "Now for the turkey."

He smiled and took a forkful of crispy skin, white meat, and then dark meat from each turkey, and put them on their little saucer. He turned toward the tables.

Oh, fun. He knows how to sensationalize this. Those ranger talks are good for stage presence.

He took a mouthful of the first sample of dark meat and chewed thoughtfully. "The dark meat is fantastic. It's moist but not rubbery. Perfect." Then tasted the white meat. "This is also great. It's moist without being watery, and I love the traditional spicing. Nothing too strong, but there's definitely at least garlic and rosemary." Finally, he picked up the skin and tasted that. "This is wonderful. It's wonderful without being too salty. A traditional roast turkey."

He changed out his plate for the other turkey samples and took a forkful of the dark meat. "Wow, this is something completely different. The spices are definitely non-traditional but pretty subtle in this part. Juicy, though."

He sampled the white meat and rolled his eyes. "Oh my goodness. I'm getting the flavoring now. It's basil along with some ginger." Finally, he tasted the skin and wrinkled his brow in concentration. "I got it now. It's a subtle Asian combination with an unusual onion flavor as well."

Miranda laughed. "You're having way too much fun with this. Get on with it. Which one is the best roast turkey?"

"It's the Asian one here. It's creative and also delicious. What could be better?"

"That's that, then. Which team made that one?"

"We did," said Carol. She stood and high fived with each of her team members.

Miranda shooed Austin back to his seat. "That gives the Firehawks a real chance. Only two more events to go. The pies and the moonshine. Enjoy your dinner. We'll be having a couple of extra guests for the pie competition. I've received a call from Sheriff Larson. He has informed me that he will be stopping by with his wife, Felicia, to give us the final resolution of the Terry Burns case."

"What for?" said Mr. Tobin. "There's no need for that. It's just going to waste more time when we could be on the road before this storm hits."

"He would be here now but ran into some difficulty reaching the family due to storm damage. There's plenty of time to get back to Lexington, but if you want to abandon the rest of the workshop, that's fine with me."

Mr. Tobin slammed his phone down on the picnic table. "Not on your life. This needs to run its course."

"As you say," said Miranda. "Let's enjoy our Thanksgiving feast."

Lily and Iris passed the platters and bowls around to both tables family style and, in general, hovered like broody hens to make sure everyone's plate was loaded with each and every side dish.

Miranda dug in and enjoyed the best meal ever produced in the short history of Paint & Shine. It seemed to lift everyone's spirit, and for a moment she thought everything seemed completely normal.

After serving themselves and eating in the kitchen, Lily and Iris asked for two volunteers from each team to clear the tables and wash the dishes. Carol, Jeffrey, Eileen, and Oliver sprang up and helped them.

"The rest of you, please reset the table for our pies. We're going to do something different for judging them."

"Like what?" Mr. Tobin clipped his words and drummed his fingers on the table. "We don't have all day. I thought you said we'd be gone by three o'clock."

"Right," said Miranda. "We're right on schedule." Everyone return to their seats. "Carol and Jeffrey, you're going to judge the pies."

"But we know what they look like!"

"Yes, you do, but Lily and Iris are going to give you six small pieces of pie from samples that have been cut back in the kitchen. You won't be able to tell which team made what pie."

"Fine," said Carol. "But how will you be able to identify the winner?

Miranda smiled. "That's my secret. You and Jeffrey choose the best pie of the bunch." She called down to the kitchen. "We're ready."

Iris and Lily came into the living room, each with a tray that had six tiny plates holding six tiny samples of pie. Lily set her tray in front of Carol, and Iris did the same in front of Jeffrey.

Oliver raised his hand. "Excuse me for a bit. I'll be right back." He wriggled his way out of the picnic table bench, saying "Sorry" a few times, then headed for the back of the house in a trot.

Carol and Jeffrey plunged into their task with relish. They didn't speak, and a quiet peace settled over the farmhouse.

Mr. Tobin's cell phone rang. He glanced at the number and got up. "This is important. Let me through." He punched the Answer button and yelled, "Hang on. I've got to find a private space." He pointed to Miranda's office, and she nodded permission. It was an uncomfortable squeeze for him to get by everyone, but he finally made it and slammed the office door.

Miranda turned back to the tasting. "How's it coming? Have you each chosen a winner?"

"Wait for a second," said Carol. "I'm undecided between these two." She pointed to one of the chocolate pie samples and one of the pecan pie ones. "Just one more taste." She did that, then placed her spoon down. "I've decided." She looked directly at Jeffrey and pretended to be annoyed, but everyone saw right through that.

Miranda stood between the tables. "Great. Hand me the plate the winning pie was on."

"I made up my mind ages ago." Jeffrey handed Miranda one of the pecan slice plates. "This is the winner." Not a single morsel remained on the plate.

Mr. Tobin came out of the office and stood in the doorway between the dining room and the living room. His face was flushed and his arms were folded across his chest.

Miranda took the winning plate from Carol, also eaten clean. "The team names are taped under the plates, and it looks like this win goes to . . ." She paused to let the tension build. "Firchawks by the unanimous choice of the two judges."

The Sweatsocks team cheered but stopped when they

saw the frown on Mr. Tobin's face. He grumbled under his breath, "Making pies is not a management skill I'm looking for."

Miranda tilted her head to the side. *This comes from someone who has probably never actually made a pie.* "Congratulations, Firehawks. That means the point scores are tied. So the last competition will determine the winner. No pressure, of course." She paused for a moment to let that sink in. "Now, let's dig in."

Iris and Lily served each person at least two slices.

They were collecting plates when Lily ducked her head and looked out the front window. "Are you expecting Sheriff Larson?"

Chapter 29

Tuesday Afternoon, Farmhouse

Miranda was so focused on ensuring that everyone got at least one slice of pie she didn't understand what Lily said.

Lily cupped one hand around her mouth. "The sheriff is here!"

At that moment, Miranda heard the sheriff's vehicle pull up in the gravel driveway, and two doors slammed shut.

"Speak of the devils." She stepped out onto the porch as Sheriff Larson and Felicia walked up to meet her on the porch. "Anything new?"

Sheriff Larson's shoulders slumped low, as if he were carrying the weight of the world on his back.

In a way, thought Miranda, *he is*. Felicia also looked grim. Whatever happened next would be a life-changing event for several of the people inside enjoying pie.

Miranda held open the door. "Did my Hail Mary theory check out?"

Sheriff Larson stepped up on the porch, followed by Felicia. "Now, Miranda—"

Felicia interrupted. "Of course it did. You hit the nail on the head. But you knew that, didn't you?"

Miranda pressed her lips together. "I always hope that somehow none of this is true and that people aren't this awful. I always hope I don't need to meddle and interfere. I've been disappointed every time."

Felicia stepped forward and put her arms around Miranda. "Think of all the people who are now free and safe because you dared to meddle." She looked into Miranda's eyes. "They don't think it's nothing."

"Thanks. That helps." She held on to the door handle and asked Sheriff Larson. "How do you want to handle this?"

"I'm waiting for one last text." He pulled out his phone. "Perfect. I've got three signal strength bars. After that, I'll need to speak to the whole group."

Miranda nodded, then led them into the front room. With fresh eyes, she scanned the room and thought it looked a lot like a children's summer camp party after the cake and ice cream are gone.

Her clients were jostling one another, trying to squeeze around the picnic tables, avoid the cast-iron stove, and vying to get another slice of pie out of either Lily or Iris.

The only thing missing from the fray was Sandy. Miranda turned to Sheriff Larson and Felicia. "Excuse me for a minute. I've got to check on Sandy. He still has a puppy bladder and an even smaller puppy span of attention."

Miranda took him out from his crate in her bedroom and headed out the back way through the kitchen. As she sped by, she noticed that Iris and Lily had everything well in hand. For once, Sandy didn't dawdle over his potty break. He looked up at the threatening sky nervously several times and scurried back to Miranda and waited by her feet.

I bet he can sense the oncoming storm. She tucked him back into his cage and returned to the crowded and noisy living room.

Miranda tapped her knuckles on the nearest picnic table. "Because of the incoming storm, I've had to modify our last competition. Our judge was going to be the owner of the Limestone Distillery over in Lexington. He canceled because of the storm. Congratulations, not only are you all going to be the judges, but because the teams are tied, this event will determine the overall winner."

Lily and Iris came into the living room, each bearing a tray. The trays had tiny, two-ounce mason jars filled with a light, ginger-colored liquid. Lily's jars were labeled with a bold A, and Iris's jars were labeled with a bold B.

Carol frowned. "That's hardly fair. My team will vote for mine, and Jeffrey's team will vote for his. It will be a useless tie."

Miranda tipped her head. "I can see where you might think that, but the taste profile between the two brews is quite close." Then she pointed to Austin. "Plus, Austin, Rowena, and Mr. Tobin will give us an odd number. That is my lucky number—thirteen."

Mr. Tobin butted in. "There's no way I'm voting. I loathe moonshine."

Carol twisted her lip into a dry smirk. "Well, that's okay, then."

Miranda continued. "Fine. Lily and Iris are the only ones who know which moonshine is which, and they're not tellin'." She paused and started passing around voting slips. "In order to save you from drinking straight shine, they've added Ale-8 as a mixer to each sample. Everybody gets to taste the two samples and markdown their vote on these slips of paper. Lily and Iris will collect them, and I'll count the votes."

Lily and Iris finished handing out the jars, and then they stood on each side of the wide doorway to the dining room. Miranda stood in front of them. "After the voting is done, we'll announce the winning team and get you guys back to Hemlock Lodge as quickly as we can."

The participants started tasting both samples, and immediately there was a ruckus of different discussions.

"They're both great!"

"Can I have more?"

Finally, everyone settled down to make their vote and pass the slips up to their captains to collect. Lily and Iris collected them and handed them to Miranda, who took the slips and tallied the votes. A puzzled look crossed her face, and she counted the votes again.

She raised the voting slips over her head and announced, "I can't believe it, but I've counted them twice. It's a tie!"

Miranda heard the sheriff's cell phone ping and watched him check the message.

He gave her a positive headshake.

"Before we head back to Hemlock Lodge, Sheriff Larson has asked that we give him our attention for a moment regarding the death of Mr. Terry Burns."

Sheriff Larson stood next to the cast-iron, freestanding stove and rocked back and forth on his heels, waiting until he had everyone's attention. It took a bit of time because everyone was a little tipsy after the tasting.

"Before y'all get back to your everyday lives, I want to pose a few last questions." He pressed his lips together. "I've had a series of communications with the Sheriff's Department in Laguna Beach, California. They gave me some interesting background on you, Oliver Young, or as you're known out there, Ollie."

"What?" His voice was shrill. "What do you mean, you called them? Why would you do that?"

"When I was investigating background checks, I found everyone's local details as well as some history on where they were from originally. I didn't find any residential information on Oliver Young, so I asked an old friend in Long Beach for names that shared those initials. They found an extensive file on an Ollie Youst."

"You had no business doing that." Oliver stood and shouted so loud he showered spit all over his teammates.

"Hey, chill, Oliver," said Jeffrey. "This is probably just a paperwork snafu. I'm sure—"

"Don't you dare try to manage me. That's not your job." Oliver was beet red and on his way to turning purple with rage. "Your department has no clue what is happening in BigSky. You're the worst kind of clueless to everything that's happening right under your nose."

Mr. Tobin looked up at Oliver. "You don't have anything to worry about." Then he glared at the sheriff. "It was an accident. Remember, that's what you said. You assured me that Mr. Burns died in an accident."

Oliver reached behind his back and pulled out a thin-bladed knife. He pulled at Mr. Tobin's arm to draw him up into a standing position. "I've got to make myself scarce and you're my ticket out of here. Stand up!"

Mr. Tobin's face drained of all color, and his eyes focused on the sharp blade that Oliver held pointed at the base of his throat. "What are you doing? Are you crazy?"

"Shut up! You're coming with me." Oliver pointed the knife at the sheriff for a moment, then realized that he needed to keep it on Mr. Tobin. "If anyone tries to stop me, I'll gut him like a trout." He looked at Mr. Tobin. "Get your keys out. You're going to drive me outta here."

"But," Mr. Tobin began to sputter, "y-you can't do this."

Oliver pressed the point of the knife against Mr. Tobin's throat and scanned the shocked faces of his peers. "Everyone get out of the way. We're going out the back."

Everyone around the table scrambled out of his way, and he had a clear path to the dining room.

Sheriff Larson put one arm around his wife and the other in front of him. "Just be calm. You don't have to hurt anyone. We're going to all get out of your way." He motioned for everyone to come over his way near the front door.

"Move out of the way." Oliver shifted the knife, alternating between Miranda and Austin.

Miranda moved to one side of the double doorway to the dining room, and Austin scooted to the other side. "Don't hurt anyone," said Miranda. "There's no one in your way. Stay calm."

Oliver pulled Mr. Tobin into the dining room by one arm and turned to go into the kitchen.

Miranda exchanged a look with Austin, and as soon as Oliver turned his head toward the kitchen, they each stepped into the dining room, grabbed the tail end of the runner rug, and pulled with all their might.

The scream bounced around the walls of the tiny room, and Miranda grabbed Oliver's slender wrist in both of her hands. She squeezed for all she was worth.

Austin sat on his chest so that he couldn't breathe. In seconds, Oliver dropped the knife.

Sheriff Larson pulled out his handcuffs, and in moments, Oliver was facedown, cuffed, and sobbing. "I'm sorry. I'm sorry. I'm sorry. I didn't hit him that hard. Burns shouldn't have died. No way. It was a warning."

Mr. Tobin was sitting on the floor, gulping air and with his head between his knees. His head was wobbling in small circles, and it looked like he might pass out.

"Lily, Iris! Get the smelling salts. We've got another fainter over here." Miranda massaged the feeling back into her hands and stepped into the kitchen. Lily handed her the small, old-fashioned bottle. She removed the dropper and held it under Mr. Tobin's nose.

"Whew! What is that?" Mr. Tobin shook his head like a water dog.

"It will keep you from passing out. You've had a shock."

"Don't do that again. I'm fine."

Sheriff Larson pulled up on Oliver and searched his pockets for additional weapons. He didn't find any. "Let's get you over to the jail before the weather closes in." He looked at Miranda. "Thanks for letting us know about Ollie. I'm not saying we wouldn't have figured that out, but you handed us a shortcut."

"Did I guess right? Was Mr. Burns using Oliver's access to the BigSky's financial accounts to siphon off the cash for a competing startup?"

"Yes, you guessed it. Apparently, Mr. Burns tried to

cut Oliver out of the new deal. I do believe that Oliver only meant to warn him, but he's got a good throwing arm," Sheriff Larson said. He glanced out the window. "In fact, it's probably a good idea to get all these good folks up to the lodge."

Miranda and the entire household stood on the porch and watched the sheriff's patrol car make its way down the snowy road into town.

Miranda turned to Carol and Jeffrey. Carol was sobbing into Jeffrey's chest, his arms holding her in a protective embrace. He patted her on the back and kissed the top of her head. "It's over now. We can start to build a better life for the two of us by quitting our jobs and finding a company we want to work for."

Miranda raised her voice. "Get your teams in the van. This team-building workshop is officially completed, and I'm declaring an unbreakable tie in the competition. I'll help Rowena with the reports."

She looked around for Rowena and found her struggling to help a pale and trembling Mr. Tobin get into the passenger side of his car. Miranda rushed to get him a warm blanket to tuck around his legs.

"Thanks," said Rowena. "I'm going to drive him home. I'll come back on Friday." She dug into a pocket and gave Miranda her keys. "I'll have someone from the company drop me off to get my car." She beamed a broad smile. "Thanks for everything." Rowena drove Mr. Tobin's car away.

Lily grabbed the keys to the van from Miranda and hopped in. "I'm driving everyone to the lodge. I know every crook and dip in the road."

Iris yelled from the cab of their ancient truck, "You're still a greenhorn around here. But you're our greenhorn now. Happy Thanksgiving!"

Austin came out and brought Sandy with him. Miranda put her arm around his waist, and they all watched the red taillights make their way down the road.

Chapter 30

Wednesday Evening, Lexington

Miranda touched the antique pearls she had inherited from Grandmother Della at her throat. They were special, but she rarely wore them. This was the perfect occasion, and they looked fantastic with her little black dress. Her only dressy dress.

She began to memorize every detail about this moment—the crisp, white linens on the table, the tall, white candles in a sterling candelabra, the shining cutlery arranged in formal simplicity, and the enormous leather book that contained the menu.

She looked across their cozy table for two and caught Austin doing the same. At least she thought he might. Maybe. Maybe not. She realized that she really didn't know that much about him after he graduated high school. She knew he went to college. You have to do that in order to be a forest ranger, but where did he go?

Miranda scanned the menu for her favorite classy meal and found a filet mignon served with a sauce Bordelaise. Perfect. She closed her menu. "Where did you go to college? You did, didn't you? I mean, I thought it was a requirement for forest ranger."

Austin closed his menu and leaned forward with an open smile on his face. "I knew I wanted to be a forest ranger when I was ten. We didn't have much money, of course, but I studied hard in high school and made it to the top of my class. I applied to in-state universities and was awarded a full scholarship to the University of Kentucky for their Department of Forestry, which is part of the College of Agriculture."

Their waiter arrived for their wine order. Austin waved a hand toward Miranda. "She's the connoisseur. I enjoy wine, but you're the expert. I'm having the New York strip—rare."

Miranda smiled. "We're both doing steak." She looked up at the waiter. "Do you have an Australian or New Zealand Cabernet Sauvignon, or maybe a Shiraz?"

"Yes, ma'am. I have a 2018 Shiraz from Bulletin Place in Southeastern Australia."

"Perfect. How pricy?"

The waiter cracked a small smile. "It's a good value for a bold red."

Miranda cracked a smile back. She had deciphered the waiter code of wines while she was living in New York City. A value wine meant fairly cheap. But they carried it, so it was probably quite good.

"I'll be right back with that."

Miranda was going to stop him and go ahead with their order, but she didn't. *I want to enjoy this meal. I haven't been out for a fancy dinner for a long, long time. I need this.*

Austin shifted in his chair. Miranda reached across the table and held his hand. "You look uncomfortable. I know this isn't your cup of tea, but you went to university here in Lexington. This isn't your first fancy date. Is something wrong?"

Austin smiled and started to say something, but the waiter returned with their bottle of Shiraz. When he showed the label to Austin, he raised his eyebrows. "She's the expert, remember?"

The waiter quickly recovered. "Yes, sir." He turned to Miranda. "Ma'am, please forgive me."

Miranda smiled up at him. "Definitely forgiven."

He served her a sample, and she swirled, looked at the color, and tasted. She looked up at him. "It's perfect. I adore Australian reds." He bowed slightly, filled their wineglasses, and left.

Austin watched the waiter return to the kitchen. "No, this isn't my cup of tea. I would really rather be on your front porch swing sampling another local recipe or new moonshine cocktail. But you've had a rather stressful few weeks here, and I wanted to give you an uptown experience for a change."

"Oh, I checked my account this morning. Rowena worked some administrative magic and I've already gotten the balance due from BigSky. Isn't that wonderful?"

"That's a relief."

"Absolutely. She said the remaining executives at Big-Sky are going to appoint her as the acting manager until they replace Mr. Burns. They're also keeping me on their qualified subcontractors list for more team-building workshops in the spring."

"Are you going to shut down for the season? Most of the other guided tours have closed."

"I've shut down everything but the distillery. Now that I've got Uncle Gene's recipe nailed, I'm going to investigate small batch distribution and special events. That way, I can keep Lily and Iris employed."

"What about your mom?"

"I'm so happy she's decided to move back to the farmhouse. She really is more connected to her family and friends in Wolfe County than up in Dayton. Plus, she'll be a big help in running the distillery tastings."

Their waiter returned with two tiny plates and added a little fork to their already impressive array of cutlery. "Chef has sent you an amuse-bouche. It is a pastry bite with melted brie cheese, cranberry sauce, walnuts, and honey, nestled in puff pastry cups. Enjoy." He disappeared.

Austin squinted. "We didn't order this. How much does this cost?"

"Don't worry. It was sent by the chef free of charge. It's a sign of favor. We must look like a special couple. 'Amuse-bouche' is a French word that translates as 'mouth amuser.' It should be heavenly."

Austin watched Miranda take the little fork, slice the pastry in half, and then in half again. She took a bite, and her eyes rolled up, and her head tilted back. She savored it slowly. "Oh my goodness. This is what I miss about New York City. If this is any indication about the rest of our meal, I'll be saving my pennies to come back here."

Austin followed her lead. "I've never eaten anything like it." He tucked in, and they finished their treat in silence.

Their waiter returned. "Would you care to start with a salad? Maybe a bowl of our locally grown pumpkin soup?

What about our new butternut squash soup with ginger and coconut?"

Miranda sat a little taller. "That sounds fun. Let's do that."

They gave the waiter their steak orders and chose a side dish of cheesy baked asparagus to share.

Austin leaned over to talk low. "We've ordered a lot of food, but you absolutely must save room for dessert. The macarons here are incredible, and I believe that's one of your favorite desserts in the world."

"You're on." Miranda smiled. "How did you know that? Did my mom tell you that?"

"Yep. Your mom is your biggest fan." Austin lifted his wineglass. "Let's toast to the success of Paint & Shine in its first two months of operation and especially the completion of that dreadful team-building workshop. Welcome to eastern Kentucky—according to some, the land of storybook hills, stunning sandstone arches, and drawls. Good luck and continued success with Paint & Shine."

"Cheers," said Miranda as they clinked glasses and took a sip. "It is an incredibly difficult place to catch on to."

"What do you mean? You've spent a lot of time in Wolfe County over the years."

"Well, I like the contrast between the country life and the urban life that we can get here. In just an hour away, we've got all the sophistication of Lexington whenever we need it. But I find the generations-long systemic intolerance difficult to understand."

Austin smiled through his eyes, registered a sad look, and nodded his head. Their waiter delivered the delicious soup. After that dish was removed, he delivered the steaks, which were prepared to absolute perfection.

"You're not saying much." Miranda drank the rest of her wine after their empty steak plates were taken away. "Is anything wrong?"

Austin pressed his lips into a strained smile. "Everything is fine. Perfectly fine." He refolded his napkin for the tenth time and looked back towards the direction where the waiter appeared. "I just hope you like your dessert."

"Not a problem. I've never had a bad macaron." Then Miranda laughed and shook her head. "I take that back. I actually tried to make them once in my little New York apartment. What a disaster. Mine tasted horrible. Rubbery. Cardboard."

"But you're a great cook," said Austin. "What went wrong?"

"That's right. I'm a great cook, but baking is more like chemistry. Everything is based on ingredient reactions with precise measurements. An old stove in the middle of a humid, sweltering city with no air conditioning—not good for baking. Macarons are extremely sensitive to humidity. After dozens of ruined batches, I've learned to let others make them. It doesn't diminish my eating pleasure one bit."

Austin looked at her with a mildly surprised expression. "Accepting a failure? I didn't think that was in your nature."

"It is for macarons."

The waiter returned with the chef to present a small box in front of Miranda. She looked up and quizzed Austin. "What's this about? Aren't you having any? I thought you liked macarons."

"These are special." His voice was tight, and he was sitting tall and stiff.

Miranda was quite puzzled but opened the pastry box. It revealed a selection of pastel macarons that surrounded a little velvet box. She inhaled a nervous breath and looked across at Austin. "What is this—"

Austin, the waiter, and the chef all said at once, "Open it!"

Inside the box was an antique locket on a delicate silver chain.

Miranda tilted her head to the side and opened the locket. Inside was Austin's picture and a tiny handwritten note that said, "I love you."

Miranda caught her breath and felt her heart leap. She looked into Austin's wide eyes and calmly spoke. "And I love you."

Moonshine Cocktails Recipes

Honeysuckle Fizz

Equipment:
Cocktail shaker
2 champagne flutes
Jigger or measuring cup
Citrus hand juicer
Cocktail stirrer

Ingredients:
Ice
2 limes
¼ oz. simple sugar
¼ cup clear moonshine
Prosecco
Rosemary stalks (optional)

Directions:
Fill shaker with ice.
Squeeze juice from limes into shaker.
Add simple sugar and moonshine to shaker
Shake thoroughly and pour into flutes.
Top up flutes with prosecco, then gently stir.
Garnish with stalk of rosemary (optional).

Serves two

Lemon Shine

Equipment:
2-qt. pitcher
Vegetable peeler
Lemon juicer
Spoon
4 mason jars

Ingredients:
6 lemons
Mint leaves
½ cup turbinado sugar
1 cup clear moonshine
2 cups water
Ice

Directions:
Peel skin off four lemons for curl.
Muddle mint in bottom of a 2-qt. pitcher.
Squeeze lemons, add juice to pitcher.
Add sugar, stir all until sugar dissolves.
Add moonshine and water to pitcher.
Fill mason jars halfway up with ice.
Stir and pour mixture into mason jars.
Garnish with mint and lemon curls.

Serves four

RC Shine

Equipment:
  2-qt. pitcher
  Knife
  Spoon
  4 mason jars

Ingredients:
  1 fresh lemon
  Mint leaves
  ½ cup turbinado sugar
  1 cup clear moonshine
  16-oz. bottles RC Cola (or any cola on hand)
  Ice

Directions:
  Peel off four lemon skin curls.
  Muddle mint in the bottom of a 2-qt. pitcher.
  Squeeze lemon, add juice to pitcher.
  Add sugar, stir until all the sugar dissolves.
  Add moonshine and cola.
  Fill mason jars halfway up with ice.
  Stir mixture in pitcher and pour into mason jars.
  Garnish with mint and lemon curls.

Serves four

Homemade Herb Crackers

Equipment:
Parchment paper
Baking sheets
Mixing bowl
Measuring cups
Measuring spoons
Spatula
Rolling pin
Pastry brush
Pizza cutter or sharp knife
Dinner fork
Cooling rack
Airtight container

Ingredients:
3 cups all-purpose flour, or a mixture of all-
   purpose and whole grain flours
2 teaspoons sugar
2 teaspoon salt
4 tablespoons extra-virgin olive oil
1 cup water
1 tablespoon herb seasoning

Directions:
Preheat oven to 450 degrees. Position bottom rack to lower third of the oven. Cut a piece of parchment paper to fit the baking sheet.

Mix the flour, sugar, and salt together in a medium-sized mixing bowl.

Add the oil and water to the flour mixture. Stir until the flour is incorporated. If flour remains in the bowl, add more water a tablespoon at a time until a sticky dough ball is formed.

Divide the dough in half and shape one portion into a flat square. Sprinkle your work surface as well as your rolling pin with a little flour.

Roll out the dough working from the center out shaping it into a $\frac{1}{8}$-inch-thick or thinner rectangle. The thinner the dough, the crisper the cracker.

Brush the surface of the dough very lightly with water. Shake the herbs onto the surface of the dough in an even coverage. See Notes for topping ideas.

Using the pizza cutter or knife, cut the dough into individually shaped crackers. You can make squares, diamonds, rectangles, or use cookie cutters.

Transfer the crackers to a baking sheet, then prick each cracker with the tines of the dinner fork to prevent them from puffing up too much.

Bake the crackers for 12–15 minutes, until the edges are browned. Thinner crackers will bake quicker, so you can remove them and continue baking the thicker ones. While the first batch is baking, roll out and cut the remaining dough.

When the crackers are browned to your preference, transfer them to a wire rack to cool. They can be stored in an airtight container for 3–5 days. If they turn a little less than crispy, reheat in a 350-degree oven for a few minutes.

Makes about 50 crackers.

Notes for the Cook:

My husband and I love these crackers with chili, and also with soup. They look fabulous on a charcuterie board of meats and cheeses. For a variation, I top the crackers with kosher salt, chili powder, or a Greek seasoning. This recipe is extremely flexible and very forgiving. It also lends itself to experimentation. Another variation is to make flatbread instead of cutting into crackers. Have fun!

Chicken Noodle Soup

Ingredients:

For the homemade stock:
3 lbs. whole chicken
Water just to cover (or use stock for richer flavor)
2 large pinches of kosher salt
1 celery rib with leaves, cut into large chunks
1 large carrot, cut into large chunks
1 medium onion quartered
1 large bay leaf

For the soup:
8 cups reserved homemade stock, or 2 (32-oz.) cartons of chicken stock/broth
1 tablespoon chicken base (like Better Than Bouillon), optional
3 garlic cloves, chopped
2 stalks celery, halved lengthwise and sliced
2 carrots, sliced
1 parsnip, chopped, optional
½ large onion, diced
2 tablespoons diced fresh ginger, optional
1 teaspoon dried thyme
Freshly ground pepper
Large handful frozen peas
Large handful frozen corn
Optional veggies: mushrooms, diced potatoes, diced turnips, chopped leeks, sliced scallions, green beans, etc.
2 tablespoons dried parsley, plus additional for garnish
Cooked egg noodles or cooked rice

Directions:

Cut up chicken coarsely, splitting back and breasts. Place the cut-up chicken in a tall stockpot, add the water or chicken stock only to cover chicken plus about an inch. Cover pot and bring to a boil, reduce heat, remove the lid, and simmer uncovered, skimming off any foam that accumulates. When foam subsides, add the salt, celery, carrot, onion, and bay leaf. Cook, uncovered, at a steady, slow simmer for about 2 hours.

Strain, but reserve the broth. Discard the vegetables. Put the broth back into the stockpot and set the chicken aside to cool. To the stock, add in the chicken base, garlic, celery, carrot, parsnip, onion, and ginger. Sprinkle in thyme and pepper. Allow to slow simmer until vegetables are tender.

When cool enough to handle, remove and discard the skin and bones from the chicken. Tear the chicken into bite-size pieces and add back to the broth. Add the peas and corn and any additional veggies you like; add parsley and simmer until tender. I prefer to cook the noodles or rice separately from the soup itself so that the noodles do not absorb most of the soup broth.

Spoon cooked noodles or rice into a serving bowl and ladle the soup on top. Sprinkle each serving with a bit of additional parsley.

Notes for the Cook:

You can use a variety of chicken parts you've saved up for this (wings, backs, etc.). However, you'll want some additional chicken to add to the soup since the parts have done their job! Throw a few chicken thighs in the pot along with the parts—they give a great flavor to the soup. Avoid boneless, skinless chicken breast, however, as it lacks flavor and tends to overcook and be too dry. Save those for a shortcut version. The chicken base is optional if you're making homemade stock, but I like the richness it gives to the soup. If you use the base, you will not likely need to add any additional salt to the soup. If you don't use the base, you may need salt. Either way, be sure to taste it before adding salt.

Serves 16

Side Dish—Three Bean Salad

Equipment:
   Large mixing bowl
   Small mixing bowl
   Mixing spoon
   Can opener

Ingredients:
   1 16-oz. can green beans, drained
   1 16-oz. can yellow wax beans, drained
   1 16-oz. can red kidney beans, drained
   1 cup chopped sweet onions
   1 cup chopped celery
   1 cup chopped green bell pepper
   1 jar (4 oz.) chopped pimento peppers, drained
   ½ cup vinegar
   1 teaspoon vegetable oil
   ¼ cup white sugar
   ¼ teaspoon salt
   ¼ teaspoon black pepper

Directions:
   Mix green beans, yellow wax beans, kidney beans,
onion, celery, green bell pepper, and pimento peppers in
a bowl.

   Combine vinegar, oil, sugar, salt, and pepper in a
saucepan; bring to a boil. Cook and stir until sugar is
dissolved, about 5 minutes. Remove saucepan from the
burner and pour dressing over bean mixture, toss to coat.
Refrigerate until flavors blend, 8 hours to overnight.

Chicken Pot Pie

Equipment:
  Large saucepan
  Large skillet
  2 9-inch pie plates
  Medium saucepan
  Colander
  Knife
  Mixing spoon
  Mixing bowl

Ingredients:
  2 cups diced, peeled potatoes
  1¾ cups sliced carrots
  1 cup butter, cubed
  ⅔ cup chopped onion
  1 cup all-purpose flour
  1¾ teaspoons salt
  1 teaspoon dried thyme
  ¾ teaspoon pepper
  3 cups chicken broth
  1½ cups whole milk
  4 cups cubed, cooked chicken
  1 cup frozen peas
  1 cup frozen corn
  4 sheets refrigerated pie crust

Directions:
  Preheat oven to 425 degrees. Place potatoes and carrots in a large saucepan; add water to cover. Bring to a boil. Reduce heat; cook, covered, 8–10 minutes or until crisp-tender; drain.

In a large skillet, heat butter over medium-high heat. Add onion; cook, and stir until tender. Stir in flour and seasonings until blended. Gradually stir in broth and milk. Bring to a boil, stirring constantly; cook and stir 2 minutes or until thickened. Stir in chicken, peas, corn, and potato mixture; remove from heat.

Unroll a pie crust into each of two 9-in. pie plates, trim even with rims. Add chicken mixture. Unroll remaining crusts, place them over the filling. Trim, seal, and flute edges. Cut slits in tops.

Bake 35–40 minutes or until crust is lightly browned. Let stand 15 minutes before cutting.

Freeze option: Cover and freeze unbaked pies.

To use, remove from freezer 30 minutes before baking (do not thaw). Preheat oven to 425 degrees. Place pies on baking sheets, cover edges loosely with foil. Bake 30 minutes. Reduce oven setting to 350 degrees; bake 70–80 minutes longer or until crust is golden brown and a thermometer inserted in center reads 165 degrees

Serves 4–6

Candied Sweet Potatoes

Equipment:
   Potato peeler
   Kitchen knife
   9" x 13" casserole dish
   Medium saucepan
   Wooden spoon
   Aluminum foil

Ingredients:
   4 medium-size sweet potatoes
   1 tablespoon salt
   1 cup butter, cubed
   ½ cup white sugar
   1 cup brown sugar
   2 tablespoon cinnamon
   1 tablespoon nutmeg
   ¼ cup orange juice

Directions:
   First, preheat your oven to 350 degrees.
   Grab your four medium-size sweet potatoes (about 2 pounds) and wash, peel, and cut them into slices, about ½ inch thick. Then lay them flat in the casserole dish. Sprinkle the sweet potatoes with salt. Set aside.
   Then in a heavy-duty saucepan, melt your butter over medium-low heat. Add sugars, cinnamon, nutmeg, and stir until your butter has melted and your sugar has dissolved. Remove from heat and add the orange juice. This slight hint of citrus adds a lovely brightness to the dish.
   Pour the butter mixture over the sweet potatoes, mak-

ing sure every single sweet potato is covered. Cover tightly with foil and place in your preheated oven.

Bake for 30 minutes with the foil on. After 30 minutes, remove the dish from the oven, remove foil, and stir the sweet potatoes. Place back in the oven and bake uncovered for an additional 30 minutes or until the sweet potatoes are tender. I usually poke a few pieces with a fork to ensure they are tender to my liking.

Remove from the oven and allow the sweet potatoes to cool a bit. It'll give that syrup a little time to thicken up.

Notes for the Cook:

You'll absolutely want to make sure that every single potato is covered in that butter-sugar mixture. If not, it may result in some sweet potatoes being very tender and others not so much. That would be the worst.

I don't add marshmallows to this recipe as I feel it's sweet enough as is.

Chocolate Creme Pie

Ingredients:

Crust
1½ cups King Arthur Unbleached All-Purpose
   Flour
½ teaspoon salt
¼ cup vegetable shortening
4 tablespoons cold unsalted butter
⅛ to ¼ cup ice water

Filling
2 tablespoons unsalted butter
1⅓ cups semisweet chocolate, chopped
1 teaspoon vanilla extract
⅔ cup granulated sugar
3 tablespoons cornstarch
2 tablespoons unsweetened cocoa, Dutch-process
   or natural
1 teaspoon espresso powder, optional; for richer
   chocolate flavor
⅛ teaspoon salt
3 large egg yolks
1 cup heavy cream, divided
2 cups milk

Topping
1 cup heavy cream
¼ cup confectioners' sugar
½ teaspoon vanilla extract

Directions:

To make the crust: In a medium bowl, whisk together the flour and salt. Work in the shortening until it's in lumps the size of small peas.

Dice the butter into $\frac{1}{2}$" pieces, and work it into the mixture until you have flakes of butter the size of your fingernail. Add the water 2 tablespoons at a time, mixing with a fork as you sprinkle the water into the dough.

When the dough is moist enough to hold together when you squeeze it, with no floury patches or bits of dry pastry in the bottom of the bowl, transfer it to a lightly floured work surface. Fold it over on itself three or four times to bring it together completely, then pat it into a disk $\frac{3}{4}$" thick, rolling the disk to smooth its edges.

Wrap the pastry in plastic and refrigerate it for 30 minutes before rolling.

To pre-bake (blind bake) the crust: Preheat the oven to 400 degrees. Lightly grease a 9" pie pan that's at least 2" deep.

Roll the pastry into a 13" circle. Transfer it to the pre-pared pan and trim the edges, so they overlap the edge by an inch all the way around. Tuck the edges up and under, and flute or crimp them. Put the lined pie pan in the refrigerator to chill for 10 minutes.

Line the crust with foil or parchment paper and fill it with pie weights or dried beans. Bake the crust for 20 minutes. Remove it from the oven, and gently remove foil or parchment with the weights or beans. Return the crust to the oven for 10–20 more minutes, until it's golden brown all over. If the edges of the crust start be-coming too brown, cover them with a pie shield or strips of aluminum foil. Remove the crust from the oven and cool completely.

To make the filling: Place the butter, chopped chocolate, and vanilla extract in a 2-quart mixing bowl; set aside.

In a medium saucepan off the heat, whisk together the sugar, cornstarch, cocoa, espresso powder, and salt. Add ½ cup of the heavy cream, whisking until the mixture is smooth and lump-free. Whisk in the egg yolks.

Place the saucepan over medium heat and gradually whisk in the remaining ½ cup cream and milk. Bring to a boil, whisking constantly as the mixture thickens; boil for 1 minute. The temperature of the mixture will be around 200 degrees after 1 minute.

Remove the pan from the heat and pour the mixture over the reserved chocolate and butter. Whisk until the chocolate is melted and the mixture is smooth.

Pass the filling through a strainer into a bowl to remove any lumps. You can use the back of a ladle, a flexible spatula, or a wooden spoon to stir it through the strainer. Scrape the underside of the strainer once in a while with a clean spatula to help the process along.

Place plastic wrap or buttered parchment paper on the surface to prevent a skin from forming, and chill thoroughly. A shallow metal bowl with more surface area will chill the filling most quickly.

To make the topping: Place the heavy cream in a chilled mixing bowl. Whip until the whisk or beaters begin to leave tracks in the bowl.

Add the sugar and vanilla and whip until the cream holds a medium peak.

To assemble: Spoon the cooled filling into the cooled, baked pie crust. Level the top with the back of a spoon or an offset spatula. Spoon or pipe the whipped cream on top. Note: If you're not planning on serving the entire pie at once, top individual slices with a dollop of whipped cream just before serving.

Chill the pie until ready to serve. For best slicing, refrigerate the pie overnight before serving.